ROOKE

Callie Hart

ROOKE

Copyright © 2017 Callie Hart

ROOKE

"I am not young enough to know everything."

— Oscar Wilde

ONE

THERAPY

SASHA

D rowning is a peaceful way to die.
There's the panic at first, of course. Your lungs screaming for oxygen, your mind revolting, blinding flashes of light stealing your vision, every muscle in your body burning and on fire as your cells begin to die. And then the terrible moment when you can no longer keep your lips pressed shut, can no longer deny the primal urge to inhale, and you do it, you open your mouth, knowing what it means as the cold water floods your lungs: *this is the end.*

That's when everything slows. A kind of calm settles over you, and the panic and the fear melt away, dissolving as your limbs begin to fall numb. It doesn't take long. The thrashing stops. The hammering in your ears stops. The mundane, silly things that plague your everyday life are no longer important. And then you simply...leave. At least that's what it was like for me, anyway. Every night, when I close my eyes, I relive the morning five years ago when the Chuck Holloway Moving Co. truck with the splintered windshield and the green, frayed piece of rope tied around the handle of the driver's side door careened across the freeway, hitting my sedan, sending my car tumbling over the side of the Brooklyn Bridge with me still inside it. I remember the weightlessness of the fall, and the terror as the nose of the car impacted with the water, and then the seeping cold and the violent scramble to escape.

I wasn't ready to die. Moreover, I wasn't ready for my six-year-old son strapped into his car seat in the back seat to die. I knew I had to get back there before the car submerged, to unclip him, to drag him into my arms, to force open the door and kick us both free of the sinking wreck. It wasn't possible, though.

"Start again, Sasha. What did you do the moment the car hit the river?"

Again, we're going through this. Again, we must rehash the finest of details, assessing and measuring each of my actions. Dr. Hathaway smiles softly as I tense in my seat. It's a very comfortable seat, I'll admit, but I despise this chair. Having to sit in it once a week, five years after the accident, is a self-enforced prison sentence I will never be free of. Dr. Hathaway, in his late forties, his still-thick hair shot through with steel, in his immaculately pressed shirt, and his designer thick-rimmed glasses, folds his hands in his lap and waits for me to begin.

"Well. I hit my head. On the steering wheel. It made it really hard to see properly."

Dr. Hathaway nods. "What were you feeling as the water started to fill the car?"

"I was frightened. More than frightened. I couldn't breathe. And Christopher..." I look away, out of the seventeenth-story window of his Manhattan offices, not really seeing the other high rises or the cold, stark white-blue of the New York winter sky on the other side of the glass. "Christopher was screaming," I say softly. "He was always so quiet. He never made any real sound, but *that* day..." Christopher was deaf. He never quite understood that when he opened his mouth and he breathed over his vocal chords that he produced sound, so he just never did it. The day our car went over the bridge and into the river was the first time I'd really heard him scream since he was a baby.

Silence hovers over us like a suffocating blanket in Hathaway's office. I know he won't prod me any further. He won't ask me any more questions. It's up to me to go through every split second of the accident until I reach the end now. The sooner I begin, the sooner it will be all over. I clear my throat.

"He was screaming. I couldn't think straight for a moment. I was so dazed from hitting my head that I just sat there, trying to figure out what the hell was going on. And then everything began to tip sideways and I realized something really bad was happening. Something really, really bad." I can still feel the weight of that terrible realization settling in my stomach. I feel it at least three or four times a day, no matter how well I might be coping.

I continue with my account of the story, experiencing it all over again as I relive the murky water swallowing the car. "I unfastened my seat belt. It was hard to climb into the back. It felt like the car was spinning over as it sank beneath the water, like it was almost on its roof. It was hard to move. My arms and legs felt strange. They didn't want to work properly. Christopher was reaching out to me. He was so afraid. He kept signing for me over and over again. He was trying to get out of his chair by himself, but we'd bought a really good car seat for him. Andrew insisted we get something strong, something hard wearing. Something he couldn't just let himself out of. The button was really stiff. He couldn't press it. His fingers weren't strong enough. I eventually managed to pull myself through to the back, and I unclipped him. He climbed into my arms. I don't know how long that took. It felt like it was a long time. A really long time. The fire department said it couldn't have been more than ten to fifteen seconds, though, that the car couldn't have sunk that far if I could still see the lights from the bridge overhead through the back windows, but I don't know. It felt like forever.

"I tried to open the door to the car then. The one beside Christopher's car seat. It was jammed shut, though. It wouldn't open, and I couldn't do anything to move it. I kicked at it. I used both feet to try and smash the glass. I saw a show once that said you should use your belt buckle or something, that you should wrap your belt around your shoe and use the hard metal part to break open the glass, but I wasn't wearing a belt. I couldn't find anything hard to use. Nothing. Christopher was frantic. He was shaking all over. He was clinging to me, burying his face in my shoulder. I kept signing to him that everything was going to be okay, but I knew it wasn't. I knew I was laying to him, and I felt...I felt so guilty. I failed him. I couldn't save him. The water kept pouring into the car, and I couldn't stop it. It wasn't long before the car was almost full. Christopher—" I choke on his name. This part of the story is always so hard to relive. The sharp edge of pain that lances through me is enough to steal my breath away, even now, after so much time has passed.

"Christopher kissed me on the cheek, and he signed that he loved me. He was six years old and he knew he was going to die. A child shouldn't have to...god, no child should ever have to face that knowledge. It's just not right."

Hathaway nods. His expression is impassive. There's no judgment in his eyes. No emotion whatsoever. Just once I wish he would let something slip. I wish I could see the condemnation in his eyes. The pity and disgust he must surely feel whenever I tell him about the time I allowed my only son to die.

"I held his hand," I whisper. "It was so cold. He was

4

freezing. I held onto him so tight. As the water rose over our heads, I crushed him to me, and I told him I loved him, too. And then...everything went black."

"You don't remember the police officer who jumped from the patrol boat into the water after you? You don't remember him smashing the rear window?"

I shake my head slowly. "I remember letting go. I remember hoping I was going to see Christopher again. That's all." I tell this lie every time I sit in front of Hathaway. It seems wrong to admit that I did see the shadowy shape of the man swimming toward the car. I recall with perfect clarity how he repeatedly beat and thrashed against the window of the car, until eventually he managed to shatter it with a jagged-edged rock. I was half crazy from holding my breath, but I remember his hands reaching into the car and tearing at me, trying to drag me out of the wreck. I didn't shove myself out of the vehicle, though. I did nothing to help the guy to save me. I already knew by that point. I already knew Christopher was dead. I also knew I couldn't live a day on this earth after letting him down so terribly.

Never in all of our sessions together have I admitted to Hathaway that I wanted to die. I wanted to stay inside the water-filled shell of the car I'd had since college, and I wanted to go with my son. I fought against the brave man who was trying to save my life. I struggled from him, ripping myself free from his strong hands; I closed my eyes and I opened my mouth. I let my life go.

That's when everything truly went black. *That's* when I lost consciousness and I allowed the void to take me.

"I woke up in the hospital two days later suffering from hypothermia and a broken collarbone," I say. "And that was it. Christopher was dead."

I always find it so hard to say those words. Saying them is owning the fact that I will never hold my boy again. Acknowledging the fact he will never see his seventh birthday, or his tenth, or his twenty-first. He will never grow up and have adventures in Europe, children of his own who will make his heart burst with warmth every time he sees them smile.

"And what do you think you could have done differently, Sasha? What do you think you could have done to save Christopher? To prevent the accident in the first place?"

I stare blankly at the floor. My hands are chapped from the cold. I've forgotten my gloves yet again, and the wind outside has been biting for weeks now. "I don't know," I say quietly. "If I hadn't been so confused after I hit my head..."

"The doctors told you it was a miracle you were even conscious, didn't they? Didn't they say the force of the blow should have snapped your neck?"

"Yes. They said that."

"Then how could you have been more alert?"

I say nothing.

"What else? What else could you have done to save Christopher?"

"I could have taken a different route to drop him at school."

"Christopher's elementary school was in Brooklyn, wasn't it? You had to cross the bridge to get him there. There was no other way."

Again, I say nothing.

"What else?"

There are thousands of ways in which I could have altered the events of that day five years ago, but I know how ridiculous they sound to a reasonable person. They're happenstance, what-ifs only divine premonition could have brought about: I should have had some sense that something terrible was going to happen. If I had, I could have left later to drop Christopher off at school. I could have kept him home altogether. I could have called and said he was sick, and we could have stayed in the house all day, reading, tucked up under a blanket, pretending to be space warriors or robots.

Hathaway sighs, tapping the end of his pen against his

desk. "You know you weren't responsible for your son's death. You know deep down in your heart that it was just an awful accident. Both the police and the fire department said there was nothing you could have done."

"How many times do we have to do this?" I ask, finally looking back at him. "How many times are you going to say that before we can move on to something else?" I'm rude. My tone is sharp and angry, but Hathaway merely shakes his head.

"As many times as we need to, I suppose. As many times as it takes for you to realize that it's the truth. To *feel* that it's the truth."

I blink at him, pressing my thumbnail into the fine skin over my index finger knuckle, holding my breath. "I'm never going to feel that way."

Hathaway places his pen down on his desk in front of him, followed by his notebook. He doesn't seem annoyed by my words. He doesn't appear to be affected by them one way or another. "Then I guess we're going to be doing this for a very long time."

TWO

BLEEDING HEARTS

SASHA

"Why don't you just sell? It's so big. It must be costing you a fortune just to heat the damn place. You're here on your own. You do not need four bedrooms."

"I'm not selling the house, Ali." Today seems to be a day for repetitive conversations. I can't remember how many times my best friend has tried to convince me to part with my brownstone, and I can't remember how many times I've sighed and told her it's not going to happen. "I grew up here," I say, throwing a tea bag into the chipped mug I've just taken down from the cupboard. I have my back to Ali, so she can't see the strained look on my face, or how furrowed my brow is. I don't need this today. I can't handle arguing over whether I do or don't need four bedrooms. Of course I could easily downsize to a two or even one-bedroom place, and yes, it would mean I could buy something else and still have close to a million dollars left over to do whatever the hell I wanted with, but she'll never understand. This place is full of memories for me. I gave birth to Christopher in the damn hallway, for crying out loud. I'd gone into accelerated labor before Andrew had been able to get home, and I'd been alone. I'd been the first person to see him, to take him into my arms, to hold him to my body. His room is just as he left it—toy trucks and decapitated Lego Stormtroopers all over the floor, his sheets mussed and pushed back where he bounced out of bed on the morning of his death.

I won't leave this place. I will *never* leave it.

I make Ali her cup of tea and I hand it to her, hurrying from the kitchen through to the formal dining room.

"Are you sure you're in the mood for book club today?" She gingerly takes a sip from her drink. She has no patience, she knows the hot liquid is going to burn her mouth, and yet she can never seem to wait for her tea to cool before she drinks. I get a bottle opener down from the shelf behind me, placing it next to the three bottles of Malbec I bought earlier from the liquor store.

"It's okay. The distraction will do me good."

Ali pulls a face. "I don't even understand why we're reading this book. It categorically makes no sense."

"Of course the book makes sense, Al."

My friend sticks out her tongue. She's thirty-three, the same age as me, but she acts like a twelve-year-old sometimes. She looks younger than her years. Her thick red hair is always wild and crazy, like she just stuck her finger in a power outlet, and for the most part her makeup looks like a teenager applied it—bright pink blushes, and shiny, glossy lip balm probably called bubble gum or cotton candy. She's always giving me hell about my makeup, or the lack thereof. She thinks I should dye my long dark hair blonde. If she had her way, I'd lose my jeans and sweaters and I'd wear skirts and low cut tops an awful lot more. We met in college, back when we were still teenagers and still very much alike. We used to misbehave together on a daily basis, getting ourselves into trouble with boys and with our workload until I met Andrew, a business major, and I buckled down. I think she's spent the last eleven years trying to get her old friend back.

"What about this makes any sense?" She tosses a dog-eared paperback onto the table I'm trying to prepare for the other members of our book club, who will be arriving in less than half an hour. She nearly hits a bowl filled with assorted crackers and I scowl at her. Picking up the book, I set it to one side, rearranging the cheese plate.

"It's a romance story. You know. Boy meets girl. Boy does something monumental to fuck up their relationship. They fight and go their separate ways. Boy works hard to regain her trust and her love, and they live happily ever after."

"Real life isn't like that. Well, apart from the boy doing something to fuck up the relationship. That's actually pretty close to real life. But what kind of guy sells everything he owns to prove a point to his spoiled-ass rich bitch girlfriend? *Gabriel's Way* was just too far-fetched. I wish I'd never read it."

"Save it for book club," I tell her. "If you start complaining about it now, you won't have anything to complain about once the other girls get here."

"Oh, I'll still have plenty to complain about, trust me. That book was garbage. I don't get why we even let Kika pick books anymore. They're always so saccharine."

"We're a romance book club. These books are meant to whisk us away from our lives, to make us swoon and feel that flush of love for the first time again. What do you expect but saccharine?"

"There are other kinds of love stories, Sasha. Something a little darker every now and then wouldn't kill any of us."

I lay out a stack of small plates along with a couple of small cheese knives, and I notice my hand shaking. It's been shaking since I left Hathaway's office six hours ago, and it probably won't stop shaking for a couple of days. Some of my sessions with him are harder than others, no matter that we always go over the same thing every time we meet.

Ali sips more of her tea, grimacing when she burns herself further. "I don't even know why you're still running this book club."

My hand stills on the knife I'm setting down. "Why wouldn't I?"

"Because...I don't know. I don't mean anything by it. I just...I mean, *romance,* Sasha? You haven't looked sideways at a man since Andrew. And I get it, I really do. I don't expect you to be out bed-hopping and having the time of your life. I'm just surprised that you're still interested in this stuff is all."

"I'm not a nun."

"I know you're not a nun. Nuns get more action than you do."

"Ha! You realize how absolutely ridiculous your last statement was, don't you?" She just raises her eyebrows. "My vagina isn't a dusty old relic yet. I'd date if I came across the right guy. Maybe."

She snorts.

"What? I would."

"No, you wouldn't. You'd flip if a guy even asked for

your number right now and you know it."

"I work too much to go out on dates. That's the problem."

"The problem is that you're afraid of your own shadow."

"And I suppose you'd have me approaching guys in coffee shops, asking them if they want to hook up later or something?"

"It would be a step in the right direction. Or maybe setting up an account on a da—"

"Do *not* tell me to set up an account on a dating app. I will lose my fucking mind if you tell me to set up an account on a dating app."

"Would it really be so horrible? You're acting like I want you to go trawling the back alleys of the ghetto for a good time. The guys on most of these sites are professionals. They're short on time, just like you. They're normal. They earn a paycheck." She gives me a stern look. "A lot of them even own suits and cover their own bills."

"I'm sure they do. I'm sure they're all great guys. I don't want to just fall into bed with someone, though. How is a meaningless connection going to be of any benefit to me?" I have to place the wine glass I'm holding down on the table with the utmost care; if I don't, I'm liable to smash the thing.

"So you're looking for something more serious? You want to find a guy to marry and have a brood of kids with? Is that it?"

I jump, an awful, bottomless agony slamming through me, deep as a ravine, wide as the ocean. The wine glass I just set down so carefully topples over. It rolls, tumbling from the edge of the table before I can catch it, hitting the floor and smashing into a thousand pieces. My heart is stumbling all over the place, stuttering like an engine almost out of fuel. "I'm never going to have another child,

Al. How could you even suggest...?"

Pain flashes across my friend's face. "But why not? You're still young. You're a great mom. There's no reason you shouldn't—"

"There's *every* reason—"

The doorbell cuts us both off, the bright, cheerful sound chiming throughout the lower hallways of the house. I grip hold of the edge of the table, trying to calm myself. Ali and I stare at each other, and can see that she knows exactly how painful her suggestion was just now. I can see the remorse written into the lines of her face, but there's defiance there, too. It's a familiar look on her. After Christopher died, she wrapped me in cotton wool just like everyone else did, brought me meals, cleaned my house, my clothes, and my body when I couldn't even muster the energy to do that for myself. But there came a point, months after the accident, when she decided enough was enough and she challenged me to start doing things for myself again. This feels like one of those times, but she's pushing too far.

"Go and get the door," she says, breaking the tension. "I'll clear up the glass."

There are a thousand things I'd rather do than get the door right now, but it beats standing here, continuing this conversation. I step over the mess on the floor and hurry down the hallway, nervously wiping the palms of my hands on my jeans. I can see the warped shapes of three heads through the frosted pane of glass in the front door even before I open it. Kika, Kayla, and Tiffanie: always on time, and always together, no matter what. The book club has been going for a long time, maybe seven or eight long years. There hasn't been a single instance these three women haven't shown up joined at the hip.

Tiffanie squeals when I open the door; she rushes forward, clapping her hands. "Oh. My. *God*. I am so excited.

13

This book was *life*. I can't wait to show you the edit I posted on Goodreads. Where's Ali?"

"She's in the back."

Tiffanie bustles past me, grinning from ear to ear. Kayla and Kika are hot on her heels. Kayla plants a kiss on my cheek, while Kika gives my arm a squeeze. She hangs back, allowing the other two women to go on ahead of us.

"You're pale," she tells me. "Have you eaten anything today? I'm not going to sugar coat it, babe. You look like shit." This is Kika all over: very perceptive, but also very blunt. I like this about her, but others have been known to be less appreciative of her honesty.

"I'm fine. And, yes, I've eaten, thank you very much, Mother Theresa."

"Hey. I didn't offer to cook you a meal or anything. I just pointed out that you could probably use one. Don't go giving me more credit than I deserve."

"Wouldn't dream of it."

"Good. Come on. Let's go drink a gallon of wine and stuff our faces with cheese."

THREE

YELLOW PAGES

SASHA

eing a curator at the American Museum of Natural History might not seem thrilling to most people, but I love it. The dioramas, the dinosaur exhibits, the crocodiles, and the space exhibition. Every single one of the museum's levels holds something of interest to me. I'm excited every single time I jog up the steps towards the grand entrance, dodging tourists and people taking pictures, leaning against the columns and posing with the lit-up dinosaur topiaries. Work is all I do get excited about these days. What a sad, sad thing to admit to. There once was a time when family vacations and cross-country trips would have me bouncing off the walls, thrilled by the prospect of adventure, at the prospect of experiencing something new. Christmas was my favorite time of year, and spring in the city would make me delirious with the promise of t-shirt weather, cold glasses of Sauvignon Blanc, and rooftop barbeques. Now the seasons all seem to blur into one another. I haven't left New York in years.

As I climb the steps, avoiding a row of people wrapped up warm with coats, hats and scarves, who all appear to be involved in a mannequin challenge, I think about the day ahead of me. Morning meetings are unavoidable, as are answering a litany of emails. Midmorning, I have to conduct three interviews in the vain hopes of finding a replacement for Shun Jin, my intern, who has basically been saving my life for the last six months. God knows how I'm ever going to find someone to fill her shoes. Shun Jin's the kind of girl to assess a situation and gauge whether or not I need to get involved. If the answer is no and it's something she can take care of herself, then she does exactly that without so much as mentioning it. She doesn't sweat the small stuff. I know my calendar is entirely safe in her hands, along with all of my exhibition timelines. I can hardly begrudge the fact that she's been given a pay raise and a junior position within the museum, I recommended her for the post after all, but now that I'm having to find someone who will be as diligent and professional as she is, I'm starting to feel like I've totally sabotaged myself.

In my office, a stack of envelopes has been left on my desk for me by the museum's internal mail service. I hang my purse on the back of the door along with my jacket, and then I leaf through the mail, discarding advertising material in the trashcan and setting aside any invoices I come across. The second to last piece of mail is a small white envelope. My hands go still as I stare down at my name written in black, blocky ink above the museum's address. I recognize the handwriting. In my mind, I remember the very first time I ever saw that awkward, no nonsense, yet somehow childish handwriting. It was years ago, back in college, when a boy slipped a note inside my Fine Arts of the 20th Century textbook. The note read:

> You ever need a live model, feel free to hit me up.
> *310 962 5177*

Underneath the number, the boy had drawn a crude smiley face, which appeared to be winking and sticking its tongue out.

I drop the envelope into the top drawer of my desk, swallowing hard. My mouth is strangely dry all of a sudden.

"Sasha? Ahh, Sasha, there you are. I'm glad I found you." Oscar Blackheath, the oldest curator on staff at the museum, blusters into my office without knocking, a whirlwind of tufty white hair, brown tweed and Davidoff Cool Water. From observing him on the street, you'd be right in placing him as an octogenarian, and yet upon speaking to him you begin to suspect you're the victim of some weird reality TV show prank. His attitude, his energy levels, and his general outlook on life are more in line with someone in their late twenties. He's tech-savvy, but his fashion sense is all over the place. In the summer, his go-to outfit is a crisp button-down shirt coupled with a pair of khaki shorts that expose his ghostly white, incredibly knobbly knees. Beyond polite, he speaks like a Victorian gentleman from Saville Row, London, but I know for a fact he was born and raised in New York.

"Been looking for me, Mr. B?" I ask.

"I have indeed. I wondered if you might be around this afternoon? I'd like to ask your opinion on the new Theory of Evolution program we're hosting next year. A number of school programs have expressed their concern over some of the planned exhibitions."

"Concern?"

"Yes. Well, I believe a number of Catholic and Baptist schools are upset that we've missed the word *'theory'* from our promotional flyers."

"Oh god."

"Yes. Exactly. I've penned a very expressive email in response to their missives, but I'd love for you to cast an eye over them before I hit send. Don't want to go upsetting anyone unnecessarily now."

I laugh. "Of course. I can swing by your office around three if that suits you?"

"Excellent." Oscar vanishes, leaving behind a cloud of cologne and a pair of wet footprints on the polished floorboards where he was standing a moment ago.

******

"What made you apply for the job here at the museum, Carl? You say you're primarily interested in linguistics. You realize you won't be able to further your ambition in that field here at the museum?" The kid across from me looks at me blankly, like I'm speaking Swahili. Ironic, given that he should be able to understand me even if I am, in actual fact, speaking Swahili. It says he has a working knowledge of the language on his resume.

"I know. Honestly, I just thought it might be fun. I have a couple of months before school starts again. I figured it might be interesting to do some part-time work here."

"Part-time? This is a full-time position, Carl. It's for six months in the minimum."

"Oh, for real? I thought maybe that was flexible or something."

"Definitely for real. Definitely not flexible."

"Huh. Well, okay then. Thanks for seeing me, I guess." The twenty-year-old punk gets up, shrugging his arms into his down jacket, picking up his incredibly hipster-looking bag and gives me a thumbs-up. "It was great to meet you anyway, Ms. Connor."

I watch him go, trying not to let my jaw hit the floor. What in the actual hell was that? *A thumbs up? It was nice to meet me anyway*? Damn it all to hell. Of the three interviews I've just sat through, none of the applicants were suitable. Not even close. The first girl was rude and kept snapping her gum. The second kid was severely shy, to the point where I couldn't hear a word he mumbled in response to my questions. And my third interviewee, Carl, well... Carl was obviously something else entirely. I slam my laptop closed, sighing heavily.

Out in the marble-floored bustling corridors and hallways of the museum, I can hear men and women talking in groups, the high, excited chatter of children, and the never-ending echo of footfall. These sounds have been a comfort to me for so long now. It's the background noise of a life I've always had yet a life that now seems distant and strange, like I'm a visitor here and I don't really belong anymore.

Back here, amongst the stacks and the high shelves, laden with treasures from previous exhibitions—stuffed coyotes, life-size jellyfish, celestial maps of the heavens—I find that I *am* still me, though. Just about.

My interviews were pointless and a waste of time, but somehow it seems they took forever. I've missed lunch, it's well passed two, so I make do with a coffee instead. In my office, I sip the dark black liquid slowly as I give myself the luxury of a ten-minute break. In my purse, the new book club novel glares at me malevolently, taking up too much room. Lord knows why Kayla picked this one. *The Seven Secret Lives of James P. Albrecht.* Doesn't sound like a romance to me. Not in the slightest. The blurb on the back of the book doesn't give anything away, either. Just that the male protagonist of the story is a kleptomaniac and a thief who descends into madness as his crimes worsen in nature.

I can't see anything about a woman in the story's description. No sense that James P. Albrecht is going to be rescued from his life of crime and insanity by some sweet-natured do-gooder. It's what I've come to expect. It's what I crave when I read these days, because the knight in shining armor never lets his princess down. The caring, redemptive heroine never fails her broken beau. These books are my escape from real life. Because you know what? Real life fucking sucks.

The book starts out slow: a man in his early thirties, trying to figure out where he belongs in the world now that the love of his life has left him. The language is trite and frankly a little weird in places. Bizarre descriptions of a Chicago landscape that clearly doesn't exist in real life. A couple of brief emotional internal monologues that strike me as odd, since as far as I can tell James is neither an empathetic nor sympathetic man. By the end of the first chapter, I'm convinced James is a sociopath and the reason the love of his life left him is because he's actually murdered her and buried her body in his newly paved back yard.

Weird, though. I'm sucked in. By the time I glance up at the clock it's already ten past three. Shit. My meeting with Oscar. I'm late. I *hate* being late, especially when I've agreed to help someone. I hurry out of my office, pulling the door closed behind me, and it's not until I reach the other side of the building that I realize I've brought my book with me instead of putting it back in my bag.

I slip unnoticed through the sea of people inside the museum, people's eyes skating over me indifferently as I weave between gatherings of grandmothers and foreign exchange students, Hasidic Jewish men, and fathers with their sons. I might as well be invisible; the name badge I'm wearing on my shirt, simple, black and inconspicuous, sets me aside from the other museumgoers. I am an employee, a member of staff, and therefore not even a real human being. I'm a part of the grander diorama of the museum, the bigger exhibition. People don't bother me, especially when it looks like I'm on my way somewhere as I am now.

Oscar's domain is an assault course of obstacles, designed to keep the unworthy out. His office is on the third floor, tucked away behind the crocodile exhibit, down a series of drafty hallways that are always cluttered with cardboard boxes so old and rotten that they spill their random contents out onto the chipped terracotta tile.

I duck around a crooked tower of telephone directories, smiling when I see their splintered, cracked spines clearly advertise when they were printed (1981 to 2002 respectively), and promptly collide with another obstruction, this time of the human variety. I drop my book as I crash into the person lurking behind the telephone books, yelping out loud as I reach out to steady myself. Very unladylike and most certainly not graceful in any way, shape or form.

"Whoa. Holy shit. You okay?" A hand reaches out and grabs me, and not a moment too soon. I haven't fallen down since...I can't remember the last time I fell down, it was so long ago. I'm saved from the indignity of doing so now, but only by the grace of the strong arm that's snaked its way around my waist. I find myself looking up into the face of a kid. Dark hair, dark eyes... No, wait. Not a kid. Not really. He's young, but he's made the transition through that awkward, gangly teenage stage that makes young men appear so uncomfortable inside their own skin. He's broad shouldered, and his hands feel huge on me. His hair is shaved at the sides, slicked back on top in that oh-so-fashionable cut nearly all twenty-somethings in New York seem to be wearing these days. His jaw is marked with a smattering of stubble, and his left front tooth is delightfully crooked. The flaw isn't something I would have noticed normally, but being this close to his face I find I have a prime view past his full lips, and his teeth are right in my line of sight.

"Last I checked, murder's still a felony," he growls.

"What?"

"Crushed to death by a stack of Yellow Pages," he continues. "That's not how I plan on going out."

"I'm sorry, I didn't mean to—"

He laughs, boisterous and surprising, scaring the shit out of me. He doesn't look like the kind of guy who laughs like this, like he doesn't care who hears him. He lets go of me, raising both eyebrows as he clearly checks me out. "I'm just fucking with you," he says. "Don't worry about it."

"Oh. Glad to hear it." I shake my head, regaining a little poise as I straighten my shirt. "Why are you lurking in the hallway back here? Are you waiting on someone?"

The guy, this James Dean-esque stranger whose dark eyes are glinting wickedly in my direction, makes a gun out of his fingers and fires it at me. He blows the imaginary smoke from the end of his index finger. "My grandfather. My mother said he needed to see me." The guy watches my mouth as I fight back the urge to smirk. "What? Why's that funny?"

I look him up and down. "Well. I think you probably went to a great deal of effort to look so...disheveled—"

"*Disheveled*?" He smiles a reckless smile. A dangerous, predatory smile. A smile that undoubtedly gets him into an awful lot of trouble.

"Yes."

"Why? Because my jeans are ripped? Because my

shirt's faded?" he says in slow, measured words. Damn, his voice is so deep. I can hear the amusement in it, though he's trying to hide it. He's enjoying this far too much.

I stand my ground. "Yes. Because your jeans are ripped and your shirt is faded."

"Fair enough. What of it?"

"You're obviously trying to exude some kind of bad boy persona, dressing the way you do, and then you're out hovering in the hallways of museums, doing as your mother tells you."

He looks at me in a way that makes my insides twist. "Don't all good sons do as their mothers tell them?"

A sharp twinge daggers me in the chest. I shouldn't have brought up mothers and their sons. What was I thinking? I do my best to hide my discomfort by glancing down at the floor. "Not in my experience, no."

"Then you've been spending time with some really shitty guys," he informs me.

Oh, how little he knows. In the past five years, I haven't been spending time with any guys at all. It's not as though I've been avoiding contact with men. I've just been avoiding contact with everyone, period. That's not something you tell a stranger, though. "I'm assuming Oscar's your grandfather?" I ask, sidestepping his comment. Oscar is the only faculty member old enough to have a grandchild this old, despite that being not very old at all.

"Bravo, Sherlock."

"Well, his office is three doors down. Right now you're standing outside..." I peer over his shoulder. "You're standing outside a disabled bathroom."

"I'm fully aware," James Dean tells me. "I'm preparing myself."

"Preparing for what? Oscar's the sweetest man alive."

"Maybe to you. But to wayward grandsons who don't

23

visit very often and who cause..." he clears his throat, "*trouble* on a regular basis, he can be quite the opposite, I promise you."

"Maybe you should cause less trouble." I don't know why I'm engaging with this kid like this. It's none of my business how he behaves, or *mis*behaves for that matter. And it's certainly not like me to blurt out obvious suggestions like the one I just gave him. The guy just smiles, though, apparently not noticing how strange or bossy I'm being.

"Where would the fun in that be?" he asks.

"Rooke?" A voice rings out down the hallway, echoing dimly. "Ahh, yes, Rooke, I thought I heard someone laughing like a madman out here. You're an hour early." Oscar shuffles down the hallway towards us. His pants are pulled up so high that his waistband must be chafing his nipples, and his hair is even poofier than before; it looks like a small cloud of cotton candy perched on top of his head. He catches sight of me and nods.

"I see now why you've been held up. I should have known *you* were behind this somehow." He casts a scathing yet affectionate glare in his grandson's direction.

"She tried to kill me, actually," he says mildly. Rooke. His name is Rooke, and for some reason I find the name instantly fitting. A rook is a chess piece, but it's also a kind of crow. Dark, mysterious, clever, wily and brazen. I can already attribute all of these traits to the tall man standing next to me and I only met him a second ago. "I thought I was going to have to defend myself. Now you're here I'm sure I'm safe, though," he says, biting back a smirk.

"Good lord, Sasha," Oscar exclaims. "I thought you were a capable woman? What's all this '*trying to kill him*' business? If you need some help getting the job done, I'd be more than happy to assist."

Rooke pretends to growl under his breath. "Traitor.

You're meant to be on my side."

Oscar stops in front of us, puffing a little. He takes a pair of extraordinarily fragile looking wire-framed glasses from the breast pocket of his shirt and hooks the narrow arms over his ears. Squinting, he assesses his grandson, his mouth hanging open slightly as he takes stock of him. "You got taller," he says.

"You got shorter," Rooke retorts.

"Yes, well, I suppose gravity has been kind of getting me down of late." Oscar slowly reaches out and places his hands on Rooke's shoulders. He seems emotional all of a sudden; his voice is thick when he speaks. "I'm very glad to see you. And I'm very glad, despite my jape with Sasha here, that you weren't callously and coldly murdered moments ago."

I begin to feel as though I'm encroaching on a deeply personal family moment. "You know what? Rooke's early and I'm late. I think maybe I ought to come back—"

Oscar shakes his head violently. "Nonsense. Our meeting won't take long. Rooke, why don't you wait upstairs for me in the gift shop? I should only be fifteen minutes or so. Sasha, come now. I appreciate you lending your expertise to me for a while." He tucks his hand into the crook of my arm and leads me back toward his office. I can sense the guy behind me smiling. I can feel his amusement somehow, burning into my back, skating across my skin, making my ears burn, and for a very brief moment I'm spun around by it. Why should a kid at least ten years my junior make me feel so...*odd*?

"It was nice meeting you, Sasha," he calls after me, that maddeningly deep voice booming down the corridor. "I'm sure I'll see you around."

I cast a hurried glance over my shoulder, considering what kind of response would be appropriate. For some unknown reason, it feels like I should tell him to go fuck himself. While the words that made up his farewell were civil enough, it felt like he was mocking me, and now I'm gripped by the need to tell him where the hell to go. Instead of heading up to the gift shop, Rooke leans heavily against the wall, tucking his hands into his pockets, smiling at me, and I feel the scowl etching itself into my features.

Oscar squeezes my arm. "Don't worry. You don't need to hurl such sharp daggers at him. The boy makes a habit of carting around enough rope to hang himself with and then some. He won't be coming to the museum again. I'll make sure of it."

"I'm sorry, I didn't mean to be rude. He just caught me off guard. He has...quite the personality."

Oscar chuckles. "Personality. Attitude. Call it what you will. I love the boy dearly, but he is his own worst enemy. I'm sure it's his age. One day he'll mature, I'm sure of it. Until then, I'm afraid the world is just going to have to tolerate the madness and machismo of Rooke Idlewild Blackheath as best it can."

FOUR

DARK SHIT

ROOKE

*H*e drew her closer, wrapping his arms around her. *She felt insubstantial inside his embrace, like she might dematerialize at any moment, and that scared him. She'd been his for such a short time. Not months. Not weeks. He'd possessed her for a mere matter of days, and yet the prospect of continuing on with his life without her made a cold, dead weight grip at him from the inside. There was no life without Isobel. There was no rhyme or reason, no up and no down. He would do whatever he had to in order to make sure she was safe from the men who would hunt her down and cause her harm. More than that; he would do whatever he had to in order to make her his forever.*

"What the fuck are you reading, bro?"

I nearly drop the book I'm holding, the sound of Jake's amused voice sending a jolt through me. The fucker's always sneaking up on me, always trying to make me jump. I hate it at the best of times, but now? Being caught with a romance novel in my hands? Yeah, that ain't good. I consider launching the book at his head, but then I decide against that particular course of action. There's a half naked dude on the cover of the book, for fuck's sake. Why give Jacob even more ammunition to mock me? I bend the pages back, cracking the book's spine so I can conceal the image of the dude with the ripped abs caressing the side of an anonymous woman's face.

"None of your damned business." I pick up a dirty sock from the floor (his) and toss that at him instead. He sidesteps the missile, laughing like a hyena.

"Forgive me," he says. "I just didn't know you could read."

"I read. I read plenty."

"Graphic novels do *not* count as reading, my friend."

"Of course they do."

Jacob shakes his head, collecting a shirt from the living room floor (also his) and sniffing at it dubiously. "My folks are coming by in a couple of days. How long do you think it'll take to make the apartment fit for parental consumption?"

The house is normally immaculate. The only clutter in the living room right now is Jake's, and I plan on burning whatever the fuck he doesn't tidy up soon. "For anyone else's parents, I'd say we were good. But for yours...I'm gonna say it'd take longer than either of us have left on this earth."

"Gee. Thanks for the vote of confidence."

"I do my best."

Jacob shrugs his way out of the ball tee he's wearing

and slips on the black button-down shirt he just collected from the floor. As he does up the buttons, he squints at me like he's trying to read my mind. "What's wrong with your face?" he asks.

"What the fuck are you talking about?"

"I'm talking about that weird, guilty twitch you've got going on."

"I don't have a weird, guilty twitch."

"Oh, but you do. Give me the book."

"Fuck you, asshole."

He holds out his hand. "Don't make me fight you for it."

I let out a bark of laughter. "You think you can take it from me, come on over here and try." No way he'll be able to. All through high school Jake tried working out, dietary supplements, protein powders, basically anything he could get his hands on that might help him bulk out a little. Suffice it to say, nothing worked. He's still as rail-thin as he's always been. He was adamant he would weigh a hundred and ninety pounds by the time he was twenty-one, and yet here we are, both of us creeping up on our twenty-fourth birthdays, and he can't weigh more than a buck forty soaking wet.

Jake rolls his eyes. "Fine. If you wanna be all secretive and weird, then so be it. But know this. If that piece of literature in your hands has anything to do with those psychos in waiters' outfits handing out free personality tests in the city, then you and I are no longer friends."

"I'm not joining a cult, dude. It's just some book this woman dropped. It's nothing."

"Some woman? What woman?" He narrows his eyes again.

"I don't know. Some chick that works at the museum. She was kinda hot."

"Oooh. Librarian type. I like it. Is she interning or

something?"

Jake seems to have entirely skipped over the part where I called Sasha a *woman* and not a *girl*. I choose not to bring it up again, though. "I don't know. Maybe. We only spoke for a few seconds."

"And you stole her book?"

"Like I said. She dropped it."

He waggles his eyebrows in a comical way. His face is made of elastic. Has to be, the way he can contort and manipulate the way he does. If he wanted to, he could easily be the next Jim Carrey. Jake's more interested in becoming the next Damien Rice, though. "I get it. You're reading the thing from cover to cover so you can take it back to her and impress her with your knowledge of its contents, right?" he says.

"No. I'm not going to see her again. My grandfather doesn't want me back there any time soon. And besides...she's not exactly...suitable."

Gathering his bar blade and apron from the dining table, Jacob makes a derisive sound. "What the fuck does suitable have to do with anything, man? She's a chick, right? You think she's hot. Do what comes naturally. Take her out for some drinks. Charm her with that ridiculous fucking face of yours. Bring her home and fuck her. The end."

I could take the time to explain that Sasha's not the bring-her-home-and-fuck-her type, but Jake wouldn't understand. Not until I also explained that she must be in her early to mid-thirties, that she looks like she has her shit together, and that screwing around with a guy like me is undoubtedly very low on her list of things to do. Instead I give my friend the dirty, rakish grin he's expecting from me and I shrug my shoulders. "Yeah, you're right," I tell him. "I do have a ridiculous fucking face, don't I?"

"I'm gonna be late for work. I have a crazy early shift.

If you wanna bring this mystery hottie by the hotel later, I'm sure I can slide you guys a couple of free martinis."

Jake works at The Beekman in Lower Manhattan; it's classy and stylish—the kind of place I probably would take a woman like Sasha, if I was planning on taking her on a date. Since Jake is there every night, making an obscene amount in tips and flirting outrageously with anyone who sits at the bar irrespective of their gender or sexual orientation, I won't be doing that any time soon, though.

"Yeah, dude," I tell him, lying through my teeth. "Maybe."

Jake leaves. I return to the book in my hand, smoothing back the pages, flexing the spine, trying not to laugh at the blatantly sexual cover before me.

"Don't you dare hurt me," Isobel snapped fiercely. She had every right to warn me from bruising her heart. I'd hardly shown myself to be anything close to reliable since we'd met, and yet her words still stung a little. How could she not see what she meant to me? How could she not know that I would crawl over broken glass for her? Defend her always. Even die for her if I had to?

The crush of her breasts against my chest was enough to drive me mad with desire. My erection was rock solid and painful. I was in severe need of release, but my physical desires were nothing compared to the painful need I felt deep in my chest. Was this what it felt like to love someone? In all my years, I'd never experienced a sensation like it before. Warm, enveloping and comforting, yet terrifying at the same time. The feeling was a drug, an addiction, a craving that only seemed to intensify every time I drew breath around her.

This woman had the power to own me. She had the power to destroy me if she wanted to. Fighting it seemed futile.

My parents bought the two-bed walk-up in Brooklyn Heights where I live back in the mid-nineties, back when the 11201 zip code wasn't quite so coveted. In fact, back then, the area was rough and more than a little run-down, and it wasn't smart to walk the streets alone after dark. For years they rented it out to tenants until I turned twenty-one and "came into my inheritance" as they put it. I frequently get the impression that giving me real estate in what they considered a rough, violent area was a passive aggressive way of telling me what they thought of me: that I wasn't worth much to them; that they thought I was cut from a certain type of cloth; that I wasn't going to amount to anything.

It's ironic that Brooklyn Heights is now fast becoming one of the most sought after areas to live in New York. Where dilapidated seven elevens with grated windows caked in dirt used to stand, now Kombucha shops staffed by pretty little hipster girls with thick-rimmed black-framed glasses are doing a booming trade. Where once stood empty thrift stores and soup kitchens, fixed gear bicycles are now sold, along with beard maintenance kits and quirky unisex clothing lines that look like they're made for androgynous space aliens.

As I make my own way to work, heading north into Williamsburg, I think about the shitty fucking email I received from my mother this morning:

Rooke,

Dad says you came by like you said you would. Thank you. It's about time you went out of your way to see more of your family. When you come by at Christmas, I'll write you a check for your efforts. In the meantime, don't steal anything if you go over to his place.

Mom.

Don't steal anything? Don't fucking *steal* anything? From my own grandfather? And she's planning on cutting me a check? Bitch can shove her Bank of America special where the sun don't shine. When I read the brief message this morning, I nearly smashed my fucking hand through the screen of my laptop. The only thing that stopped me was the knowledge that laptops are not cheap and certainly don't just unexpectedly fall from the fucking sky, so I bit the inside of my cheek instead, snarling at the stark black and white of the words in front of me.

In fairness, I suppose some people could say she's well within her rights to give a warning like that. I *have* been known to steal things in the past. Cars, mostly. I spent two years in juvi for borrowing a vehicle that didn't belong to me and ever since then I've been Rooke the thief. Rooke the bad influence. Rooke the black sheep. My father won't even look me in the eye. Five years, and I've forgotten what it's like to be properly addressed by the man. Not that that's any great shame. He's always been an asshole. Being ignored by him is a blessing as far as I'm concerned.

I roll up to the shop at eight thirty with a piping hot coffee in my hand. I'm half an hour early, but I like opening and setting myself up for the day before anyone else arrives. I like the quiet. I like sitting in the back and arranging the tools I'll need for the day, making sure I have everything I require. If there's a particularly difficult mechanism I need to repair, I might get a head start on that and see if I can't have the watch ticking by the time Duke, the shop's owner, arrives, whistling loudly while complaining halfheartedly about the temperature in between refrains.

"You're a problem solver, boy," Duke always tells me. *"Your brain doesn't work like anyone else's. You can tell what's wrong with a watch or a clock just from holding it in those hands of yours. I've been running this shop for close to eighteen years now. I never met anyone like it."*

It's not just watches. I can fix nearly anything mechanical or electrical, given a few hours and a vat of coffee to keep me chugging along. Before the whole juvi thing, Dad was grooming me for a spot at MIT. He was convinced I was going to graduate early and that I'd be designing spacecraft for Nasa by the time I was in my early twenties. Then, when I was arrested, all hopes of attending such a prestigious school went flying out the window and so did any interest he had in me.

I plant myself at my desk, quickly going through the paper packets that are overflowing from my in-tray, each packet stapled closed and marked up with Duke's messy, barely legible cursive handwriting: *Cracked face; remove four links; water damage; change battery; pressurize.* All easy fixes for the most part, newer watches that simply need a little maintenance. Boring jobs that can be completed without my full attention. I look for something a little more interesting to work on this morning, though. Something that will challenge me, allow me to stretch my mental legs, so to speak. Stiff workings. A slow mechanism. Something that will take longer than five minutes to finish.

There's nothing too mind blowing for me to tackle, so I settle on a beautiful antique silver pocket watch that an old woman brought in earlier in the week. It just needs a service, a cleaning of the inner workings and a treatment for the metal work—tiresome, boring stuff that I'd normally find dull, but the sheer beauty of the piece makes the task rewarding. By the time Duke shows up, I have the pocket watch in pieces, laid out before me on a velvet cloth, and my fingers are nimbly cleaning.

"Freezing out there," Duke states as he appears through the door from the main shop. "Free-*zing*. I don't think I can recall a November this cold in, well now, let's see, must be twenty-five years at least." He's always trying to remember the last time it was this cold, the last time it was this windy, sunny or rainy. As far as I can tell, it's been twenty-five years since Duke can recall most, if not all meteorological events taking place. Personally, I seem to remember that it was cold as fuck *yesterday*. Duke unwinds a thick grey scarf from around his neck, revealing yet another scarf underneath, red this time, with a fine white stripe. This red scarf he leaves in place, bolstering it up around his ears, tucking his chin into the material as if trying to warm himself.

His family came to the States from Antigua when he was just a baby. The only language he's ever spoken is English and yet his speech is heavily accented, as though it isn't his mother tongue at all. "Well, look at you, already hard at work and all. I wondered if you'd even come in today," he tells me.

"Why wouldn't I come to work?"

Duke slaps his hands down on my shoulders, laughing. "Because it's your birthday, young man. People shouldn't have to work on their birthdays."

For a moment I act stunned, a look of shock spreading across my features. And then... "It's not my birthday. It's not my birthday until March."

"Oh. Oh my." Duke rubs the back of his neck with both hands, pacing up and down. I stop what I'm doing, covering the pocket watch's internal workings with a piece of velvet, and then I turn on my swivel chair to face him.

"The fuck is up, man? You're freaking out."

"My memory's going," he moans. "It's definitely

someone's birthday today. If it's not yours, then I don't know whose it is!" He's practically wailing. In his green corduroy blazer and his dusky grey slacks, he cuts a rather theatrical figure as he wears a hole in the carpet, frantically pacing from one side of the room to the other.

"Fuck, dude. Stop. Stop. *Here*." My leather jacket's hanging over the back of my chair. I reach into the pocket and pull out the small white envelope I stashed there before I left the house. "Happy Birthday, you miserable cunt. I hope you got breakfast in bed this morning."

Duke damn near snatches the envelope from my hands, eyes filled with excitement. Christmas, New Year, his birthday: Duke's like a kid when it comes to celebrating holidays of any kind. He tears open the envelope, making short work of the paper. Inside his birthday card, he pulls out the two tickets to The Book of Mormon I bought for him, holding them aloft like they're two golden tickets to Willy Wonka's chocolate factory. "Yes!" he shouts. "Fucking *yes*! Now he can't say no. Now my miserable Grinch of a boyfriend *has* to go with me to see a show. Thank you, sweet boy. Thank you, thank you, thank you." He rains a shower of kisses down on my head, and I hunch my shoulders, screwing my eyes shut, growling out loud. Duke gets the picture and stops. He's the only man in the world who'd get away with doing something like that. Anyone else would lose a motherfucking testicle.

"Do you know what he bought me?" he wails. "The man I have lived with for nearly fifteen years? The man who I cook and clean for on a daily basis? The man who makes me clip his toenails because his back is too bad for him to reach his own damned feet?" Duke pauses. He clearly expects me to take a guess.

"I have no idea."

"He...bought   *me*...a   toaster   oven.

Agoddamnmotherfuckingtoasteroven! He knew I wanted a pair of brand new red patent leather Spats. Instead he gave me something that I will never use. I mean, who uses a goddamn toaster oven these days? Go to Subway, you cheap ass, miserable, ungrateful, half deaf..."

Duke continues to rant about his boyfriend's general ineptitude in very colorful language for at least another five minutes. I sit and pretend I'm listening, while I'm really watching him flail his arms around wildly like a maniac. How the fuck did I come to know such a bizarre, outlandish, wonderfully over-the-top human being?

"And then," he says, leaning forward, sticking a pointed finger in my face. "He tells me that I have to take my own damn car for an oil change today. *On my goddamn birthday.* Can you believe it? Can you seriously, honestly believe the gall of the man?"

"I seriously, honestly can't."

"Thank you. Thaaank. *You.* Mmm. I thought I was going to have a heart attack on the way over here this morning. Oil change my ass. Whew. Would you like a top up on your coffee, sweetheart?" On the days that I'm surly and grumpy, Duke calls me Eeyore; he says I'm just like the sad donkey in the Winnie the Pooh books. On days I buy him tickets to The Book of Mormon and I console him on the pains of having such a thoughtless partner, I get called sweetheart.

"That would be great," I tell him, holding out my coffee cup. "Thanks."

Duke lets his arms fall limp by his sides, my mug swinging in his hand. His head falls back as his eyes turn toward the ceiling. "Lord have mercy. I can't even *remember* the last time Simon said thank you to me."

I feel like suggesting that it might have been twenty-five years ago, but Duke storms out of the room in a flurry of arms and scarf before I get the chance.

*****

She could taste herself all over him. It was an unmistakable flavor that made her head spin. Why was that so exciting? Why did tasting her pussy all over his mouth make her heart beat so fast? It made no sense. Guys had gone down on her before plenty of times. She'd lain on her back constructing to-do lists and thought about the groceries she needed to pick up the next day, and when the guys were done she'd told them thank you very much and then thanked god even more the experience was over. It had never been fun. But with James, everything tilted on its axis when his head was between her legs. The things he could do with his tongue were criminal. She trembled just thinking about the unfathomable depth of her orgasm a moment ago. She'd had no idea it was even possible for her body to react that way, shaking and convulsing, her hands clawing at the skin of his back. It had left her more than breathless, and now, kissing him, tasting her pleasure on his lips, she could already tell that—

It's really hard to turn the page of a book when you're jerking off. I didn't know that until today, when I finally hit the juicy part of Sasha's book. Jake's still at work, and since I've been home I've done nothing but flick through the pages of *The Seven Secret Lives of James P. Albrecht* and stroke my dick. It's absolutely fucking crazy. I've watched my fair share of porn, let me tell you, but I had absolutely no clue reading about sex could be a turn on. It made me feel kinda stupid at first, reading scenes that contained words like *wet*, and *pussy*, and *throbbing cock*, but after a very short while I realized I was getting a hard-on. Next thing I knew, my pants were unbuttoned and I was having to stop myself from coming.

I can't help but ask myself the question: is this what

Sasha does when she reads books like this? Does she pour herself a glass of wine and sit on her couch, growing hotter and hotter under the collar as the characters get closer and closer to one another? Does she pretend the guy, James, is kissing *her* mouth with *her* pussy all over his lips? Does that make her wet? Does that make her touch herself, slowly sliding her hand beneath her panties so she can tease her clit as she reads? Fuck. The image is too hot for words. Call me ignorant, but I had no idea this sort of thing existed. I know chicks get horny. I know they get turned on enough that they'll lynch you for sex sometimes, especially if they've got a few drinks in them, but that's different. This is a grown woman, a sexual woman, seeking out her own pleasure. And fuck me if the idea of it isn't driving me insane.

An hour later, I'm still teasing the fuck out of myself when I receive a text:

Corner of 2nd and 5th. Black Mercedes. DROP OFF AFTER MIDNIGHT.

It's 11:15 now. Well, shit. That's that, then. Looks like my fun is over. I toss the book underneath my pillow and grab my go-bag from underneath my bed. I'll be back to finish what I started here later. Outside, huge puddles of water flood the sidewalk, reflecting the sodium orange burn of the streetlights. The location that was texted through to my phone isn't far away, but I usually like to stake out a boost before I commit. Smart to wait, smart to watch. You never know if someone's going to show up all of a sudden and ask why the fuck you're jimmying open the driver's side door of their car. It starts to rain again while I'm walking. When I reach the corner of 2nd, I stand in the shadows of a doorway, pop the collar of my leather jacket, and I light up a cigarette.

People see me leaning in the doorway, but they pretend they don't. Conversations stop as nervous eyes take me in. The jacket. The tattoos. *Especially* the tattoos. Hipsters all over the city have full sleeves these days, but full throat tattoos? Hands, covered in ink? That takes a certain level of dedication most pretty boys shy away from. Passersby notice me, and they recognize danger. I'm not a safe person to acknowledge. Even a gang banger quits shouting into his cell phone and speeds up a little when he sees me.

I hover, and I take my time. It's almost twelve by the time I decide it's safe to make my move. The Mercedes is right where the text said it would be. It's a new model, bound to be alarmed, so I don't go for the obvious. I hold off on sliding the length of flat steel down the gap between window and door and instead I use a long-bladed knife to force open the hood. Takes less than a second to cut the necessary electrics and slam the hood closed again. *Now* time to pop the door.

To say I have experience at this would be the understatement of the fucking century. There are fools out there that take a full thirty seconds to get a car open. Me, on the other hand? Two seconds. Three maybe, if I'm off my game. An onlooker seeing me approach the driver's side of a car would see the vehicle's owner letting himself in and driving away. I'm *that* fucking good.

I make short work of the Merc's interior electrics. The engine purrs as I start it up. I drive away calmly, responsibly, the way a normal person would drive. Thirty minutes later, I pull up outside my destination feeling pretty fucking smug. I passed three cop cars on the way over and not a single one of those bastards paid me any attention.

A tall, shadowy figure emerges from the garage I'm parked outside, hood pulled up against the rain and prying eyes. A tap on the window.

"Jericho ain't here, man," the guy by the window tells me. Tall. Skinny. High as fuck, by the looks of things. He twitches nervously. "He told me to drive the car 'round back when you got here. Said he would pay you tomorrow if you come by at four."

I narrow my eyes, staring at the guy. He twitches some more, then scrubs at his nose with his palm, shivering. "Okay, man. Sure." I get out of the car, and I brace myself. I know exactly what's coming next.

Sometimes, I'm not the only person to get a text like the one I received earlier. Sometimes, the message is sent out to two or three people, depending on the job. If someone shows up at a boost after someone else has already arrived, it's expected that you'll move on and find another job. Common courtesy among thieves, if you will.

This guy doesn't look familiar, I didn't see him over on the corner of 2nd and 5th just now, but I'm willing to put money on the fact that he was there. He saw me and bailed, only he didn't want to walk away from the paycheck. He figured he'd come here and wait for me, then snake the job right out from underneath me. It's not the first time it's happened. Won't be the fucking last either, I'm sure.

He's desperate.

I make a point of turning my back on him as I close the door of the Mercedes—*I'm not scared of you, motherfucker.*

When I turn back around, he does not look happy. "Hey, man, what are you doing? I told you I got to move it 'round back."

"I'm not giving you the car, you stupid piece of shit. I'm going to give you three seconds to get the fuck out of here, and if you're still standing there when I'm done counting then I'm gonna beat you so hard your face is going to cave in."

The guy in the hoody sneers. His teeth are a mess. His eyes are bloodshot. He needs a fix, and he needs it bad. The last thing he's going to do is walk away from me. He reaches into his pocket and slowly draws out a long flick knife, the silver of the wickedly sharp blade glinting in the darkness. "Pushy rich boy. You think I don't know who you are? This is *my* job. I already told Jericho I'm bringing it in."

I eye the knife. It's a savage thing. Looks like its brand new, never been used, though. Either that or this tweeker takes exceptionally good care of his steelwork. "How are you gonna use that thing on me?" I ask.

He frowns. "What?"

"How? How exactly are you going to use that blade on me? Are you going to try and stab me in the ribs? Neck? Stomach? How's this next part going to go down? I'm interested."

"I don't know, asshole. It'll land where it lands. However I get you with it, you're gonna end up dead. Better you just walk away."

If there's one thing I learned in juvi, it's that you don't walk away from a fight. No fucking way. It's stupid, I'm aware that it's stupid, but my pride just won't allow it. I take a step forward, and the tweeker laughs. It's an ugly sound that echoes down the abandoned street.

"All right, man. All right. If this is what you wa—"

I lunge forward, my index and middle fingers bent at the first knuckle, hand outstretched. It's a quick, sharp movement, a jab that takes the guy by surprise. My knuckles drive deep into his throat, crushing his larynx in one brief, explosive movement. See, this is the thing. These shitheads take one look at me and they see this huge, hulking dude, broad-shouldered and so very fucking still, *unusually* still, and they make assumptions. They think I'm slow. They think, 'man, this one's going to come down

42

hard.' Only problem is that I am actually lightning fast. I'm not what they expect at all. I'm like a goddamn snake when I strike, and it's usually fucking fatal.

The tweeker goes down. His head makes a sickening cracking sound as it connects with the sidewalk. I suck a breath in through my teeth, shaking my head. "Ooooh. That sounded like it hurt."

"Fuck...you...man." He can't breathe properly, he's clutching at his throat, and I find myself wondering absently if I've done some serious damage. You can collapse a man's oesophagus if you hit him hard enough in the throat. He can sustain serious damage that will leave him eating through a tube for the rest of his life. Do I care if this bastard needs a tracheotomy right now, though? Is my conscience bothering me in the slightest? That's a resounding hell no.

"Help me...up, man," the guy gurgles.

I fold my arms across my chest and I study him for a second. He's flailing on his back like a bug. The knife he was holding a moment ago is on the ground three feet away, still rocking on its hilt as raindrops hit the blade. No sense in hitting him again. He's well and truly down and out. I take a step forward, and I hold out my hand. He takes it, and as I'm pulling him to his feet, he does something profoundly stupid. He swings wildly with his other arm, snarling like a wolf, aiming a sloppy right hook at the side of my head.

I let go of him and block his strike, then I'm on him. He should have accepted the help and fucking disappeared. He should have bailed and chalked this one up as a bad experience. Instead, he's tested my patience. I hit him hard enough to feel bone crack. The tweeker's legs buckle, but he somehow manages to straighten himself out and remain on his feet. Not for long, though. I slam my fist into his face again, and he slumps to the ground, lights out. I slowly stand over him, and I consider taking hold of a handful of his hair and repeatedly pounding his head against the concrete.

"Rooke?" I look up. Jericho's right-hand man, Raul, is standing in the now open doorway of the garage, staring at me with his mouth open. "What the fuck, man? You're kicking the shit out of someone right outside the place? Bad fucking form."

I spit, shrugging my shoulders. "Some people just don't know when to leave well alone. This one's on him."

Raul sighs, scowling hard. He tosses a black zip-up bag at me, and I catch it out of the air. "Better get out of here before the boss sees," he says. "He's not in a very forgiving mood tonight. I'll take care of this. Go on. Go."

I leave on foot, ten grand richer, soaking from the rain.

FIVE

SELF-DESTRUCT

SASHA

There's nothing more frustrating than having to buy a book twice. I was too embarrassed to go hunting through that huge pile of telephone directories for *The Seven Secret Lives of James P. Albrecht* after I left my meeting with Oscar four days ago, so now I'm having to stop in at a Barnes and Noble on the way home from the museum. Good job I'm a fast reader. There are only two days left between now and Friday when book club meets up, and I can't just *not* read the book. Kayla would take it personally, guaranteed, and she's not the type of person to forgive a slight like that easily. She would assume I hated her choice of book, that I was trying to personally insult her by not only not completing the read but subsequently misplacing my copy as well. All in all, it would not go down well. The thing is, I really hate buying romance novels in bookshops. There's always some pimple-faced English lit student standing at the register, ready to silently judge you for your choice of reading material when they have such wonderful, awe-inspiring, Pulitzer prize winning tomes readily on hand instead. And don't get me started on the creepers who lurk around the erotica section of the store, waiting to pounce the moment you pick up something that looks like it might be a little racy. Is a bookstore the best place to ask someone if they would like to come swinging with you and your wife? I think not, sir.

So I find the book, and I buy the book. I sidestep around the weird dude with the long white hair in a ponytail, wearing what looks like a set of white pajamas, and I ignore the judgmental twenty-year-old behind the counter who looks down on me with such pity. I decline the offer of a plastic bag, and I shove the novel into my purse along with the receipt, and the next thing I know I'm standing outside in the cool, calm night air, and I look up to see that the rain that's been persisting for the past few days has now turned into snow.

A woman with a Santa hat perched jauntily on her head rings a bell, shaking her Salvation Army bucket, smiling at me warmly as she bounces around to Christmas music blaring out of a portable speaker. I give her the change from the book, three dollars and a penny, and I hurry off down the street in the direction of home.

When I get back, I grab some leftover salad from the fridge and I pick at it with a fork as I stand at the kitchen counter, staring at my purse. The book is in there, waiting for me to finish it. I'm about halfway through, but I just can't seem to muster up the energy to crack it open right now. It's not like I hate the story or anything. I just...I don't know. I'm not focused when I try and read at the moment. My mind wanders. I find myself revisiting events in the past instead of seeing the words on the page, and the past is not a place I want to spend my free time. The past is dangerous, full of potholes and darkness. Losing myself there is damaging beyond belief.

Hours later, I'm in bed when I finally pick up the damn book. I can't avoid it forever, and the couple of glasses of wine I drank as I watched television earlier seem to have comfortably numbed me.

She held the glass in her hand, and pieces of the shattered bottle dug into her skin. Small pearls of blood blossomed out of nowhere, swelling and swelling in size until they were too big, hanging like teardrops before falling to the earth. "Is this what you meant?" she asked me. "Is this the kind of pain that will remind me I'm alive?"

I nodded. The wind whipped and pulled at her coat and her hair, and the blood continued to fall to the concrete below. "I'm not cut out for this," she whispered, her voice tremulous. I could easily see the tears welling in her eyes. Perhaps I should have given her an escape route at this point, it would have been the gentlemanly thing to do, but I was not a gentleman. And the sight of her emotions spilling out of her, the same way her blood was spilling out of her, for some reason made my dick hard in my pants. "I need you to take me home," she whispered.

"No, Isobel. No, you're not going home." I stepped forward, and, like a mirror of my own movements, Isobel stepped back at the same time. She looked afraid.

"I'm not your property," she told me, her hand shaking, fingers still curled around the glass. "You can't make me stay."

"I don't need to make you stay. You want *to stay."*

She swallowed hard. "You're wrong. I have to get back to—"

"To your husband? The man who beats you senseless every night of the week?"

47

Isobel flushed, her cheeks reddening against the cold and the sharp sting of my words. "You don't know what you're talking about. You have no idea what kind of man—"

"I know exactly what kind of man raises his fist to his woman. A coward. A weak piece of shit who doesn't deserve the right to walk the streets."

Her hand tightened around the broken glass. "I don't want to do this anymore, James. We're done, okay? I just...I have to go home."

"And I told you—"

"God, please. Just let me go. I can't stand this anymore. I'm being torn apart. It's too much to deal with right now. Maybe in time—"

"What? The past will suddenly no longer matter? You think there'll come a time when you don't wake up screaming in the middle of the night? When you're not looking over your shoulder every time you walk down an unfamiliar street?" I laugh, shaking my head. "I'm disappointed. I thought you wanted to be brave. I thought you were ready to let go of everything that happened."

She visibly shrinks before me. My words are harsh, I know, but she needs to hear them. She can't go on living like this, jumping every time a car backfires.

I slam the book closed, slowly closing my eyes. It's becoming apparent why Kayla picked this specific book. She's not particularly known for her subtlety, but I really do have to give it to her this time. The female protagonist in the book hasn't lost her child, she was kidnapped and held against her will by a demented man who escaped from prison, and yet there are startling similarities between myself and the fictional girl in the book: she's haunted by her past; she can't seem to get her life back in order after her ordeal; persistent nightmares plague her every time she closes her eyes; and she finds it hard to trust men. Especially the dark-haired rogue who refuses to cease and desist in his borderline stalker-esque pursuit of her.

Somehow, I think Kayla is trying to show me that a brooding, sarcastic asshole in my life is exactly what I need to break me out of my melancholia. I can't seem to understand her logic. And who is she to speak, anyway? She's been professionally single for the past three years, ever since she caught her ex-husband fucking his secretary in the basement of their house, and have I given her a hard time about her personal life choices? No, I have not. I don't judge. I don't comment on anyone else's decisions, mistakes or general quirks. All I ask is that I'm afforded the same treatment in return. With Kayla, it never really matters what anyone else wants, though. She'll do whatever she thinks is right, irrespective of who it might piss off.

I set down the book, thinking about the main guy in the story, James. He's from a broken home. The thought of having a long-term, committed relationship with a woman has never occurred to him until he meets Isobel, the female lead, of course. He's a reprobate, a criminal, a dangerous gun-toting kind of guy you wouldn't want to meet in a dark alleyway. He has very little going for him when you consider him as potential boyfriend material, and yet when I think about him I can almost feel the touch of his fingers against my mouth. I can almost imagine how it would feel to be locked inside his arms, half afraid and half melting with desire as he breathes heavily against the sensitive skin of my neck.

Why is it that the idea of a reckless, frightening man like him is enough to get my heart racing, and yet the idea of a sensible investment banker from Hoboken makes me want to vomit?

Maybe it's because Andrew was an investment banker

from Hoboken. Maybe sensible, reliable men with no psychopathic tendencies are always going to remind me of him, and in turn what we lost. Or maybe it's the fact that edgy, dark, moody men with hidden pasts are bad for women like me, and I hit my self-destruct button a long time ago.

SIX

PAYDAY

ROOKE

A nother text message this morning. Another car. This time the boost is an easy one. "Fifteen grand. You're not getting a cent more from me, Rooke. I don't need to remind you how badly you ripped me off with the other night, do I?"

"I'm not exactly popping the hood on these things to check the engines, Jericho. If it runs when I cross the wires, I take the fucking thing. You can't blame me if the vehicles I bring you aren't in pristine working condition sometimes."

Apparently the Merc was a dud. He fucking wanted it, though. He was the one who told me specifically where it

51

was. Jericho uses the nail on his little finger to scratch at the corner of his mouth, frowning deeply. He curses under his breath, using language that would make a sailor blush. "How about a wager? Double or nothing, my friend. Spice things up a little."

"No, thanks. I'll stick with the twenty you promised." I've learned my lesson with Jericho. He never places a bet he knows he can't win. His coins are double-sided. His decks are stacked. If I chose to go head-to-head with him every time he proposed a bet, I'd be the poorest car thief in the tri-state area.

"All right, man. Twenty," he says. "But I'm telling you now, if I lose money on this thing I'm coming after you for the balance. And I don't want to have to get on a bus to Brooklyn, asshole. That would be some bullshit right there." Despite his role as mechanic and "used car salesman," Jericho hates driving cars. He prefers to sit on the back seat of a bus whenever he has to get around, generally falling asleep with his mouth hanging open and missing his stop at least twice. There's no reasoning with the man, though. No matter how many times I try to persuade him it would be more efficient to use one of the many cars he has on hand in his garage, he refuses to budge on the matter.

"How do I get pulled over by the cops if I'm riding a goddamn bus? How do I get caught for some stupid small shit like speeding, only to get dragged down to the station on an outstanding warrant, if I'm minding my own damn business at the back of the Q54, huh, Cuervo?"

He calls me Cuervo because he thinks I'm ignorant to the fact that it means crow in Spanish. He has no idea how I spent my time in juvenile detention, though, my adult-sized legs concertinaed beneath a child-sized desk as I pored over high school AP Spanish textbooks, mouthing the translations to phrases, verbs, adjectives and nouns silently as my eyes hungrily skipped over the pages. I'm pretty much fucking fluent these days.

"You won't have to come looking for me," I assure him. "It's perfect. It's last year's model. No problems with the head gasket on this one, I promise. And even if there was a problem, you could always take it into a service center. It's less than a year old. I'm sure it's still under warranty."

The broad, mildly overweight Mexican man now leaning against the driver's side door shoots me a withering look that's made lesser men turn tail and run in the past. He doesn't say it: *how am I supposed to take a car into a manufacturer's service center if it's been stolen and I don't have any of the paperwork?* He just lets the look hang between us for a moment, searing into me, doing the talking for him. I'm probably getting sunburn from the intensity of his glare.

"Funny man," he says eventually. "I always forget how funny you are. And then you show up here and remind me, and I find myself wanting to forget all over again."

"That's a little harsh."

He shrugs. "You're funny. I'm harsh. We all have our crosses to bear." I follow him as he leaves the metallic blue Land Rover I've boosted for him and heads into the back of the garage, where his office is located. I've spent half my life in places like this—mechanic's shops, choked with car parts, everything covered in grease, stinking like sweat and cigarette smoke. Jericho's place is unique, though. There are no pictures of naked women on the walls. Not one single poster. According to Raul, Jericho has seven older sisters who raised him after his mother died, and as such he won't hear a bad word spoken against a woman. He beat a guy with a tire iron once because the guy in question called a hooker standing outside on the street corner *puta*.

Inside Jericho's office, he gestures for me to have a

seat. He turns his back to me while he opens up his small wall safe, entering digits into a keypad hidden behind an old photograph of a stern looking Mexican dude with a moustache in full military dress. Porfirio Diaz. I know the guy's name because I made the mistake of asking Jericho about him once. Forty minutes later, I'd been well educated in the history of Diaz, including the fact that he served seven full terms as president of Mexico. He died in 1915. Jericho doesn't appear to have gotten over the tragedy of it just yet.

I can hear him counting to himself as he retrieves my payment for the Land Rover. My phone goes off in my pocket but I leave it where it is. Jericho and I are on good, if a little spiky, terms. He's a guy that demands your full attention, though. Texting in his office would no doubt be considered disrespectful on my part.

"There," he says, turning around. "Twenty thousand. I don't have any small bills I am afraid."

Great. Hundred dollar bills are a nightmare to get rid of. Try to pay with a Benjamin in most of the establishments Jake and I frequent and you'll get a suspicious look in the very least. At worst, the bill will be returned to you and you'll be told to go break it somewhere else or they'll call the cops. Still, money is money. It's not like I'm planning on spending it anyway.

I take the small black carrier bag he's holding out to me. "Any idea what you might like next? And don't say a fucking Tesla." I don't normally grumble, but fuck. That's all he seems to ask for, and those cars are virtually impossible to misappropriate.

Jericho half closes his eyes, thinking deeply by the looks of things. "Ferrari. Bugatti," he says slowly. "Sports cars. I have people asking me for sports cars."

"No one drives a Bugatti in the city. What would be the point? The average speed a car travels here is fifteen miles an hour and that's if you're lucky."

Jericho shakes his head sadly, skirting around his desk, which is overflowing with paperwork and empty takeaway coffee cups. He descends the two steps from his office and meanders in between the sleek fleet of expensive cars that are parked on his garage floor. "You asked me what I would like and I told you. Do I expect you to bring me a Bugatti? No, I do not expect you to bring me a Bugatti. I expect you to bring me a Prius or some other bullshit."

Cheeky motherfucker. "I have *never* brought you a Prius."

"And so what? Perhaps it would be easy to sell a Prius." He looks indifferent as he points me in the direction of the exit. "You'll bring me something I can sell, I'm sure. Thank you for stopping by, Cuervo."

When he smiles at me, I notice for the first time that he's had some dental work done: a gold-plated grill over his top row of teeth. On his grill, the word: *Arrepiente.*

Repent.

******

Twenty grand in a black plastic shopping bag. Twenty grand, banging against my shinbone as I walk across the Brooklyn Bridge. The long struts of the support wires look like long, skinny fingers stretching up towards the sky. The sun's been down for hours already, and the thick layer of clouds overhead break occasionally, revealing the brief, sharp pin prick point of some unknowable star. It's so cold, the air hurts as I draw it into my lungs. I think about a lot of things as I cross the bridge.

I start by thinking about what I'm going to do with the money swinging from my hand as I walk towards home. It would be really easy to flag a taxi down and pay to be taken to my front doorstep once I'm off the walkway, but I know I'm not going to. The cold feels like it's restarting my heart, and walking always helps to clear my head.

Jacob. I could give the money to him. He has student debt up to his eyeballs just like everyone else, and struggling to make it as a musician in New York is pretty much the same as struggling to make it as an actor in Los Angeles. Nine times out of ten it just ain't gonna happen. If I give the money to Jake, though, he's going to want to know where I got it from. He's too curious. He'd never be satisfied with the knowledge that it's his to do with as he pleases, no matter where it came from. There would be questions, questions I obviously won't be able to answer. We'd end up arguing or falling out, and neither of us need the drama in our lives right now. If I had a sibling, a brother or a sister, I could give them some of the money. I wallow in the strangely comforting idea of having an older brother to look up to. A younger sister to protect. Only those who are born as only children can know and understand the longing most of us have for a brother or a sister. I'm an adult, and even now I wish things were different.

I think about Lola, the last girl I fucked. Would I spend any of this money on Lola if we were *still* fucking? Probably. I'd take her for dinner. Maybe buy her some flowers. I'd do clichéd, pointless things like take her to see a movie, and afterwards we'd get steaming hot salted pretzels from a bodega near my place. Would we disappear off on a plane to South America together, to adventure through Argentina and Patagonia? Abso-fucking-lutely not. She wasn't that kind of girl.

Bicycles zip past me in blurs of blinking red bike lights and puffy black down jackets. I don't hear their bells ringing. I listen to a heavy rap playlist on my phone, earphones blocking out the world, and I have one of those bizarre, out-of-body, *how-is-this-my-life?* moments.

It really is a surreal kind of life, y'know. Weird, unexpected things happen all the time. Twenty grand continues to thump against the side of my leg as I walk across the bridge, taking my time, in no hurry, even though everyone else seems to be rushing like their lives depend on it.

It takes me two hours to get back home. I find myself staring up at the building from the sidewalk, considering the yellowed light that's on in the living room, shining out into the darkness. My father's voice echoes inside my head, worn out and frayed a little, as though he can't really decide why he's even bothering to ask me the question he then posed. *Why, Rooke? You have everything you could ever possibly need. Why would you do it? Why would you steal someone's car?* The bastard wasn't really mad I'd been caught stealing. He was embarrassed that I'd been caught stealing cars specifically, that I'd committed such a pedestrian crime. If I'd been discovered red handed insider trading or performing some other white-collar misdemeanor, it would have been less humiliating to him.

"*Because cars are a solid,*" I'd told him back then. "*You can mistreat a car. You can drive it too fast. Too dangerously. You can scratch the paintwork. You can crash it into a guardrail. You can set it on fire, until it's just a burned out, unrecognizable shell.*"

My father had paled at how uncivilized I'd turned out to be. Him in his fresh pressed, snow-white shirts and the set of seven plain, conservative ties he rotated through depending on what day of the week it was.

I knew it even then; I was never going to please him, no matter what I did. He wanted conformity. Obedience. Respect.

And all I wanted was something I could fucking destroy.

SEVEN

MOTHERFUCKER

ROOKE

5 Years Ago.

Goshen Secure Center

"You've lost weight."

I look at my mother, sitting across the other side of the table from me, and I have to literally bite back laughter. What does she think this is, the motherfucking Ritz Carlton? "I'm in juvenile detention, Sim. The food here is dog shit. The guards aren't exactly giving out seconds either."

"All right. No need to be rude."

There's every reason to be rude. I told her not to

come. Back when they locked me away in here eighteen months ago, I told her very fucking specifically not to come and see me. She's adhered to my wishes all this time, so why the fuck has she shown up now? I know my mother is an attractive woman. I've had friends tell me they want to fuck her my whole life. So having her come here, where my cell mates have nothing to do all day long but try and find ways to get underneath each other's skin, is just fucking perfect. Honestly. I know exactly what's going to happen the moment I walk back onto the block. Someone is going to say something. Someone's going to make some kind of suggestive comment about my mother, and I am going to murder them.

"Where's Dad?" I ask quietly.

"He couldn't get away from work, I'm afraid. This is a very busy time of year for him, Rooke. You know that."

Yeah. I know. I know that she wouldn't have been able to drag him here kicking and screaming if her life depended on it. Richard Blackheath is a stubborn man. If he says he intends never to see you again, you'd better believe he's going to be ghosting you for the rest of your natural life. I shake my head, laughing under my breath. Sim pointedly ignores me. "Your grandfather wants to visit you, though. He wants to come every other week and play chess. I told him you wouldn't want him here, but—"

"He can come."

She looks shocked. "He can come, but I'm not allowed?"

"*He* won't look at me like I'm a criminal when he occupies the chair you're currently sitting in."

Sim sighs. "You *are* a criminal, Rooke. How am I supposed to be looking at you?"

"I don't know. Like I'm your son? Like I'm a human being?"

She fiddles with the clasp on her purse. Unshakable

Sim, shaken. She's probably thinking about her own work she must get done when she gets back to her office. Either that or just counting down the seconds until she can leave. "I'll let him know," she says. "In the meantime, is there anything I can do for you? I can try and talk to Judge Foster. See if he can—"

"*No.*" The word snaps out of me like a gunshot, violent and loud. Leaning against the wall ten feet away, Rawly, one of the nicer guards, puts his hand on his nightstick, giving me a warning look. "No. Leave me in here," I say. "I don't want your help. I just want to finish this, get out and start over again. That's it. No appeals. No more lawyers. No more judges. Just *no.*"

She doesn't understand. I can see it in her eyes. "Okay. If that's what you want..."

"It is."

Nodding, she pushes her chair back from the table, clearing her throat. "I added some money to your commissary account. You should be able to get whatever you need, whenever you need it."

She doesn't have access to my inmate trust account, so she can't see that I haven't spent a cent of the money she's loaded onto my EZ card. There's over two grand sitting on the damn thing right now. Impressive when you consider that you're only allowed to deposit a hundred bucks at a time. I'd rather give the money away than benefit from it myself. I'll go without smokes, snacks and all that other bullshit before I let her think that she's somehow taking care of me in here.

It's rare that a family member leaves before the end of visitation, but I don't try and stop Sim. I refuse to ask her to stay. She gives me an almost apologetic look, then walks from the visitation room, her heels clicking loudly as she goes. A number of guys follow her with their eyes as she passes their tables. I try not to notice. I hate the woman most days. I will resent the fact that she didn't try and defend me when the cops came to arrest me until the day I die. But fuck. She's my mother. It feels like having razor blades dragged down my back to have these bastards checking her out the way they are right now.

Rawly escorts me back through a series of long, winding, narrow hallways with one hand on my shoulder. "Don't let it faze you, kid," he says. "Even my parents are assholes."

I say nothing. He slams the door closed behind him as soon as I'm safely deposited back on my block, and then it's just me and them—thirty other teenagers who beat their high school teachers, set fire to municipal buildings, or stole cars and torched them like I did.

For the most part no one fucks with me in here. I have a short fuse, so everyone steers clear. Everyone except Jared, that is. Jared Viorelli, eighteen, serving three years for assault. He's as tall as me. As broad. As quick to temper. Maybe that's why he will not quit trying to fuck with me. He feels like he has a point to prove. He sees me from the other side of the room and gets up from the game of poker he was playing, heading straight for me.

"Don't start, Viorelli."

"What?" He smiles, flashing uneven teeth. "I just wanted to congratulate you. I saw your mamma on the wa—"

My fist connects with his face before he can even finish his sentence. I knew it was going to happen. I fucking *knew* it. I could have bet money that it would be Viorelli making the comments, too. My knuckles split open as I hit him again. Blood sprays across the bleach-clean tiles and Viorelli goes down, hitting the ground hard. I hear the satisfying clink and bounce of one of those uneven teeth of his as it flies out of his mouth.

"Ahhh! Fuck you, Blackheath. You are a fucking dead

man." Viorelli turns his head and spits blood. Rawly's back, then. He lays into me with his nightstick, striking me square between the shoulder blades, and I drop to my knees.

"Down, down, down! Get down on the ground, Blackheath!"

I oblige him, because laying on the ground is far more enjoyable than another blow from the hollow piece of steel he has in his hands. Jared continues to spit and swear and curse me out, but I don't hear him. The sound of the other guards' thundering boots as they hurry to help Rawly detain me is missing. I'm deaf to the whoops and cries of the other inmates. In my head, all is silent. All is peaceful. Strange how violence is the only thing that will calm the raging storm inside me these days. I feel like I'm fucking drowning in blood and I don't seem to mind one bit.

Jared continues to scream threat after threat at me. I smile at him as I'm bodily lifted from the ground and carried away; my smile spreads even wider when I see that it's not just any tooth I've knocked out of his head. It's his two front teeth.

That's right, motherfucker. Prod an incarcerated guy about his mom. See what fucking happens.

EIGHT

INTERLOPER

SASHA

Two glasses of Sauvignon Blanc into book club, the doorbell rings. Alison, Kayla, Tiffanie and Kika are arguing over James's anti-hero status—is he or is he not a redeemable character—and none of them have seemed to register the *otherness* of the doorbell ringing. We're all here. We're not expecting anyone else, and I'm shot through with a wave of anxiety. This isn't good. People don't just walk up the steps to my house and ring the bell. The place is too imposing and severe from the outside for sales people to ever try their luck shopping their wares, and, after many years of curt "no-thank yous" and slammed doors, the Jehovah's Witnesses know better.

"Did you hear that?" I ask the question incredulously, my eyes wide, hand tightening around the stem of my wine glass. Ali looks up from the battered book in her hand, arching an eyebrow at me.

"Hear what?"

"The doorbell. The doorbell just rang."

"It did?" Confusion appears on her face.

I nod.

"Well go and answer it then, you weirdo."

"Definitely not. I'm going to ignore—" The bell rings again, almost intuitively, as though whoever is standing out there on the front doorstep knows my game and doesn't plan on letting me get away with it.

"For god's sake, Sasha, just go and answer the door. And grab another bottle of that Ridge & Sons white while you're up, would you? We seem to be out over here."

I get to my feet, unsure about what will happen next. It's been a really long time since I've interacted with people in this kind of setting. I have no idea how to be polite anymore. I'm just as likely to scream at whoever is at the door, as I am to invite them inside for a cup of coffee. My hand shake is back as I reach out for the door handle. I'd hoped that maybe this interruption to book club was a case of neighborhood kids playing knock-a-door-run, but I can see this plainly isn't the case as I observe the dark, tall shape waiting to engage me in some way on the other side of the frosted glass.

I open the door with my heart pin-balling around the inside of my ribcage—the most unpleasant, worrying feeling. And there, waiting grimly on the doormat, is a face I didn't think I'd be seeing again. Rooke Blackheath? Oscar's grandson? He looks older than he did under the stark strip lighting of the museum's hallway. His hair is slicked back again, and he's wearing a black button-down shirt with the sleeves rolled up, revealing a confusion of colorful ink on his forearms. Black jeans. Black boots. No jacket. There's a bottle of red wine nestled in the crook of his right arm. Who the hell shows up to a house at eight thirty in the evening in November, in New York, without a jacket? What the—

He smiles sharply, angling his head to one side, as if he's waiting for me to say something. When I don't, he shrugs one shoulder and sighs, looking off to the left, down the street.

"Rooke?" I manage.

"Yes, my name is Rooke," he replies. "Well remembered." He points the bottle of wine at me accusingly. "You're Sasha."

"Sasha. With an A. No H."

"I didn't say it with an H."

I snatch the bottle of wine out of his hand, stepping through the doorway and out of the house. "You did. I could hear it," I snap.

His face contorts, like he's trying not to smile. "My apologies, then. Ask me inside."

I blink at him, utterly bewildered. "Why would I do that? I'm hosting a book club here tonight. It's not...*wait, how do you even know where I live?*"

A cloud of fog billows into the air as Rooke laughs. I'd forgotten about his loud, unashamed laugh. I can feel it in the soles of my feet. He holds up his other hand and in it is *The Seven Secret Lives of James P. Albrecht.* "Your address is inside," he informs me. "On the..." He turns the book around and flips back the front page. "...*Bleeding Hearts Book Club* sticker that's pasted inside. It also has your name and a best telephone number to reach you at. I thought showing up unannounced would be better than spoiling the surprise, though."

"Where the hell did you get that?" I try to grab the book, but I'm grasping onto his bottle of red and I'm also still holding my own glass from before, so the action is entirely impossible.

"You threw it at me in the hallway remember? Outside my grandfather's office?"

"I didn't throw it at you. I dropped it."

"Could have fooled me."

"You should have returned it if you found it."

"I am returning it. I'm returning it *now*. At book club."

"Sasha, who—" Footsteps thud down the hallway, and then Ali is peering over my shoulder, trying to get a look at Rooke. He seems extremely entertained by this whole situation. "*Who* is your friend, Sasha? Jesus, young man, you are not wearing a coat. You must be freezing. Come in before you die of pneumonia."

"He's not going to die of pneumonia. He's going to go home before—"

Ali gasps, shoving me to one side. Her eyes are locked on the novel in Rooke's hands, and she looks pleased as punch. "Wait a minute. Did you read this? Are you a new member of book club? Say it ain't so."

Rooke grins, slapping the book into his palm. "I did read it. I hoped Sasha might let me join the group. She doesn't seem very happy I'm here, though."

Ali rounds on me, her jaw almost scraping the floor. "No. No, no, no. You're not making this poor guy go all the way home in the cold with no coat on when he's read the book and he wants to join book club. *What the fuck is the matter with you?*" There's an awful lot being said in that "What the fuck is the matter with you?" She thinks Rooke is hot. She thinks I've been holding out on her. She's severely distressed that I don't seem willing to let him inside the house, and she's also threatening physical violence if I don't.

Basically, I am screwed.

Slumping, I lean back against the doorjamb. I'm

suddenly exhausted and unwilling to spend anymore time trying to figure out how this bizarre situation has come about. "All right. Fine. Come in. But this is a book club. There will be lots of questions about the book. You're going to be in trouble if you haven't actually read the thing." I plan on making sure of it.

He just smiles, nodding his head as he walks into my house like he's been here a thousand times already. "Don't you worry yourself," he says over his shoulder. "I'm ready for you."

******

"The first kiss scene. What did you think of that?" Kika asks, leaning forward across the dining table toward Rooke. "Wasn't it just *so* romantic?"

I wait for Rooke to look uncomfortable. I wait for him to say something stupid. I've been waiting for the past thirty minutes while the girls have each taken it in turns to stump the guy, if only out of pure surprise that he is here, and he's done nothing but eat cheese and answer all of their questions easily and without embarrassment.

"Romantic?" he asks, chewing. "It wasn't romantic. It was awful. They were down some dark, stinking alleyway. There were garbage bags spilling out of the dumpster, and there...oh my god. The rats!"

"The rats!"

Kika and Rooke say "the rats" at the same time, both of them laughing, and I want to punch a hole through the table. Who the hell is this strange alien creature who has invaded my comfort zone, and when, pray tell, is he planning on leaving? I would love to know, but I can't ask because all four of the other girls appear to be completely smitten.

"How *old* are you?" Kayla asks. She sounds perplexed,

like she can't wrap her head around this young guy sitting at the table with us, spreading Roule onto garlic and herb crackers and drinking Pinot Noir like he's some kind of goddamn grownup.

"I am twenty-three years old," he answers. "Nearly twenty-four, if you want to get technical."

God. I remember the days when I actually wanted to round my age up, too. Seems like forever ago. Kayla presses her hands flat against the dining table; it's a weird thing to do, almost as if she's trying to stop herself from reaching out to touch twenty-three-year-old Rooke. "That's a great age," she says, giggling. "I was dating this amazing keyboard player when I was twenty-three. He told me his band was going to be huge. He had the worst mullet *ever*. I believed him, though. I let him go down on me at the movies and my mother and father were sitting in the seats in front of us. It was really hot, and pretty fucked up."

"Kayla!" Ali looks stunned. "No way you did that."

"I did so. Jeffrey Saunders. My dad told me if I married him, our children would be mentally compromised and we wouldn't be allowed to use the beach house in the Hamptons on account of Jeffrey's Depeche Mode tattoo, so I dumped him."

I watch the conversation ping pong around the table, the girls firing questions at Rooke, Rooke answering confidently, as if being grilled by three women in their mid-thirties isn't daunting to him at all. It's certainly not how I assumed book club was going to go this evening, that's for sure.

"What do you do for work?" Alison asks.

"I'm a watch maker. Actually I should say I *repair* antique watches, but sometimes I get to make watches too. If something is too broken to fix, or the owner never returns to collect their watches, then I can cannibalize parts to create something new."

"Why would someone not return to collect their watch?"

Rooke speaks around a mouthful of cracker. "They die. Old people own antique watches. They have a peculiar knack of dropping down dead a lot of the time."

Silence falls over the table. Then, one by one, the girls all start to titter into their wine glasses. Who *are* these people, and what have they done with my friends?

"Did you go to college?" Ali asks.

Rooke shakes his head. "No. I was on track to admission at MIT, but then I got arrested and that goal kind of went up in flames." He says it so matter-of-factly that I almost forget to process it. *But then I got arrested...*

Alison gawps. "Why were you arrested?"

Rooke's been careful not to glance in my direction— I've been paying specific attention to how many times his eyes meet mine across the table—but now his gaze flickers to me and remains on me, and I get the feeling he's uncomfortable for the first time. "I did something stupid. I took something that didn't belong to me."

"What did you take?"

"An Audi R8. I stole it from the parking lot at the Yankee Stadium. I crashed it into a cop car parked outside a Rite Aid in the Bronx a couple of hours later." This time no one laughs. Rooke doesn't seem to care. Or perhaps he just doesn't notice. He takes a healthy slug of his wine. "Don't worry. No one was hurt. I was a stupid sixteen-year-old kid who was angry with his father. I've grown up since then."

Sixteen years old seems very young, but it was actually only seven short years ago for Rooke. I take a deep drink from my own wine and clear my throat. "Why don't we discuss the end of the book? Isobel decides to keep the baby. Who else thought that was pretty reckless on her part? James is hardly father of the year material."

"I actually think it was the only way they were going to be able to stay together," Rooke announces. "James was still too hard. Too damaged by the things that happened to him when he was a kid. He loved Isobel, but it was only a matter of time before he did something to fuck up their relationship. As a father, he had to get his shit together. In his mind, he couldn't *ever* let down his own child."

No one speaks. Slowly, Alison leans across the table and asks very gravely, "Rooke? Are you gay?"

"No. Do I seem very gay?"

Alison tilts her head to one side. "It used to be easier to tell, y'know. I'm not so sure these days. Even straight guys spend an awful lot of time doing their hair. But no, you don't seem very gay."

"Is that a good or a bad thing?" He seems genuinely interested, not in the least bit offended that she's asking about his sexuality.

"It's neither. I just don't know that many straight twenty-three-year-old males who like to read romance novels. Let alone any twenty-three-year-old guys who've taken the time to analyze the storyline so much."

"I'll admit, it's not a genre I'd get caught dead reading typically."

"Then why did you read it? Why did you come?" I ask. I can't help myself. It's the first thing I've said in a while, and it feels like my cheeks are blazing. For a moment, everyone is looking at me like I have three heads and no nose. Rooke sets his wine glass down and just...*looks* at me.

"I read the book because I wanted to know more about you. What interests you. What excites you. What turns you on. I came here tonight because I wanted to see you again. Okay?"

I stand. My legs are shaky, barely able to support my

weight. "No. It's *not* okay. How could you think it would be?" I don't think I'm going to make it out of the room before I burst into tears. My eyes are stinging, burning, blinding me. I bang my hip on the doorframe as I hurry to escape and pain spirals through me like a jangling set of keys. Taking the stairs two at a time, I don't stop my frantic scramble until I'm in my bedroom, my back pressed up against the sealed door with my heart banging manically in my chest.

No one follows me.

No one calls out my name.

NINE

DUE DILLIGENCE

ROOKE

People always say they want to know the truth. They make big speeches about how important it is to them and they harp on about the consequences of deceit, but when they're faced with the truth, they suddenly don't want it anymore. The truth requires you to be brave. The truth requires you to face awkward situations. The truth requires you to stand your ground, to bear it, not run away and hide from it.

That's what Sasha did. She ran. I have no idea why, either. It would have been very easy for her to tell me politely that she isn't interested in pursuing a romantic relationship with me. Fuck, I wasn't even suggesting we *have* a romantic relationship. I don't know her. I don't know the first fucking thing about her. I was merely trying to change that. I was also just giving her a straight answer to her question. I could have lied to her, made up some bullshit excuse for coming across town to come see her, but it would have been pointless. Why else would a guy read a fucking romance novel that a beautiful woman dropped in front of him?

Downstairs, I can hear Jake playing guitar. He's pretty fucking good, been playing for as long as I've known him, and that's coming up on ten years now. He gets morose when he plays, though, so I give him his space and stay in my room. I'm not in the mood to make friendly, unimportant conversation anyway. I'm *brooding.* My mother tells me I've perfected the art, but Sasha Connor is causing me to really master my technique. How can she be so closed off? Fair enough, she's older. Eleven years, to be exact. But what the hell does her age matter? She's a beautiful woman, and I'm seriously fucking attracted to her. There's something about her, some look or smell or idiosyncrasy of hers that keeps gnawing at me, demanding I think about her, and I can't put my finger on it. It could be something as simple as her perfume. It could be the way her lips purse as she forms her words. It could be something more complicated, like the way her pupils fix and dilate as she listens to me speak. It's plaguing me day and night, and I fucking know myself. I'm not going to be able to let the idea of her go until I understand why I'm so drawn to her. To do that I need to know everything there is to know about her.

I open up my laptop, galvanized. If she won't sit down at a table with me, I'm just going to have to do things the underhanded way. Facebook. Twitter. Instagram. MySpace, if she used to have an account. I'll ransack every single social media profile she has online if I have to. I'll trawl through her awkward family photographs. I'll run her name through a search engine. I won't stop until I find what I'm looking for, and when I do find it, that one thing that is drawing me so intensely to her, I'll jettison it from myself and I won't care about the woman anymore. That will be that.

Only, Sasha has no Facebook account. No Twitter or Instagram, either. How can that even be possible? In this day and age, everyone has a handful of social media profiles. Everyone. Even Oscar is on Instagram and Snapchat; the old boy has the funniest fucking feed I've ever seen. So how can Sasha be a complete non-entity online? It must be a mistake. I try Facebook again, scrolling through the profile pictures of a million Sasha Connors before I finally have to accept defeat and give up.

Google has nothing on her, either. She's like a goddamn ghost. I'm about to give up altogether when I'm struck with a bolt of inspiration, however, and I decide to type in her name along with the museum's name:

Sasha...American Museum of Natural History, New York City.

One point eight million responses returned. Well shit. That's a lot of responses. There are only three links that look like they might be relevant, though. The link at the very top is an academic article about a deep space exhibition that was held at the museum nearly six years ago. Sasha Varitas, though. Wrong name. I skip over that and click on the second link down: *How species adapt and evolve. A new theory of evolution that has scientists rethinking the engineering behind the human eye.*

The internet connection up here isn't stellar. As my laptop thinks about loading the page, I take a swig of the beer I've been nursing for the past hour. When the information appears on the screen in front of me, I don't bother reading the text. I scroll down, down, down until I hit the bottom of the page, on the hunt for referencing data, or maybe even a photograph of the contributing author. Sure enough, just as I'd hoped, a tiny professional headshot of Sasha stares back at me from the screen. Her dark hair is much shorter, almost cropped into a boy cut, and she's wearing a slash of bright red lipstick that pops against her pale, smooth skin. Her mouth is pulled into a quirky, strange smile that makes it look like she has a secret she's trying to keep. Her eyes are sparkling in a completely unfamiliar way.

Sasha Varitas, head curator at the Natural History Museum, recently released her debut novel, *Biomechanics and the Origins of Man*. She will be signing copies at The Red Letter bookstore in Tribeca this Thursday, 17th September from 7pm.

Huh. So she *was* called Varitas. She's divorced, then. That surprises me. It shouldn't—she's old enough to have been married and gotten divorced, but it just never occurred to me. She doesn't look her age. She seems younger than she actually is, I suppose.

Sasha Varitas. Sasha Varitas. I type that name into the toolbar of the search engine, and this time I'm rewarded with an entire page of results. Page after page of results, in fact, and all of the links have Sasha's name in them.

Curator at the AMNH in tragic accident.

Sasha Varitas, 29, loses son in fatal collision.

Christopher Varitas, 6, drowned. Mother and father said to be distraught.

Car topples from Brooklyn Bridge. Woman rescued from submerged car, while son drowns.

My eyes scan over the results, the back of my neck prickling with sharp pins and needles. This is fucked. Like, *seriously* fucked.

At approximately 7:50 a.m. today, a woman driving her young, disabled son across the Brooklyn Bridge to the Carl

Gallson's School for the Profoundly Deaf was struck by a large refrigerated vehicle, launching her sedan through the barrier and sending it crashing into the water forty feet below. Motorists claimed traffic stopped immediately, and onlookers crossing the bridge by foot were screaming in panic. Local harbor patrol officer, Keaton Banks, happened to be on the river and close by at the time of the accident, and saw the whole thing take place. With little thought for his own safety, Banks entered the freezing East River and proceeded to dive down to the submerged vehicle.

One woman informed CWT News that she was convinced Banks was dead. No one surfaced from the water for a full ninety seconds. Crowds of dismayed bystanders are said to have been openly panicking and crying at the scene. Eventually Banks appeared with the body of a young woman in his arms. Banks then focused on keeping both himself and the intermittently conscious woman above water while his patrol vessel moved into position and performed a rescue.

Police trawlers recovered the submerged vehicle late this afternoon and confirmed the discovery of a deceased child inside the back seat. The victim has been named as Christopher Allan Varitas. Christopher's mother, Sasha Varitas, is currently recovering in the hospital, having sustained a serious head injury, broken collarbone, and a number of fractured ribs. Banks was treated for mild pneumonia and is set to be released from the hospital within the next twenty-four hours.

Father of the deceased child and husband to Sasha, Andrew Varitas gave a moving statement outside the hospital this evening, thanking Keaton Banks for his heroic actions. Mr. Varitas openly wept as he asked news crews and photographers to please respect the family's request for space in order that they might be able to grieve the death of their son.

Police have identified Reginald D. Whitson as the driver of the refrigerated truck that collided with the Varitases' car on the bridge, and have also confirmed that Whitson fell asleep at the wheel. Many motorists driving on the bridge have reported that the large ten-wheel truck was swerving erratically in the moments before the accident. It's yet unknown what recourse will be taken against Whitson, though State's District Attorney Helen Underwood advised us earlier that in cases such as these, penalty to the full extent of the law is nearly always pursued.

I scan the article, looking for a date, and I find what I'm searching for at the very bottom of the page. June, 2012. Five years ago. Fuck. Sasha lost her son five years ago in what sounds like the most fucking awful ordeal imaginable. Being hit by a huge truck, tumbling from the bridge, hitting the water and probably watching her son drown? Holy fucking *shit*. Doesn't get any worse than that. My chest feels like an elephant is sitting on it; it physically hurts to breathe. I don't try to overcome the feeling. I want to know it, to experience it, so I can understand. If I can feel just point one percent of the pain Sasha felt the day she lost her son, I might be able to understand her now.

I can't hold on to the pain for too long, though. It's too great to bear, even this small, microscopic, far removed part of it, and I have to shake it off. I close my laptop and set it down on the bed beside me.

How did she recover from something like that? How? It seems inconceivable that a mother could ever heal from such a brutal, tragic event. And even before all of that, her son was deaf? How did she cope with *that*? How did having a son who couldn't hear affect her life?

Suddenly, I think I understand why I've been so drawn to Sasha since I met her last week. The knowledge hits me hard—a very real, very disturbing thing. I'm drawn to that hollow look in her eyes. I'm drawn to the sadness of her, the way she seems to visibly throb with it, even when nothing about her suggests she might be unhappy. I'm attracted to the dark ache in her soul, because it's something I can understand. Something that feels real to me.

Seriously fucked up shit.

TEN

TOO LATE NOW

SASHA

I've never believed in god. Not even when I was a little girl and my mother used to take me to church every Sunday. Religiously. Pun most definitely intended. I liked the atmosphere inside the church—the smell of the incense; the echoing ring of people stomping snow from their shoes in the vestibule; the low susurrus of chatter before the priest appeared to give his homily; the way the light took on a different, syrupy kind of texture as it slanted down onto the pews from the great stained glass windows overhead. Mary, Mother of God, weeping over all of us. Jesus Christ, savior of the world, guarding his flock of lambs. Saint Peter, weeping for the sins of the wicked. I never really invested in the stories I heard there, though. Never took them on board.

As I got older, the atmosphere inside the church underwent a tragic metamorphosis, and the chatter just turned out to be gossip. The stomping off of snow in the vestibule had the ominous crack of gunshots, and the priest's homily made me progressively angrier and angrier each week. Weren't Christians meant to be kind and saintly? Weren't they meant to preach acceptance and forgiveness, not fear and hate? And I began to understand what I was being taught in Sunday school. I read the Bible, and it didn't make any sense to me. There were parts of it that were good, of course. I loved the bits about leading a morally good life. I knew it was right to respect your elders, to always be honest, to share and help and be kind always. But the other stuff? An unknowable deity living in the sky? An eye for an eye? Stoning and hell? Eternal damnation and punishment?

If I'm to believe everything the Catholic Church told me when I was growing up, my six-year-old son is now languishing in purgatory, never to know true peace or happiness, because *I* didn't have him baptized. Andrew wanted to get him baptized purely to please his own very strict Catholic parents, but I'd put my foot down. It had seemed stupid to participate in some outdated ritual merely to appease two people we only saw once a year at Christmas.

I didn't put my foot down when we had Christopher buried, though. I was too weak and broken to even register what was happening really, and so he was committed to the ground at St. Thomas's Catholic Church, five blocks from the house, less than a week after he drowned. I have to pass St. Thomas's on my way to work every single damn day. Not today, though. I leave the house and I cross over to the other side of the street, turning right instead of left. I don't ever cross the Brooklyn Bridge. I don't ever take the ferry, so I'm left with only one option to transport me to Williamsburg: the train.

The sound of the casters on the tracks numbs me quite nicely. By the time I reach my stop, I'm actually feeling better than I did when I woke up this morning, which is impressive given where I'm headed and what I'm about to do once I get there.

I *hate* apologizing. It's strange to admit that there were benefits to being locked in such devastating grief, but it's true. There *were* benefits. One of them was that I never had to apologize for anything. Late. Upset. Dirty. Hair a mess. Rude. Drunk. You name it. All sins are forgiven when you lose a child. I didn't have to say I was sorry for any of it. Time has past now, though, and those rules don't apply anymore. Alison made sure to tell me so last night, after she made everyone leave and came up to my room. Apparently, you have to start apologizing after five years of getting away with blue murder. Apparently, apologizing is what a sane, responsible, functional member of society would do, so here I am, trudging grumpily toward an antique watch repair shop in Williamsburg, wondering what the hell I'm going to say to Rooke.

I'm sorry I made you feel unwelcome in my house? I'm sorry I shouted at you? I'm sorry I ruined book club, and I'm sorry I didn't say sorry immediately last night when I acted so inappropriately? It's going to feel forced, that's for sure. He was uninvited, and he only came to create a spectacle. I still don't like that he did that.

The sky is a weary gunmetal grey over the rooftops of Red Hook as I slowly drag my heels toward what feels like my impending doom. I keep turning over the coins in my coat pocket, pressing the pad of my thumb against their flat surfaces, trying to count them as I walk. I also keep imagining Rooke's face when I walk into his place of work, though, and the smug sense of satisfaction I know I'm going to feel is very distracting. He's not expecting me. Now the shoe is on the other foot, how is *he* going to react?

The shop front of Lebenfeld and Schein Antique Jewelry, Watch Repair & Curios is just about what you'd expect it to be—dimly lit interiors behind windows that are caked with at least a couple of decades' worth of grime. Faded gold leaf lettering spells out the long, convoluted shop name, and the paintwork—rust red— that must have looked quite flashy back in the day is chipped and flaking all over the place. The glass is cold underneath my hand as I place my palm against the door. I don't just want to bull my way in here without planning what I'm going to say first. It will look rather pathetic if I saunter in like the cat that got the cream, only to open my mouth and for nothing to come out. I could quickly tell him that I feel bad for shouting at him and I could leave. Short and sweet, straight to the point. That would be the smartest thing for me to do, then I can get to work and this whole ridiculous debacle will be over.

"If you stand there much longer, my dear, your hand is going to freeze to the glass." I turn around, quickly removing my hand and stuffing it into the pocket of my pea coat. A tall, strangely dressed black man stands behind me, brandishing a takeaway coffee cup in one hand and the straps of a Louis Vuitton bag in the other. Balanced precariously on his head, a fawn skin bowler hat is knocked to a jaunty angle, and a faux mink stole is wrapped snugly around his neck, folded under his chin. He flashes me a million-dollar smile. I'd like to say I gather my wits about me and return the gesture but the truth is that I open my mouth and gawk at him.

He laughs. "Under normal circumstances, I wouldn't

mind a lovely door ornament such as yourself, sweetheart, but sales haven't been great this month and I'd really like to pay my rent. If you'd like to come on in, I'm sure I could find something very pretty for you to compliment that ivory skin tone of yours."

"I'm actually just...I'm actually looking for someone."

The smile slides off the guy's face like butter from a hot knife. "Oh, lord. Well you really had better come in then." He squeezes past me, shoving the door open with one hip, his bag clanging against the glass, and I'm left frozen to the spot, wondering if I can gracefully make an escape without looking too odd. In the fantasy where I showed up to Rooke's place of work, embarrassing him and making *him* feel uncomfortable, there was no flamboyant shop owner involved. Now I have to apologize to Rooke, passive-aggressively making him feel bad at the same time, while a fantastically dressed stranger oversees the proceedings? This is not ideal at all.

I step inside the shop, instantly hit by the musty, very familiar smell of old furniture and books that appears to be the same, no matter which antiquities store you may find yourself inside.

The guy throws his bag onto a chair behind a worn, ancient looking desk and takes off his coat. "I'm Duke," he says. His tone implies that I should somehow already know this piece of information. "And since my boy Rooke is the only other person who works here in this emporium of wonder, I assume it is he you're looking for? Oh, shit. He hasn't gotten you pregnant, has he?" Duke wrinkles his nose, shaking his head. "That would be very unfortunate."

"No, he hasn't." Should I be offended that he looks relieved when I tell him this? I suppose I'd be relieved if I were in Duke's position, although it cuts a little. "I just wanted to talk to him briefly, if he's around. I promise it won't take a moment."

Duke eyes me with open, burning curiosity. "The place is already lit up and open. He must be in the back. Let me go and find the boy for you. In the meantime, have a look around. You never know what you might find." He disappears through a moth-eaten velvet curtain into what I'm assuming is the back room, and I nervously pace the floors, waiting for him to return with Rooke.

The shop is a strange, strange place. Duke called it an emporium of wonders. I'm not sure I would go that far, but it certainly does boast some bizarre and unusual things: a Victorian era style porcelain-faced doll, whose eyes have worn off; a very creepy taxidermy of some kind of creature, half monkey, half sea monster; a replica statue of the Tin Man from the Wizard of Oz; an entire shelf of dusty tincture bottles with peeling, yellowed labels. *Cocaine Toothache Drops. Instantaneous cure! Dr. Wilson's Finest Worm Syrup. Robertson's Heroine Hydrochloride Cough Elixir, guaranteed to calm your cough in moments!*

Yeah, no joke. Heroine hydrochloride? I'll bet that did calm coughs in moments. And also render patients generally unconscious or dead.

As I wander around, peering into the vast cabinets of rings and necklaces, running my hands over the shelves, turning things over in my hands, trying to figure out what they are, I can't imagine Rooke in a place like this. His presence here wouldn't make any sense. With his slicked back hair, so closely shaved on the sides, his neck tattoos and his pressed hipster shirts, his leather jacket and his bad attitude, I just can't seem to bend his persona in my mind to fit inside a quirky, unusual place like this. He should be a barista in a pretentious DUMBO coffee shop. He should be a clothing designer in a co-op workspace in Tribeca. He should be a photographer, or some kind of beat poet.

"Sasha."

The sound of my name stills my hand on the cracked snow globe I was inspecting. Rooke's voice is hushed in the narrow, cramped space of the shop, but it seems to fill the place up from top to bottom, settling heavily into the corners of the room. I turn around and he's standing in front of the velvet curtain with his hands in the pockets of his ripped jeans. Seconds ago I couldn't wrap my head around the idea of him working here. It's funny how an idea can alter so rapidly in the space between heartbeats. He *does* belong here. The relaxed, calm way he holds himself says he spends long hours here. This is his natural habitat. It doesn't matter that Lebenfeld and Schein Antique Jewelry, Watch Repair & Curios is packed to the rafters with antiques and curios that are probably three or four times older than Rooke. He fits in here in the most unexpected way that I can't seem to put my finger on.

"Hi." I just stand there, staring at him. There's a good fifteen feet of space between us, not to mention one very tired, beaten up desk, and yet it feels like he's looming over me anyway. He smiles incredibly slowly, averting his eyes as he looks down at the floor.

"I kind of remember you screaming that you didn't ever want to see me again less than twelve hours ago. You can see how you showing up here might be a little confusing."

I nod slowly. "I can see that. I guess I just..." All desire to embarrass him and make him feel bad goes out of the window. I look at him properly for the first time since we met in the hallway outside Oscar's office, and I can tell he's holding his breath a little. He's arrogant. He's a bully in a lot of ways, but he's also a twenty-three-year-old just trying to figure out his shit.

"You just...what?" he asks. "You came here to apologize for yelling at me?"

"Yeah. I did. I'm sorry."

Rooke shakes his head. "It was a dick move, showing up at your place like that. I should have *acted with a little more decorum*." He speaks as if he's borrowing the words from someone else, as if he's heard that phrase a couple of times before. "I promise I won't show up unannounced again." He rocks on his heels, giving me a tight smile.

"I'm not...I'm not even used to talking to guys anymore, Rooke," I rush out. "It's not something I've ever been good at. And you're..."

"So young?" The look on his face is bitter now.

"Yes. You *are* young. A hell of a lot younger than me. You coming to the house, you having read that stupid book...and then saying what you did...it threw me off balance for a second. Okay, more than a second. It threw me off balance until just now, actually."

Rooke sighs. He leans forward, placing his elbows on the desk, resting his chin on his fists. He's wearing yet another black button-down shirt, this time in washed out faded denim. I pay more attention to his tattoos this time; it looks like there are a pair of matching compasses on the undersides of his forearms, both etched in black with intricate geometric patterns spiraling out from them. "Well, I'm glad to hear you're not suffering from vertigo anymore," he says softly. "What happened a second ago to make the room stop spinning? Just to settle my curiosity."

I force out a faintly nervous laugh. He seems so serious right now that I don't know how to take him. "I just realized that, I don't know...I was being stupid. You're not a threatening person. You're harmless. You're just a young guy, having fun, and for a really brief moment the idea of *me* was probably interesting to you."

He stands up straight, his back rigid, his brow creased all of a sudden. "I have more than a five second attention span, y'know. I'm not a child, Sasha. I'm not some adolescent who gets distracted by shiny, pretty things every other second of the day."

I've offended him. "I didn't mean it like that. I just meant that you're a guy, and you're hardly going grey, are you? I know what it's like to be twenty-three, Rooke."

He folds his arms across his chest. I try not to notice how strong and corded with muscle they are, or how ridiculously big his biceps are. "What was it like when you were twenty-three?" he demands.

"Well. Guys seemed to take a lot less care of themselves than they do these days."

"I mean what were you doing? You'd finished college, right?"

"Yes."

"And you'd had serious relationships with guys, right?"

My stomach rolls unpleasantly. "Yes."

Rooke tips his head to one side, studying me intensely. "You were well on your way to being married, I'm betting. You probably already owned that fancy house of yours. Were you working at the museum when you were twenty-three?" I don't answer him. I don't want to admit that he's right. About any of it. He sees the truth in my eyes, though, and he continues. "And you're here, making out that I'm incapable of maintaining focus for more than a minute? I think you've just forgotten what being twenty-three is like. If this was eighteen sixty-three, I'd probably have been married for seven years, and I'd have three kids."

"If this was eighteen sixty-three, your poor wife would have to put up with you sleeping with three or four mistresses and she wouldn't be able to do anything about it. And you'd also probably be dead from syphilis."

This seems to amuse him. "So now I'm riddled with STIs?"

"I didn't say that."

"I'm not. Just so you know."

"Good for you, Rooke. Good for you." Our conversation seems to be taking a turn for the worst. I felt magnanimous toward him a moment ago, but I'm feeling less and less generous as the seconds tick by. How old does he actually think I am? How can he say I've forgotten what it's like to be twenty-three? That's fucking preposterous. "Anyway. I'm sorry I shouted at you, okay?" I say in a clipped manner. "I have to get to work now. Goodbye, Rooke."

"If you don't think I'm a threat, you won't mind going on a date with me then, will you?" He casually tosses the words out there, stopping me in my tracks as I head for the door.

"*What?*"

"A date, Sasha. Dinner, specifically."

Frustration bubbles inside me. "I'm not an appropriate target for you to set your sights on, I promise you."

Defiance sparks in his eyes. "Because you're ten years older than me?"

"Because of a lot of different reasons. Too many reasons to even list. I have to go, Rooke. I'm already late. I—"

"You're scared."

"What?"

"You won't agree to go on a date with me because you're scared."

"I'm *not* scared. I'm—"

"Terrified? You must be if you're railing this hard against a free dinner with an attractive guy."

"My god. How do you fit your ego through the doorway each morning?"

"Don't change the subject. Go to dinner with me, Sasha. Tomorrow. I'll behave."

I can't believe what's going on right now. How he

thinks he can goad me into a date with him is sheer madness. But then, a part of me admires his determination. Most guys would give up. Most guys would walk away. Rooke appears to be cut from a different cloth.

"Tomorrow," he repeats. "*Come.*"

A red hot flush slams into me, prickling all over my body. Why was the way he said that so sexual? I open my mouth to say no, I definitely will not go out with him, but I catch the challenge in his eyes. He's daring me. Actually *daring* me to be brave enough, the smug bastard. "Okay. Fine. I'll go to dinner with you. But after that, this stops, okay? No more turning up to book club. No more coming to the museum. Now if that's all, I really have to go. I'm going to be la—"

He holds up a hand, cutting me off. "*Go.*"

I spin on the balls of my feet and I bolt out of the door before either one of us can utter another word. The cold slaps me in the face as I step out onto the windswept street, but I barely feel the sting. My cheeks are already on fire, anyway.

ELEVEN

Walk. A. Way.

Rooke

"**C**an I just say, I think that went *remarkably* well?"

"Shut up, Duke." I watch Sasha disappear from view, her long, chocolate-colored hair swaying from side to side as she marches off down the street, and I clench my jaw. *Oh you were right, baby girl. The idea of you is* very *interesting to me.*

"Are you even going to tell me who that delicious young woman was, or are you going to leave me rudely hanging?" Duke asks, taking a sip out of his coffee cup. His eyebrows are so high on his forehead that they're almost hitting his hairline.

"Her name is Sasha Connor." I refuse to give him any more information without a fight.

"Mmm. She seemed very cross," he remarks. "What on earth did you do to her?"

"I returned a book she lost. And I brought her a bottle of wine."

"Terrible. *Terrible* manners," Duke purrs. "How *could* you be so uncouth?"

"My thoughts exactly."

"Come on, boy. Sit yourself down. Burning a hole in the door isn't going to help anything now, is it? She's already gone, and my legs are tired. Why don't we take a load off while you explain this interesting turn of events to me in a little more detail?"

"There are no more details. I returned the book. I took her the wine. I ate some of her cheese. She shouted at me and told me to leave. That's all there was to it."

Duke pulls a knowing face. "The cheese. You shouldn't have touched the cheese."

"A grave error on my part, clearly."

******

Jake looks at me like I'm completely out of my mind when I explain what happened after work. I sit at the bar of the Beekman Hotel, stabbing a cocktail stick against the cool, polished marble, and he paces back and forth, trying not to laugh by the looks of things.

"You? *You* went to a book club? For *romance* novels?"

"I did."

"I knew you were up to no good the other day. I fucking *knew* it."

"All right, all right. Fuck you, man. No need to enjoy this quite so much. Give me another double." I slide my glass across the bar at him. He shakes his head, grinning, as he up-ends a whiskey bottle into my empty glass.

"You're a sly dog, dude. So what kind of baggage are

we talking about here? You said she had 'stuff' going on. 'Stuff' is never good."

"Her kid died." I throw back the whiskey quickly, slamming the glass down on the counter. I don't want to look at Jake. I've already anticipated the expression on his face, and I don't want to have to deal with it. Or defend the course of action I'm already planning out in my head.

"Rooke…"

"I know, okay. It's fucked up. *She's* probably fucked up."

"How did she tell you? About the kid?"

"She didn't. I looked her up online. It was all over the internet."

"Nope. No fucking way. You are never going to see this woman again, dude. She's too old for you, and she hasn't even told you about some majorly dark shit in her past. I can't let you do it. Walk away. Seriously, look at me. I'm not fucking joking. *Walk. A. Way.*"

"Okay." I give him a sickly sweet *fuck-you* smile.

"Goddamnit. You're such a bastard. Why are you even interested? You've got chicks slinging pussy at you from every direction every time you walk out the front door of the house."

"Has it ever occurred to you that a pussy that's being *slung* at me is pussy I might not want to enjoy?" I tap my glass, asking for yet another refill.

"So ungrateful. Some of us can't get any pussy, slung or otherwise. And you're out there, chasing down unobtainable, damaged pussy. That's pretty fucking rough, dude. And, I mean, how? She told you it's never gonna happen. And you're still planning on going back to some sexy book club for desperate housewives? You're fucked in the head. I don't know how you can even pretend to read that shit."

"I'm not pretending. I'm reading it."

Jake steps back from the bar and holds his hands up, shaking his head again. "Do you need an intervention? Because I can totally organize one. It's my favorite fucking thing to do. I promise, I'll make it a good one."

"What's wrong with a dude reading a romance novel?"

"*Everything* is wrong with a..." He trails off, looking around, as if he's searching for someone to back him up. Sadly for Jake, the hotel bar is deserted. "I just want you to listen to yourself for a moment. Listen really hard. You're talking about a thirty-four-year-old woman. A woman who's been married. To someone else. She had someone else's kid, and that kid fucking *died*. How can you think chasing after this person is a good idea? I am really trying to understand your thought process, but it's just completely and utterly fucking beyond me. You gotta help me out here, man.

I stare down at my hands, clasped around the rocks glass I'm holding, which seems to be lit up from the inside with luminous, glowing amber liquid. "It's simple," I tell him. "There *is* no thought process. It's just what's happening, and I'm okay with it."

TWELVE

LA CUCINA DEL DIAVOLO

SASHA

I'm nervous. I'm actually weirdly nervous. I may have been reading romance novels for years now, but it's been so long since I really thought about my own love life. This is by no means an ideal date situation; after all, my date for the evening is only twenty-three years old. Honestly, this whole thing feels like a bit of a joke. I feel like this is a prank that's being played on me, and for some reason I'm actually going along with it, even though I can see how ridiculous it all is.

I pick out a gold sequin dress and my favorite black heels, and I apply enough makeup to make a Kardashian proud. I wear some gold hoop earrings, surprising myself when I find that the holes haven't closed up—it's been over a year since I remember wearing jewelry—and as I

94

survey myself in front of the full-length mirror in my bedroom, I'm shocked. Looking at my reflection, I see how little I've changed in the past five years. I'm a different person since Christopher died. Beyond different. I'm not even the same species of human being I used to be before the accident. It seems odd that I should appear on the outside, for all intents and purposes, like I haven't even aged let alone transformed in the most monumental of ways.

I slowly brush a loose curl back behind my ear, studying myself. What does Rooke see when he looks at me? A stranger to win over? An older woman to charm? A challenge to overcome? A broken shell of a human being, easy to take advantage of? I don't even know what he sees, but his interest seems out of the ordinary.

I do something then that makes me question my own sanity. I head downstairs, directly to the liquor cabinet that Andrew always used to keep locked, and I take out a bottle of vodka. I crack the lid, hold the cool, beveled glass rim of the bottle to my lips, and I drink. This isn't just a shot of Dutch courage. This isn't even two or three shots of Dutch courage. This is a defibrillator to my heart, the alcohol burning intensely as it flows down my throat, gathering in a pool of fire in the pit of my stomach. I'm good at drinking like this. I'm really fucking good at it. When Christopher died, I became an expert, in fact. For long months, I would stand in the small downstairs bathroom with a bottle of something strong and inappropriate pressed to my mouth, chugging back the liquid. Andrew never said anything. He never remarked on the fact that I was literally stumbling through my own life like a disheveled, half-dead stranger. A padlock simply showed up on the liquor cabinet door one day, and that was his none-too-subtle hint that I had taken things too far.

The thing about Andrew was that he never thought outside the box, though. Alcohol lives in the liquor cabinet, ergo if he locks the cabinet, I can't drink anything. He didn't take into consideration that alcohol could be kept in a pantry. Or in a shoebox. Or under the kitchen sink, where he was never likely to look.

My drinking problem never really came to a head. It just fizzled out slowly, along with the rest of me. After so much time fighting to even get out of bed in the morning, finding the energy to drink just became too hard.

I don't seem to be having any problems now, though. I only stop pulling at the bottle when my head begins to buzz on the inside. I screw the lid back onto the bottle and put it back into the cabinet, then straighten out my dress like nothing ever happened.

The doorbell rings at five minutes to seven. He's early—a good start. I answer the door, trying not to stumble and roll my ankle in my heels. Rooke's dressed all in black—ripped jeans, another smart button-down shirt with a black crest stitched onto the breast pocket, and a pair of highly polished black leather shoes. His eyes are dark and stormy when they meet mine; I can't decipher his expression beyond the fact that he looks angry. He holds out a small, understated bunch of flowers. Nothing so obvious as roses. The blooms are simple and pretty, wild flowers, the kind that would be really hard to get in the middle of winter in New York.

I take them from him, holding them absently to my nose—they smell beautiful. I don't even know when I last had flowers in the house. They remind me of funerals. These, however, are too fresh, too innocent to bring back memories of the grand lilies, irises and orchids people had delivered to our doorstep when Christopher died.

"I'll put these in water." I head quickly to the kitchen, placing the flowers in a tall glass and filling it with water.

Rooke follows me into the house. I can feel him standing behind me, his presence searing at my skin. I know he's watching me; I can feel his eyes burning into my skin. The hair on the back of my neck stands on end.

"You look beautiful, you know," he says quietly. "So fucking beautiful. That dress..."

I turn around, leaning back against the sink, taking a deep breath. I need to calm my nerves. "It's nothing special," I say.

Rooke gives me a critical look. "Oh, but it is. *You're* wearing it." He's looking at me like he can see right through the damn dress, which makes me shift uncomfortably.

"Don't," I tell him.

"Don't what?"

"Look at me like that. It's not part of the deal."

"The deal where you get through the next few hours, and then you demand I never contact you again?"

"Yes."

Rooke sighs quietly, looking around the kitchen. "You and I both know that deal is bullshit. You're going to see me again, Sasha. You're going to want to see me again real soon."

Oh, he's going to be sore when he realizes I'm serious about that deal. I keep my mouth shut, though. It's just dinner. Like he said, I can get through the next few hours. I can. Just because he's the hottest guy I've ever laid eyes on doesn't mean I'll be dropping my panties for him and waiting for him to call me every day. I'm sure that's what he's used to, but not this time.

Rooke's voice is even and calm when he speaks. "Bring a coat. I'll be walking you home, and it's cold out."

"You're not walking me home."

"I fucking am."

"I can get a cab."

"I know you can, but you're not going to. I'm walking you back, and I'm going to kiss you right here before you invite me inside for coffee. We both know coffee means sex. From the look on your face, you obviously don't think that's going to happen, but I can guarantee you...it *will*."

I have to bite back stunned laughter. "You are *so* full of yourself. How did you end up like this? So damned sure of yourself all the time?"

He shrugs, scratching at his lip. The action makes me focus there, on his mouth; I know my eyes linger a little too long, but I can't seem to force my gaze in another direction. "Experience," he says slowly. "Lots and lots of experience in getting my own way. I'm a spoiled rich kid, after all." He licks his lips, and I can feel blood rushing to my cheeks. He did that on purpose. *Asshole.* "Are you hungry?" he asks.

"Sure." I'm not. I have a belly full of vodka. Vodka and butterflies. The bitches are drunk.

"Good." Rooke crosses the kitchen, then offers me his arm. "You know how this date thing works, right? You don't shout or scream at me in public. We enjoy a nice meal together without you trying to sabotage the night at every turn."

It would be so easy for me to snipe back with something caustic and awful right now, but he looks like he's one hundred percent serious. "I know how to behave on a date," I say.

"Great. Feel free to swoon over me. I know I look good in black."

******

ROOKE

The restaurant I direct our cab driver to isn't one

you'll find on Yelp. It doesn't have a website. You can't call and book a table. Even the president of the United States himself wouldn't be able to get a reservation unless he knew someone who knew someone. There are no huge, grand signs on the outside of the building. There are no doormen standing out in the cold with their collars popped, waiting to tell you that the place is full.

There is only a small blue neon cross lit up on the side of the dark, shadowy warehouse of a building, higher up than the average person would ever look, and a small metal grate in a heavy steel roller door. Sasha looks nervous as we climb out of the cab and into the rain.

"I really don't think there are any places to eat around here," she says. "Are you sure you've got the right address?"

I tip the cab driver and he burns off down the street without so much as a thank you; this really isn't a safe area to be loitering around after dark. If you're connected, though... If you're on the guest list at La Cucina del Diavolo, no one will dare touch you. It just so happens that I *am* on that guest list. When the Barbieri family needs an unmarked car or something fast to get them from point A to B, they have me on speed dial. They pay well, and they pay on delivery, which means I pick up their calls whenever I see their number lighting up my cell. One of the perks of occasionally working for one of the most dangerous families in New York is that I have access to places like this.

Sasha's hand tightens around my arm. She has a wired, hazy look on her face. "I think we should find another cab, Rooke. This is a shitty neighborhood."

"It's fine. I'm not going to let anything bad happen to you. Just hold on for a second and we'll be inside. You'll see for yourself." She's shocked when I walk up to the warehouse shutter doors in front of us—I can see how instantly wary she is. Someone slides back the metal grate in the shutter door, and a grim, sour-faced Italian man in his late fifties eyeballs us, first me and then Sasha.

"Name?" he demands.

"Blackheath."

He doesn't even blink. On the other side of the shutter door, a number of bolts slide free, and then the shutter is flying upward, bathing us in a shaft of pale blue neon light. "Straight through," the Italian heavy says. "Second room. We have a private function on tonight. I highly recommend you don't walk through any doors marked with an X."

"Got it." I take Sasha's hand again and lead her forward before she can object. This is probably scary for her right now, but it won't be for long. Once we're seated and we're looking at a menu, the experience will be a familiar one. A glass of wine will calm her nerves, and then we can get on with the business of the evening.

I head through another heavy steel door, and suddenly the air is filled with smoke and the sound of many conversations taking place at once. The first dining room is packed, full of New York's underground criminal elite. The men wear expensive Italian suits and smoke cigars at their tables; the women are scantily dressed with smoky eyes, dripping with diamonds that even an Arabic sheik couldn't afford. People watch us as we weave through the space, heading toward the back room.

Yet another heavy, studded door...

A long, dark corridor stretches out before us, doors on either side. These are the rooms the doorman warned us against. Small blue crosses like the one on the outside of the building glow dimly by the door handles. Sasha jerks my arm, finally trying to pull me to a stop. "What is this place?" she hisses. "I don't think I'm meant to be here, Rooke. This is a really bad idea."

She really *isn't* meant to be here. This isn't a part of

the city she will have encountered before. No doubt she would never have encountered it if she hadn't run into me. She did run into me, though, and I want her to know about this.

Maybe I'm sick, and maybe I'm deluded, but I've been thinking about this a lot. I'm going to tell her everything about me. I'm going to tell her all of the nefarious, illegal things I've done in my lifetime, as well as all of the nefarious, illegal things I'll probably do in the future. I'm going to tell her all of this tonight as we eat dinner. It'll be a crapshoot. She's probably going to get up and storm out of here without even considering what I'm telling her. But, on the other hand... she might not. She might listen to what I have to say and decide it's not such a big deal. Wouldn't that be a fucking kicker?

"Look. You're one hundred percent safe right now, okay?" I tell her. "I said I was going to look out for you, and I am. If you really want to leave, though, I'll take us to The Cheesecake Factory or something and we can have a perfectly bland, perfectly boring night instead. If you want to try something new, something exciting, then stop worrying and follow me."

It's a risk, asking her to follow me. It's the same as asking her to trust me, and she has absolutely no reason to do that. Not yet, anyway. By the end of the night, that will have changed, but for now...

Sasha glances around. We're alone in the corridor. The blue neon from the crosses on the doors reflects on the gold sequins of her dress, sending showers of pale green light skittering all over the walls every time she moves. Her eyes are round and wide. Her pupils are three times the size they should be. She opens her mouth to speak, then frowns. "Okay. Fine. I have enough problems to contend with. Don't make this another one. Deal?"

"Deal."

The second room is less busy than the first. I've learned over time that this means one of the Barbieri family members must be back here, holding a meeting or having dinner. Booths line the outer edges of the room, all of which are dark and in shadow. There's no smoke back here, thank god. The space smells like food, *delicious* food, and the sweet tang of alcohol. Sasha surveys the polished grey marble underfoot, the waterfalls of light cascading from the chandeliers overhead, and the rows of silverware glinting on the tables. She doesn't look quite so gripped by fear anymore. She's still hesitant, though, that much is very clear.

A waiter in a pristine three-piece suit seats us in a booth. Sasha looks like she wants to punch him in the face and run when he tries to take her purse.

"If you don't mind, madam. It's our policy that all bags, purses and cell phones are checked with the concierge while our diners enjoy their meals. It makes for a safer, more enjoyable evening."

"What do you think I've got in here?" She laughs, but the sound is off, a little hollow. The waiter considers her small gold sequined clutch.

"Well. A berretta would fit in there quite nicely. Or throwing knives?"

Sasha blinks up at him like he's a lunatic. I place my hand over hers, clearing my throat until she releases the clutch. "It's okay, madam," the waiter says. "I will make sure your personal items aren't tampered with in any way." He turns to me, holding out his hand. I place my cellphone, wallet and keys in his palm without saying a word. He bows, and then hurries off.

"Throwing knives?" Sasha hisses. "What the hell? Why would anyone bring throwing knives with them to a restaurant?"

"For protection." Seems fairly obvious to me. I take all

kinds of weaponry with me wherever I go. I left my gun at home tonight, though. It's frowned upon to have something like that with you when you walk through the doors of The Devil's Kitchen. The waiter comes back and gives Sasha a menu, tells us the special, offers us a complimentary glass of Sangiovese, and for a moment everything feels normal. Sasha studies the menu, picks out what she wants, orders, and I do the same. When the waiter removes the menus from the table, I reach inside my pocket and take out a different piece of paper, unfolding it and sliding it across the table toward her.

"What's this?" She studies the printout suspiciously.

"Read it and find out." I grin an evil grin as she casts her gaze over the black ink on the page. I already know what it says: Gonorrhea: negative. Chlamydia: negative. Hepatitis C: negative. HIV: negative. The list is expansive and conclusive. I'm clean as a whistle.

Sasha folds up the piece of paper and hands it back to me, mouth drawn into a tight, unimpressed line. "You think you're so funny, don't you?"

"Actually, I think I'm rather awesome. There's nothing more romantic than a guy voluntarily getting a swab shoved down his dick for you."

"How did you even get that done so fast?"

"Bribery."

She laughs—dry, scathing—as if she's brushing off my comment as an exaggeration. It isn't, though. I paid the technician at the family planning clinic five hundred dollars to process my results overnight. "You and I have very different ideas of romantic, Rooke. This restaurant, for example..."

"You're still bent out of shape that I brought you to a mob restaurant?"

"You brought me to a *mob* restaurant?"

I'm surprised she hasn't figured that part out already.

She has no part in this world, though. No experience. No reference points. She can't be blamed for her naivety. I don't allow my expression to flicker. "I did."

"*Why?*"

"Because I like the steak?"

"*Rooke.*"

"All right. I brought you here so you could see what my life is like. So you know what you're getting yourself into. So you can experience something out of the ordinary. Do you hate it?"

She sits heavily back in her seat, her eyes roving wildly around the room. "Do I *hate* it? What kind of a question is that?"

"A simple one."

"How many of these people in here are murderers? How many of them are criminals?"

"Nearly all of them are criminals. I doubt there's more than two or three actual murderers, though."

It's hard to see if she's gone pale, but I'm getting the impression all the blood has rushed from her face, relocating itself somewhere in the region of those killer heels she's wearing. "Don't panic. No one's going to murder *you* for eating dinner here."

She closes her eyes, mumbling under her breath. "God, I can't believe this is happening."

"You're making a big deal out of nothing. This is a restaurant. They serve good food. The owners are charming, so long as you don't steal from them, and everyone gets along like a house on fire." I neglect to tell her about the time the restaurant *was* actually set on fire. I don't think that information will serve my cause very well.

"We could have gone anywhere. There are literally thousands of amazing places to eat in this city, and you bring me here. And...you gave your name at the door. That guy just let you in, like he knew exactly who you were.

What the fuck was that about?"

"He knows who I am. He knows I work for the owners of this place every once in a while."

Sasha goes quiet. She picks up her butter knife and spins it over and over in her hand, staring at the dull blade like it holds answers to questions she hasn't even thought of yet.

"Ask me," I tell her. She won't look at me. "Ask me the question. Ask me what I do for them."

"I don't want to know."

"Yes, you do."

"I really don't."

"I steal cars. I sometimes drive a car from one point to another, and I don't ask questions about the why, the who, or the where. Do I beat people up? No. Not for money. Do I kill people? No. Am I good at what I do? Yes, I most definitely am. How does this sideline of business affect the fact that I want to date you? It doesn't. I'll never involve you in anything illegal. I'll never put you in a compromising position."

"Apart from this one? Apart from this *incredibly* compromising position?"

"Dinner?" I take a look around. "These people are just enjoying their meals, Sasha. There are no underhanded deals taking place. You're not meeting anyone to discuss state secrets. No one is being garroted at their table, God Father style."

This is a lot to lay on her right now. I could do this another time, but it seems that showing my hand right now is for the best. To hide this from her, knowing how far I want to take this, would be dishonest, and dishonesty doesn't feature amongst my many faults. At least not where the woman I want to forge a relationship with is concerned. The police, my family, most of my friends—they're lied to on the regular.

"This is insane," Sasha whispers. "I can't believe this is happening." She bows her head, gaze locked on the table, as if making eye contact with anyone else in the room could lead to fatalities. I suppose it might, but it's highly unlikely.

"You want to go."

She gives me a sideways scowl. "How would we be able to get up and walk out of here now, without eating our food? It will look suspicious. That would be worse than staying and eating."

"You're being ridiculous. However, if that's the case and you want to stay, you should relax and enjoy the wine. It's really fucking good."

"You know a lot about wine do you?"

She's in full spitfire mode right now. She cocks her head to one side, fixing me in a hostile stare. I can't really blame her for being mad at me. She probably wants to chew me out for admitting to what I do to supplement my income, but she's a smart woman. We're in the viper's den. Shouting at me for working for the Barbieri family would be supremely ill advised when sitting in the Barbieri family's restaurant. So this is it: she's going to rail against anything else I say to demonstrate how utterly pissed off she is with me. I sigh, putting down my glass.

"I know enough to know what tastes good and what doesn't. Am I not supposed to know anything about wine because I'm just a kid?"

"You're barely old enough to drink."

"I'm nearly twenty-four, Sasha."

Two waiters arrive, brandishing plates under cloches, white cloths folded over their arms. Our conversation grinds to a halt as they serve us our food and top up the wine. As soon as they're gone, I plant my elbows on the table and lean closer to Sasha, talking in hushed tones.

"You think the amount of days I've been alive on this

planet has any real bearing on how well I can fuck you? You think the date on my driver's license means I won't be able to make you come? That I won't be able to love you? That I won't be able to make you happy? If that's the case, then *you* are the child here, not me. You're clinging to this age bullshit like it's a life raft that's saving you from drowning, Sasha, when it's the only thing dragging you under. This moment, here, right now...*this* is the only time when our ages will ever really matter. You're eleven years older than me. Accept it. Let it go. You're fighting an unstoppable force, Sasha. I'm growing impatient...and I do very, *very* rash things when I grow impatient."

"A very mature response."

I take another sip of wine, enjoying the texture of the liquid in my mouth. "I'm going to take you across my knee and spank you soon. Is that what you want? In front of all these people?"

"You wouldn't fucking dare."

"Oh, I really fucking *would*. And no one here would mind watching, I assure you."

She bristles like a scalded cat. "This bravado thing really is a little crazy. If you're trying to impress me with how manly and domineering you are, it's not working. I can see right through the charade."

I smile. I smile like a man who knows something. I smile like a man who's just been issued with a challenge. When I don't say anything, Sasha fidgets in her seat, frowning. She picks up her fork and points it at me, stabbing it in my direction. "I'm not playing, Rooke."

"Neither am I, Sasha. *Neither am I.*"

We eat in what some might call tense silence for the next fifteen minutes. I don't find the break in conversation uncomfortable, though. I find it highly entertaining, especially since Sasha looks so goddamn hot with all of that blood flushing her cheeks. The way she stabs her steak onto her fork is admirable. I think she could probably defend herself reasonably well in a street brawl by virtue of sheer viciousness. I'm on the verge of speaking when another waiter approaches the table. Only when he reaches us, it's not a waiter at all, but Roberto Barbieri, head of the Barbieri family himself. Overly thin and overly tall, the guy has always reminded me of a caricature—an exaggerated version of what an Italian mob boss might look like if he were a villain in a graphic novel. And yet here he is, in the flesh, larger than life. He gives me a toothy grin, folding his hands in front of his stomach as he looks down at our half-finished meals.

"Ah! The steak. Yes, we do a good steak. It's wonderful to see you, Rooke. I was beginning to think you'd never bring anyone here to revel in our company. All of my other...*friends*...make good use of this place as often as they can. You, on the other hand..."

I return his tight-lipped smile. "Don't take it personally. I just don't have that many friends."

"Come now. I don't believe that for a second."

"No, it's true. It's his grating personality," Sasha says. "No one can tolerate being around him for more than five minutes at a time."

I can't help myself; I laugh out loud. She must know this guy is no joke. Who else would saunter up to a table and start talking to guests in a place like this? *Especially* in a place like this. And he knows my name... He can only be the boss.

Looks like Sasha Connor is angry enough at me to risk baiting me in front of the most dangerous of men after all. She's a fucking keeper. Roberto smirks at her, nodding his head, amused by her tone. "But you're made of sterner stuff, I see. You've been sitting here with him for at least an hour. It can only be love."

"This is our first date actually. It's definitely not love."

"And yet when you look at him, I see fire in your eyes."

"It might look like fire, but I assure you it's closer to hatred at this point."

Roberto shrugs nonchalantly. "If it burns, mi' amore...it burns."

THIRTEEN

DISASTER

SASHA

Dessert is probably the most perfect panna cotta ever created and yet it tastes like sawdust in my mouth. I swallow down a few bites, and then I discard my spoon, pushing the ramekin away.

"That's sacrilege," Rooke says. He, of course, polished his dessert off in record time.

"I'm not hungry."

"Hold out your hand."

"Pardon me?"

"You heard me. Hold out your hand." He places his own hand face up on the table, reaching for me. I stare at it for a moment. Why should I do what he's asking me? Why should I play along with this game? It's a reckless game, one that could get me incomprehensibly hurt. The very last thing I should do is give him my hand, but I'm tired and the alcohol in my veins is telling me to just give in for a second. It's only a second. How much damage can be done in a second? And we're in a room full of people, besides. It's not as if holding his hand is going to lead to raw, animalistic sex on the table.

I place my hand in his. As soon as our skin makes contact, I realize my mistake. Even in my slightly drunken, numbed state, I can feel the electricity zipping between us. The connection is undeniable. His fingers thread with mine, entangling themselves, and I can feel my resistance faltering. Even after what he's told me this evening, I'm softening toward him, losing myself a little. Without really thinking, I close my own fingers around his, returning the pressure.

"We fit well together," Rooke observes. "I think the rest of us will fit well together, too."

"Rooke, I'm not sleeping with you…"

"Why not? Don't you like fun?"

"I like fun. I love fun. Sex isn't just fun to me, though. It's a commitment you make. With your body."

"Are you super religious?"

"No. I'm just not careless with my body. It has value. If I went around, giving it to everybody, it would mean less and less each time."

He strokes his thumb up and down my curled index finger, and a rush of adrenaline surges through me. It's really crazy how he makes my head spin. "Okay, then. I can understand why you'd feel like that, even though I don't agree with you. But I am willing to propose a solution to this problem."

"Which is?"

"A proposal."

"I get that. But what is it?"

"The normal kind," he answers. "A proposal of marriage."

"Marr—" I can't even finish the word. He can't be fucking serious. He can*not* be serious. Can he? He looks like he is. I try to scoot my way out of the circular booth, going the long way to avoid him, but he still has hold of my hand and he won't let go.

"Where are you going?" he asks calmly.

"Away from you. You're a madman."

"All right, all right. Slow the fuck down. I was joking."

I don't slow down though. I rip myself free of him and I throw my napkin down on the table. I make an entirely graceless exit from the booth, leaving Rooke behind to pay for the meal. He's the one who brought me to this godforsaken place to begin with, so I don't feel in the slightest bit bad about making him fork over the cash for dinner.

I leave the dining area, exiting through the same doorway we came in through, and I find myself back in the darkened corridor. I'm not paying attention to where I'm going. I hurry blindly toward the exit, pushing through a doorway marked by a glowing blue neon cross...

...and I come to a grinding halt.

My mistake is instantly obvious.

Bodies...

There are bodies everywhere, naked, clothes scattered on the floor. The room is filled with a wash of white-blue light that highlights the curve of bare breast here, the arch of a strong, muscular back there. The scene before me is like nothing I have ever witnessed before. I stand frozen, my heart a clenched fist, risen up into my throat. A man turns around and faces me, and I do my best to meet his eyes. It's hard, though... his *dick* is hard, and he's pointing it right at me.

"If you're coming in, bella, close the door behind you."

"Uh—I—I'm not—"

"She's not coming in, I'm afraid. She can't have sex until she's married." A hand circles around the top of my arm, and I'm pulled sharply backwards. I almost stumble, but Rooke catches hold of me, balancing me so I can rush out of the room under my own steam. He pulls the door closed behind us, smirking savagely.

"And here I was thinking you were a prude, Ms. Connor."

"Jesus. There are about a hundred sanitation codes being broken in there."

"Probably more. I don't think the Barbieris need to worry about impromptu visits from the health inspector though, do you?"

A kind of hysteria rises up inside me, gathering me up until I can't even think straight anymore. This is the weirdest date I've ever been on, with the strangest man. I clap my hand over my mouth, trying to stem the laughter that's threatening to burst free from me but it's no good. It escapes me anyway.

"I think someone's drunk too much," Rooke says, leaning his back against the wall, sliding his hands into his pockets.

"Not true. I had just the right amount of wine to get me through this bizarre night."

Rooke shakes his head. "If you say so. But I think you're a little impaired, Sasha."

"I'm not."

"I can prove you are."

"How?"

"I could come over there and kiss you. Sober Sasha would never allow that to happen, right?"

"Damn straight she wouldn't."

He pushes away from the wall, his face growing very, very serious. Oh, god, he's serious. He's actually going to

113

try and kiss me. My laughter dies on my lips. "Don't, Rooke."

He's two feet away from me. One foot.

"Rooke, I mean it. Do *not* try and kiss me."

Less than a foot now. I press myself back against the wall, trying to melt into the brickwork, but it doesn't happen. Suddenly his chest is pressed up against mine, and his hands are on me, gripping my hips, pulling me toward him. His dark eyes are unblinking, locked and loaded, fixed onto me with a passion that makes me want to look away. I don't understand the way he's looking at me right now. It's as though he's been holding back before. As if every other time he's looked at me with that playful, wild grin on his face, that he's only been showing a part of himself to me. Here and now, he looks as if he's unveiling himself, showing me how fierce and dangerous he truly is.

"*Rooke...*" I sound breathless, completely unlike myself. I hold a hand up, planting it in the center of his chest, pushing a little to keep him at bay, but my strength is nothing compared to his. I feel weak and vulnerable, dwarfed by him as he leans over me, his head bowed, forehead only a few inches away from mine.

"We're only going to do this once," he says. "So really think for a second, Sasha. I'm going to kiss you. If you don't want my mouth on yours, my body against yours, then say so now and I will *never* call you again. But if you do want this, if the prospect of my hands in your hair and my tongue in your mouth makes your heart beat a little faster, then all this other bullshit has got to stop. Do you hear me? Do you understand?" He sounds angry. I stare up at him. My hand is still trapped between our bodies, pressed up against his chest, and I can feel the steady, determined tattoo of his heart thumping in his ribcage. I feel like I have a hummingbird trapped inside *my* chest, and it's frantically batting at its cage, trying to get out.

"Yes," I whisper. "I understand."

Rooke bends into me, pulling me closer to him. He leans down, his forehead resting against mine, and I'm paralyzed. Should I stop him? Should I tell him to let me go? It's not until the very last second that I make up my mind. I don't want him to let me go. I want his mouth on mine, and his hands in my hair. I want more than that. God forgive me but I do.

I'm too scared to close my eyes. Rooke's remain open, too. We stare at each other as his lips meet mine. A long moment passes, and neither of us moves. Slowly, Rooke exhales down his nose. His breathing is labored, shaky. I can tell by the sound of it that he's struggling to retain his composure. He digs his fingers into my skin through my dress, and that's it. It's been exhausting trying to keep my distance from this guy. He's taken a lot of shit from me in a very short space of time. Not only that but he's repeatedly come back for more. So I kiss him. I close my eyes, and I melt into him. Winding my arms around his neck, I reach up on my tiptoes and I commit.

He groans into my mouth as I open up for him. He tastes sweet, all the sugar from dessert cut with the tannin of the wine we were drinking. He breathes hard into my mouth as he kisses me, his tongue tasting and exploring my mouth, too, and my head spins out of control. It seems impossible that I should be feeling this swept away. It's been years since I've thought about the magic of a first kiss. This is light years beyond magical, though. It's sublime. It's incendiary. It's apocalyptic. It feels like the world is ending. The sky is falling down. I'm lost to the frantic thrum of my heart, and the feeling of my breasts crushed up against his chest.

I want him.

Damn him, and damn me, too.

This is going to be a disaster.

FOURTEEN

THE TIGHTROPE

SASHA

I fumble, dropping my keys, and Rooke stoops down to get them. I don't feel like my body is my own at this specific moment in time. I'd love to blame the alcohol—it would be easy enough to do—but I don't even feel drunk. I just feel like I'm outside of my body somehow, witness to what's happening but not really participating. Rooke glances through the keys and looks at the lock, then selects the correct key, using it to open the front door.

"How did you know?" I ask.

"I know how things work," he says. "It's my job to know."

Awkwardly, I feel like this is exactly what he has done

with me: taken one long, curious look at me and figured me out. The way he studies things, including people, is quite disturbing. He looks beyond the surface, beyond what you might want others to see, and he delves deeper. I'm not sure that I like that. There are parts of myself I've worked hard to keep hidden. Parts of me that should never see the light of day.

Rooke pushes the door open, standing back so I can enter first. He's a gentleman, I'll give him that. However, as soon as I make my way into the hallway, I'm shoved roughly up against the wall, my purse falling to the floor with a thud, and I'm quickly reassessing that thought. Rooke leans against me, hands on my hips, fingers grinding into my skin, his mouth so, so close to mine.

"Have you ever been fucked in this hallway?" he growls.

"I—no. I haven't—"

"Are you on birth control?"

"Yes."

"Good." He cups the side of my face in his palm, and then he's kissing me. It's not a subtle kiss. It's a kiss wrought from fire and iron. It's a savage kiss that steals my breath and a part of my soul right along with it. I open my mouth, allowing him in, and his tongue skates over mine, tasting me like before. I work my mouth against his, and he groans under his breath. "Goddamn, Sasha. You kiss like we're already fucking," he pants.

I could say the same of him. I don't have the breath to do it, though. I'm winded by the intensity of the moment, of the way his hands feel as they travel all over my body. I can feel how turned on he is. His erection is pressed firmly up against my stomach, and the material of my dress isn't very thick. I've never been so intimidated in all my life. He feels...*big*.

Rooke's hands move smoothly down, until he's

kneading and squeezing at my breasts. I'm not wearing a bra, so it feels like his hands are already on me, working over my skin. He ducks down, kissing my jaw, sucking my ear lobe into his mouth, then going lower still, until he's kissing my neck.

I've seen women in movies before losing their shit over a guy kissing their neck. I've always wondered what they were feeling. When Andrew thought to kiss my neck it was like bird pecks, hard and not particularly pleasant. With Rooke...

God...

My body feels like an electric current is running through it, sharp and furious. I can't stop shivering. He bites down, fastening his teeth over my skin, and I moan, my entire body going limp.

"That's it," he pants. "That's what I've been waiting for." He lifts my skirt, and for three long seconds both his hands are on my thighs, running over the sheer material of my stockings. He looks down, apparently fascinated by the fact that I'm even wearing them, a faint look of surprise on his face, and then he's tearing at them, fighting to unfasten them. He unclips the silk, and then drops to his knees in front of me.

Slowly, with deep concentration marking his forehead, he removes my pumps, left first, then right, and slides the stockings down my legs one at a time. I can't seem to get my breathing under control. My hands won't stop shaking. I can't even—

He cuts off all thought when he pushes my thighs apart and buries his face between my legs.

"*Oh...my...god.*" I'm still wearing my panties, but that isn't stopping Rooke from going to town. His teeth rip and pull at the expensive lace I'm wearing, and my head literally spins.

"You're fucking amazing," he growls. "Fuck, Sasha. You

smell like..."

I cringe. I don't want to smell like something. Smelling like anything is *bad*.

"You smell like sex," he finishes. I want to object, to stop him there, but he's gripped by something I can't comprehend. His shirt strains across his back as he bends down lower, and then he's pulling my panties aside, his fingers exploring me, rubbing, pushing inside...

"*Fuck*!"

"We're getting to that part," he growls. "Patience, pretty Sasha. Patience."

I don't want to be patient. Patience is for people who have sex every day and are bored with it. This is a whole new experience for me. I feel like I've been waiting for this my whole life, for a guy to touch me, make me feel the way Rooke is making me feel, and waiting another second for him to be inside me is a goddamn crime.

He slides his fingers further inside me, curling them a little, and my whole body bucks as he hits an unfamiliar, sensitive spot that makes my toes curl. "Oh, *shit*! Holy fucking—" He stops what he's doing, and I almost punch him in the head. He rips my underwear down my body, though, forcefully lifting my legs so he can toss the lace aside, and then he looks up at me, his mouth open slightly, his tongue wetting his bottom lip, a scandalous smile spreading across his face, and I'm stopped dead in my tracks. The man is sex. Pure, unadulterated, unfiltered sex. From the way he walks, to the way he wears his clothes, to the ink that marks his body... everything about Rooke Idlewild Blackheath screams, "FUCK ME!"

Slowly, and with the most unbelievable look in his eyes, he extends his tongue and traces it in a sweeping upward motion between my legs. It feels like I've been struck by lightning. I'm no longer myself. I'm no longer even inhabiting my own body. I feel like I'm floating on top of an endless, bottomless sea that stretches on and on forever in every direction. I feel like I have to stay absolutely still otherwise I'll drown. His mouth works over me, his tongue flicking and licking at my clit in an expert way—he must have had an awful lot of practice at this—and my legs feel like they're about to buckle out from underneath me. I need to steady myself. I need to hold onto something.

I bury my fingers into Rooke's hair, shamelessly grinding myself into his mouth. He groans—not the sound of a guy simply enjoying something. The way he groans is the sound of someone completely lost to a moment of pleasure, so swept away by it that they don't even realize they're making any noise in the first place. My skin breaks out in goose bumps.

Rooke's a huge guy. He's built like he could take on Connor McGregor. His skin is a network of tattoos that say, "don't mess with me." When he opens his mouth to speak, a litany of arrogance and charm spills from his lips. I never gave myself permission to imagine a moment like this, I never in a million years imagined I'd let it happen—but if I had imagined it, I would have pictured his back pressed up against the wall with me on my knees, pleasuring him with my mouth. I would never have dreamed that he would be so focused on making *me* feel good.

And *fuck* do I feel good.

My dress is still bunched up around my hips. Rooke pushes it even higher, then slides his fingers back inside me again. He uses his tongue and his fingers at the same time, and I can't keep myself together any longer. I need a release. I need to come or I'm going to rip the guy's hair right out of his head.

I can feel it building...

I teeter on the brink of orgasm, balancing on the tight rope between madness and sanity. Rooke has to know I'm about to go spiraling into oblivion. He's in tune with me already, able to sense just how close I am to coming. He fucks me with his fingers, stroking the inside of my pussy in a "come here" motion as he laves his tongue over me, and I'm done for.

It starts at the back of my neck: a tingling sensation, both hot and cold at the same time. The muscles in my arms and legs lock up, and the tingling spreads down between my shoulder blades, my lower back, over my buttocks and down into my legs. It hits me hard, turning inwards next, a moment of pure feeling where I am deaf and blind, completely lost. I think I scream. I think I sink to the floor. I think my back arches to painful degrees as Rooke continues to lick and stroke and fuck me with his fingers until I can't take it anymore and I'm begging for him to stop.

Only he doesn't stop. He carries on, until I feel another wave of intense pleasure building and building, sweeping over me like a tsunami. There is nothing left of me. I'm just particles and atoms, loose limbed and ruined. When I finally regain myself and open my eyes, I find myself laid out on my back on the floor, panting, and Rooke is on his knees between my legs, watching me with a very serious look on his face. He's not cocky now. Not smiling in the slightest.

"What—what is it? Are you...okay?" I pant.

He closes his eyes and looks away for a second; when he faces me, he does smile, but it's a strange, alien smile I haven't seen him wear before. "No, I'm not okay," he answers.

Oh god. Oh, holy shit, he *hated* going down on me. It was the worst experience of his life. A flood of shame rolls around in the pit of my stomach. I snatch hold of the hem of my dress, trying to yank it down my body, to cover myself and my humiliation, but Rooke grabs me by both wrists.

"Don't even fucking think about it, Connor. Don't ever pull that shit with me, okay?"

"What shit?"

"The whole, oh I hate my body bullshit. You're phenomenal."

"But you just said—"

"I said I wasn't okay, and I'm not. I'm fucked. I am completely, one hundred percent fucked."

"What are you talking about?"

"I'm going to have to quit my job. I'm not going to have time to work anymore. I just found my new favorite pastime, and I sense it's not going to leave me much time for anything else. Jesus, Sasha... Making you come is fucking incredible. The way your head tipped back. The way your thighs tightened around my head. The way my name sounded when you were panting it like a motherfucking mantra. I've only heard it once, and I can't live without it now. So yeah... I'm not okay."

"Rooke—"

He shakes his head, cutting me off. "I don't want to hear it. Not one word. You're fucking beautiful. And we *are* doing this again. You know it and I know it. Don't lie to yourself, and do *not* fucking lie to me."

I was going to be self-deprecating. I was going to tell him I didn't think it was a good idea for us to do something like this again. I close my mouth, feeling my cheeks burn. I feel like there's a fire inside me, eating me alive, and it's nowhere near as frightening a sensation as it should be. It feels exciting, more than anything else, and I'm on the brink of throwing myself onto the flames.

"Are you ready for what comes next?" Rooke asks.

"That depends," I answer shakily. "That depends on what comes next."

He straightens, kneeling properly. His fingers begin to

nimbly unfasten his shirt, slipping the buttons through the holes, all the while staring at me with a dark, sinister look in his eyes. "I'm going to fuck you, and it's going to change everything. Nothing will be the same again. The sun won't brighten your days from here on out. *I will.* Gravity won't keep your feet on the ground. *I will.* You won't want to eat or sleep without me. Every second spent away from me will be a second wasted."

Anger prickles at the base of my neck. I curl my hands into fists, ready to pound them against his chest as hard as I can. "*Why?*" I say quietly. "Fuck, Rooke. Why did you have to say that? How can you presume—"

"I'm not presuming anything. It's just what comes next. And I know, because it's a reciprocal thing, Sasha. It's not just you taking this fucking stupid, crazy-ass next step. I will be too. I can feel it. I know what's going to happen." He shrugs his shirt from his shoulders, and the material slides from his body. His chest is solid, carved muscle, covered in intricate, masculine ink. His shoulders are broad; I imagine what it would feel like to cling to him as he pushes himself inside me and my eyes almost roll back in my head.

Rooke begins to unbuckle the belt at his waist. "I'm going to be right there with you. You'll be my sun. My moon. My gravity, and my heart. I'm willing to let it happen. The question is, do you want that? Or...a better question. Do you want to risk *not* having that? This is real, Sasha. You feel that it is, I know you do. And just because it's real doesn't mean it isn't scary. Doesn't mean that we won't argue or disagree. It just means that it can be fucking amazing if we let it."

How can he talk like this? I don't understand what he's thinking. We barely know each other. There would be so many hurdles to overcome if we were to even think about being together in the way he's describing. It wouldn't just be hard. It would be next to impossible. Still…looking at him now, I can see how firmly he believes in what he's saying. Steel flashes in his eyes. His jaw is clenched and locked, every inch of him solid and immoveable.

"I'll ask you again, Sasha. Are you ready?"

My heart is in my throat. I don't know how I can possibly agree to what he's saying, but there's this part of me that wants to throw caution to the wind. I *can* agree with him. What's the worst that can happen? Things don't work out and we go our separate ways? He moves on and starts fucking some twenty-one year old receptionist? That wouldn't be the end of the world. Neither of us would die of a broken heart. It might… damn, it might even be *fun*.

I swallow, pushing down the voice of warning in the back of my head. "Okay. Yes. I'm ready. I'm ready for what comes next." But even as I'm saying the words, I know how crazy I'm being. Rooke's the most intense person I've ever met. There won't be any walking away from him. There won't be any moving on for either of us.

I wait for him to fall on me like some rabid animal—I can tell from the look in his eyes that he wants to—but he doesn't. He climbs painfully slowly up my body, until he's straddling me, his knees either side of my hips.

"You look like you're afraid," he whispers.

"I am."

"You *should* be." He leans down so slowly that I feel like I'm going to scream. His mouth gets closer and closer, and every long second that passes makes me want to reach up and grab him. I won't give him the satisfaction, though. I just won't. When he finally kisses me, I feel like I'm falling through the floor. He tastes like me. He actually tastes like *me*. I should be horrified, but I'm not. It's such an intimate, personal thing. It actually turns me on.

I go to wind my arms around his neck, but he stops me. Raising my hands high above my head, he pins them both easily in one of his huge hands. "I'm sorry about your dress," he growls.

"You're sorry?"

He takes hold of the shoulder strap and rips it, tearing it away from my body. I gasp, a sound of shock echoing around the narrow hallway. He rips the other strap, too, ripping it away from my body in one swift, cruel movement that leaves me breathless and panting. He doesn't stop there. In three quick tugs he removes the dress from me, splitting the material down the front, destroying it in seconds. I squirm underneath him, suddenly unsure of myself. He's fucking crazy. I don't know what to expect from him. He may have successfully figured me out in the most infuriating way, but I've yet to say the same of him. He's so strange and bewildering that I'm left guessing at every turn.

Rooke leans back as far as he can without releasing my hands, and he looks down the length of my body. My breasts are exposed, and my panties are gone, so that I'm totally naked beneath him. He sucks in a sharp, pained sounding breath, groaning a little.

"If you could see what I'm seeing right now..." He trails off, his eyes feasting on my bare skin.

"I do see."

"No, you don't. You won't let yourself. No woman really admits to herself how fucking perfect she is. If you did, you'd spend every waking moment of the day fingering your pussy in front of a mirror, completely in love with yourself."

Just the mention of me masturbating makes me blush. People don't talk about that kind of thing in such a matter-of-fact way. They just don't. It's not polite. Nothing about Rooke is polite, though. He sees that my cheeks are red and grins, tipping his head to one side. "Don't deny it," he whispers. "You touch yourself. You'd be touching yourself right now if I didn't have you pinned."

"No, I wouldn't."

"Yeah, you would. Because I'd ask you to. You'd do it to make me happy."

I can't fault his logic. Right now, I think I would do anything to make him happy, so long as he fucks me. I writhe underneath him, anxiety warring with my excitement when I realize just how trapped I am. I could kick and scream, shout and struggle, but there's no way I'm getting out of this position unless Rooke allows it.

"Open your mouth, Sasha," he demands.

I open up for him without even thinking. This is so new to me. If someone had told me even yesterday that I'd be allowing someone to command me like this, I would have thought they were insane. Where has this side of me been hiding all these years? Why did I not know that I would like this?

Rooke slides his index and middle finger into my mouth, probing behind my teeth, feeling around, opening my mouth wider. It's invasive yet highly sexual. I gasp as he lays himself down on me, licking at my lips, tearing at my mouth with his teeth. He rocks his hips against me, and I can't hold back. I angle my own hips up against him, creating the most intense friction, and I almost panic when I feel how hard he is again.

Scratch that. He's beyond hard. His erection is rock solid. The moment I grind up against him, something inside him must snap. A deep, tense snarl begins to build in the back of his throat. He jumps to his feet, and then he's undressing, toeing off his shoes, unfastening the button on his pants and kicking them wildly from his legs. I'm expecting underwear, but there's nothing. He's going commando. His cock springs free, and then I'm frozen in place, staring at him like a lunatic. He's *huge*. Not, *wow-you'd-really-better-get-me-ready-for-that-thing* huge. I'm talking, *you're-going-to-put-me-in-the-hospital-with-that-thing* huge. *Internal damage* huge. Rooke bends down and picks me up in his arms, as if I'm feather light, a massive shit-eating grin on his face.

"Don't worry, beautiful. It won't bite," he says.

"You do realize I am five foot two? I can't...There's no way I'm gonna be able to..."

"You *will*." He storms off in the direction of the living room, knocking the door open with one hard kick. He lies down on the floor on his back, placing me on top of him. "We're gonna do it this way for a few minutes. That's all you get, Sasha. You get to be in control for a moment while your body learns how to accept me. Once I'm inside you, that's it. *You're mine.*"

A thrill of panic rushes through me. Dear god, this is sheer madness. *How?* How the hell am I meant to—

My mind goes blank as I straddle him. Rooke guides me into place, and I can feel him almost pushing into me. I'm wet already, like, really fucking wet, but there's no way in hell he's going to just slide right on inside me. Rooke's fingers dig into my thighs as I slowly, carefully lower myself onto him.

"Fuck, Sasha. *Fuck!*"

I could say the same thing myself. My head rocks back as I try to breathe around him. I feel impossibly full. I think I'm going to have to stop, but then Rooke eases himself onto his elbows, and he takes my nipple into his mouth. He places his hand between our bodies and begins to rub my clit in small, tight circles and suddenly my body is ablaze. I begin to rock slowly against him, lost in the dizzying sensation that is sweeping through me, and little by little my body does as Rooke said it would. It learns how to accept him.

The very moment he's all the way inside me, he's true to his word. He flips me onto my back, a sharp, jagged-edged smile cutting across his face. "Feel free to scream."

He thrusts inside me, and I go still. There are fireworks going off inside my fucking head. He's everywhere, surrounding me, inside me, on top of me, his hands running all over my body, in my hair, his mouth on mine. The way he kisses me is vital, as though he's filled with the same desperate need I'm feeling right now. The need to consume him, be a part of him, be a part of something else. Something he and I alone are incapable of being, but together…

He fucks me until I forget my own damn name. He's incredible. He angles his hips in the perfect way, so that every time he pushes into me he rubs against my clit, bringing me closer and closer to my climax with every thrust. I hold onto his shoulders, and it's just as I imagined earlier: I feel vulnerable, but at the same time I feel safe.

"You're going to come for me now," Rooke tells me, grinding out the words directly into my ear. "I can feel it. I can feel you getting tighter around my cock. Are you going to come all over my dick, Sasha?"

"Shit. Oh my god, yes. Yes, I'm going to come."

"Good girl. Good girl, that's it. Show me. Show me how pretty you are when you come."

My orgasm is exactly like being sucked out of an airlock into space. I feel like I'm being yanked out of my own body, out of my own skin, and I can't seem to breathe. I dig my fingernails into Rooke's back and he slams himself inside me, and then he's roaring, his teeth gritted together as he comes with me. He crushes me to him, and it feels like we're both melting, fading away somehow. I feel numb.

"Damn." Rooke rolls over, so that I'm back on top of him. He's still inside me, still hard, still making me shiver every time he twitches, which seems to entertain him. He brushes a strand of my hair back behind my ear, then gathers it all up into his hands, holding it behind my head. "See," he says. "Your body knows now. It *knows* it's mine. There's no fucking way you can deny it."

FIFTEEN

HELP

SASHA

Living in Manhattan means I don't get to enjoy the skyline all that often. It seems as though it would be quite similar to living on the moon; everyone else gets to appreciate the silent, luminous, ghostly beauty of your home, viewing it from afar, and yet for you the vista consists of dust and rocks and not much else. Manhattan, from the inside, is just the same as any city: dirty, overcrowded and oversaturated with many different sounds, scents and colors. It's a magnificent place, though. There's something about this city that separates it from all other cities, something that inhabits the air and lives insides the very concrete and metal that forms the foundations of the place. A kind of magic that even the most desensitized, numb kind of person will recognize instantly upon stepping foot inside the boundaries of the city. The idea that people leave New York, that they up sticks and relocate to live in other, lesser places, completely without any magic at all, confounds me on a daily basis.

I still marvel at the street vendors. My blood still hums with a frisson of excitement every time I walk down Broadway. Pride still swells inside me as I look up, my eyes traveling the full height of the Empire State Building. And every time I walk through the entrance of the museum, my heart skips a beat.

It's early still. My body aches beyond comprehension from the way Rooke contorted me into a million different positions while we had sex last night. Every time muscles twinge it's the most delicious reminder of the hours we spent together. I didn't want to come to work. I would have happily stayed in bed and allowed him to explore and use my body however he saw fit for the rest of the day but he had an appointment that apparently couldn't be missed.

The only other people already working at the museum are the security guards. Amanda, a woman in her late thirties who has worked at the museum almost as long as I have, checks my purse at the front door. "Good job, Miss Connor," she says to me. "No guns. No bombs. No hairspray. You are good to go."

She says the same thing every time she checks my bag, and I always pretend to laugh, even though this charade has been going on for years now. I know for a fact she says the same thing to every other female employee that works here. I accept my bag from her and walk into the main foyer of the museum, but I only make it three or four steps before I come to a grinding halt.

The Christmas tree.

I'm always stunned the first time I see it. I had no idea they were erecting it so early this year. I stand in amazement, studying the tall, lush boughs and the pale golden lights, twinkling slowly. The rich smell of pine floods my senses, and suddenly my eyes are filled with tears. Christmas time. Just like any other six-year-old, December was Christopher's favorite time of year. Andrew and I used to go overboard, decorating the house, covering every square inch of the place in holly and wreaths, nutcracker statues and fake snow out of a can. Ever since Christopher died, Christmas has felt like a knife plunged deep into my back. Families are everywhere at this time of year, shopping, eating in restaurants, visiting aunts and uncles, moms and dads, ice skating at the Rockefeller Center, lining up to see The Lion King. I hate it.

"Beautiful, no?" Amanda calls out behind me. "They did themselves proud this year."

"Yes," I say quietly. "It really is lovely." I hurry to my office, gripping hold of my purse so tightly that I lose all feeling in my hand.

******

Thoughts of Christopher, running around in his socks and his underwear, shoulders shaking with silent laughter, Andrew chasing after him, tickle-fingers extended, trying to get him ready for school.

Last night was blissful. For a whole twelve hours, I wasn't thinking about the accident. I wasn't floundering in a deep well of pain, scratching at the walls, trying to hold on to something, to keep myself afloat. Rooke took all of that away. I never would have thought it was possible, but it was. He held me up for a moment. His hands on my body, his mouth on my skin, the feeling of him inside me...there was no room for anything else during those moments. There was only the two of us, the ghosts of my past cast far away, wonderfully absent.

Now, though, they've crept back in, lurking at the edges of my mind. Christopher eating his breakfast cereal at the same table we sit around during book club, playing with his plastic dinosaurs. Christopher sitting on the middle step of the stairs, signing a song he learned at school as I sort through the mail. Christopher watching television, mouth open in silent joy, kicking his feet against the base of the sofa. Christopher, trying to teach the little girl next door how to spell his name in sign language. Each joyful moment is a dagger in my heart.

I carefully open up the top drawer of my desk, my lips pressed together, unable to breathe as I remove the small envelope from inside. I've been putting this off forever, it seems, but now I know I can't. I have to face the past head on, and that means I have to face Andrew. My hands are shaking as I tear open the paper.

Dear Sasha,

Been a while, I know. I'm sorry I've been keeping my distance, but you know... It only seems to make things worse when we speak. I should have probably called with this news, but I'm ever the coward. I hope you'll forgive me, but I just couldn't quite seem to muster up the courage to say the words out loud to you.

Kim and I had a baby. I can imagine how this news is probably making you feel, and I'm sorry, I really am. I thought about keeping this to myself and not telling you at all, but it felt a little deceitful. Anyway, we called him Christopher.

I stop reading, the paper shaking violently in my hands. They...what? They did fucking *what?* Andrew's blocky handwriting blurs as my eyes fill with tears. He had another son? And he called him Christopher? What the hell?

I already know you think I'm a monster. Kim and I just felt like it was the right thing to do, though. I'm not trying to replace him, Sasha. I would never do that—

That's exactly what the bastard is doing. How can he not see that? How can he not see that shacking up with another woman (who looks strikingly similar to me), having a child with that woman and naming that child after our dead son is most definitely trying to replace him? How can he be so blind? So fucking hurtful?

I'm sure a small part of you, deep down maybe, will be relieved to hear that Christopher isn't deaf. We've had numerous appointments at the hospital, and as far as the doctors can tell at this young age he appears to have fully functional hearing. He's a bright, happy baby, Sasha. He's helped to heal the wounds of the past for me. In time, maybe—

I screw up the paper and hurl it across the room. My vision is flickering in a frightening, dangerous way. I feel like I need to smash something, to hurt something, to hurt myself. How can he say that? How can he put those thoughts down on paper? It's so much worse than saying it out loud, because he had to use a pen, write them down so that they exist forever. He thinks I'll be relieved that his new son isn't deaf? That makes it sound like I was disappointed that *our* son was. His disability was never a cause of shame or sadness to me. It made him special. Christopher was brimming over with happiness every day of his life. The fact that he was deaf never held him back. It makes me feel dirty inside that Andrew would even—

Crrrrrrrrrrrack!

I go still at my desk. The loud, abrupt, explosive sound that just rang out, slicing through the thick silence of the museum is still echoing down the corridor outside my office. What *was* that?

It comes again, louder this time.

CRRRRRACKKK!

What...what the hell is happening right now?

I'm suddenly flooded with panic. A gunshot? Can it really have been a gunshot? The logical, sensible part of my brain refuses this possibility almost instantly, and yet the rest of me is beginning to tremble. A gunshot. Someone's fired a gun inside the museum. Someone has a weapon in here. Why? Why would anyone—

"Hello? Is anyone down here?" a deep, slurring voice asks. Whoever the voice belongs to can't be far from my office door. Once the museum is open, the hubbub from the main exhibition areas can be heard in the administration sections of the building all too well. It's so loud you can barely hear yourself think sometimes. Right now, though, with the museum still an hour away from opening, you could hear a pin drop. The sound of boots slowly progressing down the corridor outside my room sends a thrill of adrenaline and anxiety through me.

"Hello? If there's anybody down here..."

I hold my breath. *Don't make a sound, don't make a sound, don't make a sound...*

The hallway fills with the shatter of breaking glass. I clap my hands over my mouth, forcing myself to stay quiet. A second splintering crash of breaking glass comes, closer this time. Then a third. It hits me out of nowhere—it's the frosted glass windows in the office doors. Someone is breaking them one at a time.

"*Fuck.*" I drop down onto my hands and knees,

scooting quickly under my desk. I can't make sense of what's happening. A few moments ago, I was reading, stunned by the callous, cold-heartedness of my ex-husband, and now, out of nowhere, it sounds like someone is stalking through the museum with a gun in their hands. The voice I just heard asking for help didn't sound like it came from a person in distress; it sounded like it came from someone immersed in a very entertaining game of cat and mouse. It sounded mocking and sinister. Every instinct I have is urging me to hide from the owner of that voice.

"Come on, honey. I know you're here. The woman on the front desk said you were the only other busybody in the building. You're ruining my shit," the voice hisses. I can see a sliver of the frosted glass panel in my door from my vantage point underneath my desk; I try not to scream when the shape of a tall, dark figure comes to a standstill on the other side.

"Dr. S. Connor," the voice says. "Why I do believe you're just the person I'm looking for."

Fuck. *Fuck, fuck, fuck.* I try to think, try to scan my brain, to remember what I have sitting on my desk. Any weapons? Anything to defend myself with? No. No, there's nothing. Nothing in my drawers, either. Ali bought me a tiny pepper spray canister to attach to my keys about a year back, but it was clunky and annoying so I took it off my keychain. The sound of smashing glass fills the room, and a gloved hand appears, reaching through the yawning hole in the door, fumbling for the door handle. I can't stop the startled cry that escapes from my mouth. The door isn't even locked. I mean, why would I lock it in a place like the museum? It's supposed to be a safe place. It's supposed to be under twenty-four-hour guard from the security detail. The door swings open, and a pair of dusty brown boots appear in my line of sight. The lace on the right shoe is red, which strikes me as odd, given that the left shoe is laced with black.

"Dr. S, I need a moment of your time," the voice says. "Can you help me out, or am I going to have to *persuade* you to lend me your assistance?"

I do *not* like the tone of this man's voice. I'm beyond scared. How the hell am I going to get out of this? My purse is on the floor next to me, probably knocked there when I jumped up to hide under the table. My belongings are scattered all over the floor—lipstick, hair brush, mirror compact, notebook, a silver pen my father bought for me when I graduated college. My cell phone lies within arm's reach, too. I snatch it up just as the man enters the room, snarling under his breath.

"Stupid cunt," he snaps. "You honestly think I don't know where you are? Get up, bitch. Get up *now*, before I come around there and drag you onto your feet myself."

Slowly, painfully slowly, I inch my way out from underneath the desk. My heart is hammering all over my body, my pulse erratic and crazed. I have only been more scared than this one time in my life. I have only known this kind of terror in the split second before my car hit the water all those years ago, and to feel it again now is stupefying. I can't react properly. I can't think straight. All I can do is get to my feet and hold my hands in the air.

I silently pray that the man wearing the black ski mask in front of me doesn't search me. Doesn't find the cellphone I just slipped into the waistband of my skirt in the small of my back. A for Ali, the first person in my contact list. The first person I thought of. Did the call connect? I would have called 911 myself, but there wasn't time. I barely had time to hit the number one digit—the speed dial number assigned to my friend—on the keypad, followed by the call button.

The masked man steps forward and takes me by the

arm. His fingers are tight as a vice. His breath smells like coffee. "You wanna die?" He sounds intrigued, as if he's actually curious what my answer will be. As if I might say yes, I *do* want to die, for some unknown, unexpected reason. I shake my head, unable to find my voice, and the masked stranger sighs heavily.

"Good. Do as you're told and I probably won't hurt you. Do we have an agreement?"

"What do you want?"

"I said...*do we have an agreement?*"

Panic. Fear. Terror. I nod. "Yes. Yes, we do."

"Great. Now get moving." He gives me a sharp, hard tug, and I bang my hip against the corner of my desk. Pain sings through me and I cry out, but the guy in the mask seems unaffected by my discomfort. I can't see his expression behind his thick black woolen ski mask, but I get the impression that he might even be smiling.

"Take me to the vaults," he tells me.

"Vaults? There are no vaults here."

My head rocks to the side as he slaps me. A bright sting flares inside my head, making my vision dance, and my ears take on a high-pitched buzzing ring. I try to cup my hand to the side of my face, but he still has hold of me and my hand stops short. "Don't be stupid, bitch. We both know this place is stocked to the gills with priceless art and shit. Now take me to the vaults."

"I told you. We don't *have* vaults. I can't take you somewhere that doesn't exist."

He leans forward, looming over me, and I'm gripped by the urgent and pressing need to shrink, to make myself as small as I possibly can. "You have a smart mouth on you, Doc. Don't get too clever, okay? I don't want to have to shut you up for good. Now say you're sorry."

"What?"

"Say you're sorry. For lying to me."

I stare at the blank, anonymous knit of the woolen mask over his face. I stare at the watery blue of his irises, the bloodshot threads of broken capillaries in his eyes, the white crust of dried spit in the corners of his mouth. His lips are thin, spiteful lips that are twisted into angry, narrow lines. "I can't—"

I don't finish my sentence. Lightning strikes me in the head. Or rather lightning bursts out of my head as the man takes hold of me and slams me backwards into the wall. I can't see for a second. A weightless sense of the world tilting settles in the pit of my stomach. I can hear the weird, wet rasp of oxygen trying to get into my lungs and failing.

His hand is around my throat. A strange prickling sensation creeps up around the sides of my head, over my cheeks, over my temples, hot, tight, unpleasant and frightening. Everything all at once. *"Say you're sorry,"* he growls.

"I'm...I'm sorry. I'm sorry. I'm sorry."

"Better. Much better. Now. Take your shoes off." He releases me, and the rush of blood to my head is dizzying. Slowly, I stoop down, removing the black pump first from my left foot and then from my right. I stand in my stockings, shivering despite the heat pumping from the floor vents.

"Let's go, Doc." The man holds my hand like he's my lover. He guides me around my desk this time, pulling me wide of the corner so I don't hurt myself again. His sudden care is strange, given the fact that he just slammed my head into the wall.

Out in the hallway, my stockinged feet skate on the buffed, slippery floor. The man pushes me to the left, grunting under his breath. "What's down there?" he demands.

"En...engineering. The system controls for the entire

museum. Water pumps and…I don't know. Air conditioning units."

He spins me around, facing me in the opposite direction. "And that way?"

"Storage. Old exhibit pieces. The servers for our IT systems."

"What about the money?"

"They take the money off site every night. They drop it at the bank. The night deposit. They don't keep anything here."

"Bullshit."

Something hard and round presses between my shoulder blades. The fear that I experience in this moment is all consuming. It brings me back into myself, making my vision finally sharpen. It's as if the world comes back into focus, growing lighter and brighter all at once. He doesn't want to hear the truth. Telling the truth makes him mad, which in turn causes him to hurt me. I don't want him to hurt me anymore, so I hold my hand up, quickly speaking before he can do anything. "Upstairs. Upstairs, on the fourth floor. They keep a little money up there. And some jewelry. Some of the Egyptian artifacts that were loaned to the museum from Cairo." The museum has never had any artefacts loaned to it from Cairo. There's never been an Egyptian exhibition here at all. The most valuable item in the entire building are the dinosaur remains on the ground floor, probably the most famous exhibition of all, but there's no way for him to walk out of here with a T-Rex tibia, and no way for him to make any cash on it even if he did manage to escape with it. Perhaps he knows this. Perhaps he doesn't. He's quiet for a moment, and then he says, "I'm going to let you into a little secret, Doc. That security guard downstairs? The pretty one with the glasses? I slit her throat from ear to fucking ear. She bled out all over the floor. I watched as she died. She didn't do as she was told, so I had to teach her a lesson. I want you to know this, because I need you to know what will happen to *you* if you don't do as you are told. Do you hear what I'm saying to you? Do you understand?"

The ground seesaws beneath my feet. It feels like I'm on the deck of a ship that's being pitched about in a violent storm. "Yes. I hear you. I understand." I wish I hadn't said the fourth floor now. There are no escape routes up there. There are no easily accessible emergency exits, and at this time of day there won't be any security guards either. There's nothing but meeting rooms and more storage. I may have signed my own death warrant by suggesting we go up there. It was simply the first place that came into my head.

The guy shoves me again, urging me forward. I place one foot in front of the other, holding my breath, thinking frantically. I can feel the screen of my cell phone pressing up against the bare skin of my back underneath my loose shirt. Tucked into my waistband, I know it isn't going anywhere. I have no idea if the call connected with Ali, though. And if it did, I have no idea if she can hear anything that's being said. There's every chance she thought I pocket dialed her and hung up. There's every chance that no one knows what's going on here and I am about to diE.

SIXTEEN

HEARSAY

ROOKE

You get used to the sound of sirens in New York. They are part of the sonic landscape, a staccato punctuation to the rhythm of the city. I remember just after I got out of juvi, I was laying in bed late at night, trying to sleep, and I couldn't drift off. For hours I lay there, tossing and turning, unable to figure out what was troubling me, setting me on edge, until it came to me: there were no sirens. No ambulances. No police. No fire fighters. A heavy mantle of silence rested over the city outside my window and it felt as if time had somehow stopped, and everything was frozen still on the quiet streets below my bedroom window. I held my breath and I waited. The world, despite everything that pointed toward a darker outcome, continued to turn.

That's how I felt when I woke up next to Sasha and remembered I have to meet with my mother this morning—as if some dark, impending sense of doom were hanging over me, and for no good reason. Meetings with Sim Blackheath are always shitty, though. Beyond shitty. If I could avoid them altogether I would, but she's a fucking viper. She loves to interfere, and she loves to show up unannounced to wreak havoc in my life. Ridiculous, but what the fuck. Not much to be done about it. Car thieves have mothers, too. I almost laugh out loud when I imagine telling her about Sasha.

There's ice on the boards as I walk across the Brooklyn Bridge. Ice on the thick metal struts. Ice caked like frosting on the lovelocks clasped tightly around the steel brackets that support the dim Victorian looking lights. Beneath my feet, traffic slowly rumbles, progress marked at a sluggish ten miles an hour. Great clouds of fog billow from people's mouths, and on the other side of the river, in Manhattan, a melancholy chorus of sirens is waking up Wall Street. Unlike that night after I got out of juvi, I can hear them plain as day now over the thump of the music I'm listening to, the thick pads of my (supposedly) noise cancelling headphones keeping the shells of my ears warm. Even so early in the morning, and even with the biting wind clawing at people's scarves and winding its way down the backs of people's jackets, there are tourists planted directly in the middle of the walkway, mouths hanging open in concentration as they try to capture the perfect angle of the bridge soaring up over their heads.

I stop at the halfway point to smoke a cigarette. I've all but given up—I maybe smoke one cigarette a day. Two or three if I'm particularly stressed out. I'm dragging my feet toward my destination, so loitering on the bridge while I burn my way through a Marlboro seems like a prudent way to kill a minute or two. I remove my headphones, letting them sit around my neck as I rummage in my pockets for my lighter.

"...two people. Maybe three. They've been trapped inside the building since seven this morning. Someone saw the body laying on the ground in the foyer."

"Why the hell would someone try to rob the place? It doesn't even make any sense."

Conversation swells around me as I strike the wheel of the lighter and hold the small, guttering flame to the end of my smoke.

"...cops everywhere. The road's closed off."

"My meeting's been cancelled. They're saying there's more than one shooter in there."

My ears prick at the sound of that. *Shooter?*

"I always said museums are dangerous. Crowded. So many people all over the place. A terrorist attack in a place like that would create complete chaos."

"It's not a terrorist attack, Mike. It's just some drunk. They said so on the news."

"Yeah. Right. They're not gonna come out and say it right away, are they? That would create mass panic. They'd tell us after the fact. I heard they found these huge vats of agent orange in a disused subway station last week..."

The men talking move on. I look around, searching the faces of the other pedestrians making their way along the bridge, and it takes less than a second to realize that something has happened. Something bad. I step out in front of two women, businesswomen in thick coats with hats pulled down low over their ears, their shoulders hunched up around their ears, braced against the cold.

"Excuse me. Do you know what's going on? Everyone's talking—"

It's almost as if they've been waiting for someone to

ask them. The taller of the two women nods enthusiastically. "Some psychopath broke into the Natural History Museum this morning and killed one of the security guards. There could be more people dead inside, but the police are playing it safe. They aren't letting anyone in until they've managed to search the entire building."

The shorter, rounder woman with fogged up glasses nods, too. "They showed a picture of the dead security guard's foot on the news. There was blood on the floor everywhere."

She continues to talk, but I don't really hear what she's saying; it's as though my ears are stuffed with cotton wool. The museum? Someone's broken into the museum? *Sasha's Museum?* Words bounce around inside my head. Words like *agent orange*, and *shooter*, and *terrorist*, and *blood*. My hands are cold and stiff as I pat myself down, looking for the familiar shape of my cell phone in one of my pockets.

"Are you okay? Sir, are you all right? You look a little spooked." The tall woman places a hand on my shoulder. I can't even feel the contact through my thick down jacket.

"Yes, I, uh...I'm fine. Thank you." I move out of the way, leaning against the railing as I shrug my backpack from my shoulders, continuing my search for my phone. I grip the butt of my cigarette between my teeth and I will my hands to function as I fumble with the zips. Finally I find it. I go to contacts and bring up Oscar's number, then hit call. He answers on the fourth ring.

"They called about twenty minutes ago," he tells me. "Said the museum was on lockdown and I wasn't to come into work. I don't have a clue what's going on over there but the blasted news reporters are making out like the place is under siege or something."

I'm so relieved he's okay that for a moment it feels like

I can't breathe. "Do they know who else is inside? Do people normally go into work that early? Apart from the security crew?" It was just past dawn when I left Sasha to go home and shower, but she was dressed and looked ready to leave the house. She didn't say if she was going straight to work, though.

"Not usually," Oscar says slowly. "Some of the staff do like to go in and get work done before the place opens to the public. It's so noisy during the day, you see. But I don't think anyone would have been in there at seven this morning. I doubt that very much."

"Oscar. What time does Sasha normally go into work? Is there any chance she could be inside that building?"

"*Sasha?*" I haven't mentioned Sasha to my grandfather since the first day I met her at the museum. He must be really fucking confused right now.

"Yes. Sasha."

The roar of silence on the other end of the phone is deafening.

"Oscar. C'mon."

"She *does* go in very early sometimes," he says. "If there is anyone in there, then...there's a good chance that it's her."

SEVENTEEN

ESCAPE

SASHA

My body feels like it's being tugged in five different directions. The marble floor is cold beneath me, but for some reason my body feels really hot. Scalding, in fact, like I've been laying out in the sun for too long. I really should remember to wear sunscreen. Andrew always says I'm going to really mess up my skin if I don't take better care of...

Christopher.

Where's Christopher?

I open my eyes, and my head feels like it's splintering apart. I need a drink. Goddamn it, I *really* need a drink. My tongue is stuck to the roof of my mouth, and...copper? Why does my mouth taste of copper? I try to roll onto my back, but my body feels so incredibly heavy. I'm made of lead. I'm made of stone.

"Wakey wakey, Sleeping Beauty."

I try to turn my head toward the voice, but I can't seem to manage it. I open my eyes instead, wincing against the bright light that stabs at my eyes. The light flares and then dims, not so bright after all. In fact, the room I'm in is quite dark, and smells dry, like paper or cardboard.

"I was beginning to think you might be dead," a voice says. I hear a scraping noise to my right, followed by a metallic *ting*ing sound. Out of the corner of my eye, I see him crouching there, his back against the wall, something bright and sharp flashing in dirty, calloused hands. I remember then. I remember glass smashing, and overwhelming, terrible pain. I remember climbing the stairs, and I remember the anger in his voice when he realized there was nothing up here to steal, nothing worth any real money to him. After that, everything is blissfully hazy.

"While you've been sleeping, I've been trying to decide," the man says. He's still wearing that ski mask over his head, but his gloves are gone now, and I can see the dark smudge of a tattoo on the back of his hand. Something large and black. A coat of arms? A shield of some kind? I can't make out the design, but the shape of the tattoo is familiar to me.

"I've been trying to decide if I'm going to let you live," he continues. His voice is measured and even. Calm almost, though a hint of madness lurks beneath the tone of his words. "Rich white bitches like you have big houses and plenty of money, though. I've come to the conclusion that perhaps this *wasn't* a total waste of time." He snorts, a wet, repulsive sound, and hawks phlegm into the back of his throat. He spits it onto the floor, then hums quietly to himself for a second. "You know that there's a way out of here, right? A back door or something. You need to take me to your place. You need to give me your money, Doc. It's the only way I can help you."

"Help...me?" My voice is cracked. It feels like all of me has cracked into a million little pieces.

"Yes. There are rules in these situations. They exist in order to maintain a clear line between the person in charge, and...the *other* person."

He doesn't want to say victim? He knows that's what I am, surely? He wasn't so shy about this when he was smashing my head into a wall downstairs.

"You were meant to tell me the truth," he says. "You were meant to do everything I told you to, and you were meant to tell the truth. That way, I could get what I came here for and you could go on your merry way. But now?"

That sounds ominous. I don't like the way that sounds at all. The guy in the ski mask tuts disapprovingly. "I'm supposed to kill you now," he informs me. "I can't really see any other way out of it."

"You don't have to. You don't have to kill me. Not if you don't want to."

The guy in the ski mask sighs. "Of course I *want* to. Wanting isn't relevant. I have to follow the rules, even if you don't. How much money do you have at your house?"

"I don't know. Three...three hundred dollars?"

"Three hundred? That's it?" The guy gets to his feet, hissing like a snake. "You think I can save your life for a mere three hundred dollars? You're fucked, lady. Well and truly fucked." He starts toward me, and the scuffed toes of his worn leather boots fill my vision. Panic surges inside me.

"Wait! Wait! I have...I have my mother's engagement ring at home. It's two carats. It...it must be worth at least fifteen thousand. And I have forty-seven thousand dollars in my bank account. I can get it for you. I can give you that."

"You think that's what your life's worth? Forty-seven thousand and a piece of metal and rock?"

"It's all I have." My voice is small, so quiet, but it echoes in the yawning corridor of the museum.

The man in the ski mask doesn't say anything. He stands over me, looking down at me, those cold, stark, lifeless blue eyes of his assessing me, and I know it deep down inside. This is a pivotal moment. This is where he decides if he's going to kill me or allow me to live. If I say the wrong thing, if I even look at him the wrong way, he's going to take that knife of his and he's going to drive it into my chest. There will be nothing I can do about it.

A thought occurs to me in the moments that pass. Once more I'm faced with my own death. The first time was in my car five years ago, sitting in the driver's seat, waiting for the nose of my car to hit the cold, unfriendly waters of the East River. And now, laying on my back, on the floor of the museum, staring up into the eyes of a stranger. This time, though, I'm suddenly not afraid. I survived near drowning only to die on a daily basis, every time I remembered that my son was no longer with me. If I die today, I won't have to suffer through the pain of that truth every time I wake up in the morning. I won't have to stand in the doorway of his bedroom anymore, my arms wrapped around my own body as I try to hold myself up, looking at all of his things, his Matchbox cars and his electric train sets, his neatly folded clothes piled up on the end of his bed, or his threadbare teddy bear, Javier, laying face down on the dusty floorboards in front of his window. I will just be gone, and there will be nothing left. No shame. No guilt. No loneliness. No more pain. Just the welcoming arms of oblivion.

I close my eyes.

My death doesn't arrive, though.

"I suppose that's what you're worth, then," my attacker whispers. "Forty-seven thousand dollars isn't enough for some people. But I like you, Doc. It's enough for you today."

******

I can't walk properly. I can't put any weight onto my left leg; every time I try, a searing, sharp pain stabs through my nerve endings. Not just the nerve endings in my leg, but all over my body, quick and wicked as lightning. It's breathtaking in its severity—so much so that I almost lose consciousness as the guy in the ski mask drags me by the arm down the corridor.

"You're going to take me out of the secret door," he says, ignoring my labored breathing. I'm hopping and skipping, trying to keep up with him, but he seems oblivious. "Once we're out of the secret door, you're going to wait out of sight while I hail a taxi. We'll both sit in the back. You're going to pretend like I'm your friend. You're not going to try and raise the alarm. If you do, it'll all be out of my control. I won't be able to help you anymore. Do you understand?"

"There isn't a secret door. There's only the loading dock entrance, and—"

"The loading dock entrance, then. The loading dock. The loading dock. Yes." He says the words, and it's final. I can't argue with him. I can't suggest another option. Something's not right with this guy, I can tell. Aside from being a violent criminal, I suspect he is also suffering from some sort of mental disorder that causes him to fixate on things. When he wanted me to apologize in my office, it was almost as if he was anxious. His volatile actions were driven by some desperate need for me to do as he bid me. He won't stop talking about rules—rules that I must follow, and a completely different set of rules that he needs to follow. And now, yanking me by the arm, it seems imperative that we reach the loading dock as quickly as humanly possible.

He obviously doesn't know the way, so he continually shoves me out in front of him, forcing me to stand on my injured leg, and every time I transfer weight onto it my stomach turns. I'm going to throw up soon, and I won't be able to hold back. I already know he won't like that.

He keeps me away from the windows. He stands on my right as we make painfully slow progress down the stairs, blocking the view outside so I can't see what's going on. I think that maybe there are people out there, gathered on the steps of the museum. I don't have a watch on, and I'm too scared to pull my cell phone from the waist band of my skirt to check the time on there, so I have no idea what the hour is, but it feels late. Late enough that the museum should be open now. The fact that it's not tells me he's barred the entranceway somehow, and that other staff members have been alerted to the fact that something untoward is happening inside the building. Do the police know? Dear god, I hope so.

It takes forever to reach the ground floor. My hip hurts, and so does my back. The side of my head hurts, too. My skin feels strange; I think maybe there's dried blood on my temple and further down, over my cheek.

Where is Rooke right now? My heart turns over in my chest when I think about him. If he were here… God, I can't even think about that. I'll burst into tears, and I need to stay as calm as possible. I know it, though. If Rooke were here, I already know he would have put this psycho down.

It feels like a million years ago that I arrived at the museum and saw that the Christmas tree had been erected. When I see it in the foyer now, my heart trips over itself. There, at the base of the tree, Amanda, the security guard that checked my bag earlier, is laying on the floor in a crimson pool of blood. She's face down, her head twisted to one side at an odd angle, her eyes open and unseeing. I can't see her neck, but I can imagine what it must look like. It hits me that I didn't believe the guy had killed anyone until now. I thought that he was just trying to scare me, but seeing Amanda laid out like this, clearly dead, blows that theory out of the water. Cold fear coils itself into knots in the pit of my stomach.

I am never getting out of this museum. I am never getting out of here alive.

"Hurry. Move." The guy prods me in the back, and a flash of pain lights up the inside of my head. "I don't like the way she's looking at me," he whispers.

I look around, hoping to see someone else down here on the ground floor with us, but there's no one. A second later it dawns on me: he means Amanda. He doesn't like the way *Amanda* is looking at him. Except she's not looking at him, of course, she's not looking at anyone, because she's dead. He shivers, and it's like he's seeing her body for the very first time, like he had nothing to do with her current state of being. He blocks the view through the entranceway as he leads me in the direction of the gift shop. "Where is it?" Where's the loading dock?"

Behind me, the slap of hands on the door echoes out loudly, nearly startling me out of my skin. "Hey! Hey, come out here!" Someone screams. A wall of sound erupts outside, and the guy in the ski mask curses loudly.

"They've seen us. They know where we are. It's too late."

I shake my head, knowing what too late means for me. "It's not. It's dark in here. They can only see shadows moving. They won't have any idea what's going on. Come on. Let's go before she wakes up."

He rocks back, holding the knife in his hand out toward me, his eyes growing wide. "What do you mean, *wakes up?*"

I point at Amanda. "I mean, she's sleeping right now but if we stay here for much longer, she's going to wake up, and she'll be really upset, won't she? Don't you think she'll be really upset?"

A mad look glimmers in the guy's eyes. "You mean she only pretended to die?"

This is a dangerous game to play, but I need to test out my theory. If this guy is unhinged, perhaps there's a way to trick him into letting me go. I stare at Amanda's lifeless body and sorrow wells up inside me. She was a lovely person. She didn't deserve this. "Yes. I think she only pretended," I say firmly. "I think she'll be coming back soon."

This seems to startle him. He takes a tentative step towards Amanda's body and then appears to think better of it. He swallows so hard I can see his Adam's apple bob beneath the thick wool of his mask. "I knew it," he whispers. "I fucking *knew* it." Whirling around, I think he's going to grab hold of my arm again but instead he fists a handful of my hair, snarling. "You want her to wake up," he snaps. "You want to work with her to kill me, I fucking know you do. Well I don't die, either, Doc. I'll come back to life, too. I'll haunt you for all eternity if I don't get out of here soon. I'm beginning to lose patience."

"All right, all right, let's go. I don't want her to wake up, I promise." I move as quickly as I can across the lobby of the museum, favoring my good side as I head toward the service entrance that leads to the loading dock. The noise from outside grows louder and more frantic as we move away from the entrance, a bubbling, riotous sound, and I almost scream for help. There's nothing any of them can do for me, though. With his knife so expertly held in his hand, I know this guy will stab me to death before I can even get a word out.

Amazingly, the loading dock is deserted. It makes no sense. I thought there would be people out here for sure, but there's no one. A stack of empty flattened cardboard boxes leans against a trash compactor. The wrapper from some McDonalds delicacy swirls around on an eddy of wind, trapped in the narrow, dirty courtyard. I look up, hoping to see a face in a window or the dark suggestion of a sniper on one of the surrounding building's roofs, however we are alone. No one hiding in the shadows. No one watching on from above. Just me and the guy in the ski mask. Fuck.

He pushes me out of the doorway and onto the stained concrete of the loading dock. I hear something—metal scrapping on metal—and I freeze. I'm too scared to turn around. "Go stand by the compactor over there," the guy tells me. I walk forward, holding my breath. The guy in the ski mask spins me around, grabbing hold of my wrist. He's holding onto something—a scuffed, rusting pair of handcuffs. They look like they've been used before. He snaps one side of the cuffs around the blue steel handle that is welded to the side of the trash compactor, then gives me a pointed look.

"You call for help, you die. Understand?"

I nod.

He jerks me closer to the compactor, about to circle the other cuff around my wrist, when a shrill, obnoxious ringing splits the silence. My phone. The cell phone I still have tucked into the waistband of my skirt, concealed beneath my shirt. I can feel it vibrating cheerfully against the skin of my back, letting me know I have an incoming call. The guy in the ski mask looks stunned.

"What the *fuck*?" He runs his hands over my body,

searching for the phone. When he finds it, he looks like he's just been shot in the gut. "What's this?" he whispers. Holding up the phone in front of me, I can see Ali's name on the screen, clear as day. The guy in the ski mask shakes his head slowly, his eyes unblinking. "You sneaky fucking bitch. You've had this on you the whole time? You've had this on you the whole fucking time?"

He punches me. I see his fist coming, but I'm paralyzed by fear and I do nothing to avoid the blow. He strikes me, and it feels like fireworks going off inside my head. For a moment I can't see anything. A pure white light fills my vision, followed by a dizzying blackness that threatens to swallow me up. I stagger backwards, my legs going out from underneath me. I can do nothing to break my fall. I hit the ground hard, tailbone first, the back of my head connecting with something on the way down. I can't even comprehend the pain. It leaves me winded and confused.

"I thought we were friends," the guy says softly. "I thought you knew better than to keep secrets from me, Doc." He's on top of me, then. I can't see him for a second, and panic spreads like poison through my veins. If I can't see him, how can I protect myself? The cold, hard terror of the knife presses up against my neck. "The security guard struggled. Are you going to struggle?"

Stale coffee and cigarettes: his breath is rancid. The stink fills my head, and I try to turn away from it. He has hold of me, though. He won't let go. My sight returns to me in frightening bursts of light, until I can finally see him clearly again. I almost wish I couldn't.

He presses down on the knife, and the sharpened steel breaks my skin. It's as if I've needed the shock this brings to wake me from some kind of stupor. I scream. I scream so hard and so loud that it feels like the cry is being forcefully ripped from my throat, barbed wire tearing up my windpipe. The guy on top of me hisses. He hits me again.

I have to get up. I have to get away.

Now.

If I don't...

If I don't...

If I don't...

I scramble, reaching for something, anything to defend myself with. To my left, the cardboard boxes are rocking wildly. The guy's foot is hitting them as he wrestles with me and the movement is on the verge of knocking them over. I lay my hands flat against his chest, and I push. He hardly moves. Laughing, he takes his knife and he slices slowly over my shoulder, his teeth only an inch away from my face. I register the pain, can tell he's damaging my body, but I can't really feel it. Not the way I should. My heart is surging behind my ribcage. Quickly, without even thinking, I bring my right knee up, slamming it into his body. I miss his balls, but the surprise of the movement knocks him sideways. The cardboard boxes come crashing down onto his back, scattering everywhere, and I seize the opportunity. I push him again, this time with enough force that I manage to roll him off of me. The guy doesn't fight me. He's hysterical, hacking and coughing in between his manic bouts of laughter.

I jump to my feet, and he mirrors me, getting up onto his knees first, then standing slowly, his pale blue eyes fixed on me. "What now?" he asks, wiping his nose with the back of his hand. "How fast can you run with bare feet? How fast do you think *I* can run?"

My feet *are* bare. My stockings are ripped and torn, barely still on my body. Looking down, I see that I'm covered in blood and I have no idea where it's coming from. The guy steps forward, making the small gap between us even smaller. "Are you a Sagittarius?" he asks. "My mother was a Sagittarius. She was just like you.

Arrogant. Ungrateful. She didn't see it coming, either."

I back up, knowing the move to be a mistake. I'm literally putting myself in a corner. There's no escape route behind me. No way out. The trash compactor is to my left, and there's no way to make a dash for it to my right without him catching me. I'm out of options. I don't know what to do.

He creeps forward toward me.

I take another step back. Wildly, I look around, searching for anything that might help me. Anything at all. Then...I see it: a long wooden pole, laying on the ground. There's a large metal hook on the end of the pole—I've seen the janitorial staff using it to pack down the garbage in the compactor when it's getting full. It's meant to be used to open the windows inside the museum, the ones too high to be reached by hand, or even using a ladder.

Can I reach it? Am I brave enough to even try?

It's not really a matter of bravery anymore, though. I have this one option available to me, and I have to take it otherwise I am going to die. It's as simple as that. I move quickly. I lunge, dropping to the ground, and I snatch at the pole, trying to clasp hold of it. I'm an inch short. The guy in the ski mask is moving, too. He rushes forward, presumably seeing what I'm reaching for, and he tries to get there first.

I have witnessed this moment before in countless movies. The moment where the hero and the villain are both grasping for the gun that has been kicked just out of reach. The whole situation would feel ridiculous if it weren't for the fact that I know this is it for me. When I was laid out on the floor upstairs, contemplating my death, for that very brief second I wasn't scared. I am now, though. I am really, very afraid.

I surge forward, kicking at the ground, nudging myself forward, and my hand closes around the rough, splintered wood of the pole. The guy in the ski mask is almost on top of me. I twist onto my back, lifting the pole with both hands. I hit him with it. It strikes the side of his head, and I know immediately that the blow wasn't hard enough. The guy in the ski mask tips his head to one side, smiling grimly. "You don't know when to quit, do you?" he snaps. "You just don't know when to give up."

I suppose he's right. I'm clearly beaten, but something inside me refuses to back down. I crawl backward, away from him, still gripping tightly onto the pole. I only stop when my back hits the wall. The guy approaches little by little.

"I tell you what. I'll let you hit me again. One good swing. How about that?" He stops in front of me, legs planted wide. Amusement chases pity across what little I can see of his face. "One really good, hard swing, and then we stop playing games with each other, Doc. No more fucking around. Okay?"

I can't breathe. He waits for me to say something, to move, to do something, but I'm frozen to the spot, the wooden pole held out in front of me.

He takes another step forward, and my body reacts. I'm not in control anymore. My arms are swinging, thrusting with every ounce of strength they possess, and I feel the moment that the hook hits him. I don't even hit him that hard, but metal glances off of the side of his temple and the iron sinks into his skull, and there's a moment...this long, drawn out moment where he just looks at me, like he can't really believe what's just happened. I can barely believe it myself.

He sinks to his knees, blinking wildly, and the movement rips the pole from my hands. It clatters to the ground, and his ski mask is torn from his head as the hook comes away, revealing the entirety of his face. Red hair. Weak chin. A nose that seems too large for his narrow face. I allow myself to see each of his features one by one, not taking them in as a whole. I don't want his face to haunt me. I don't ever want to close my eyes and see him there, waiting for me. I want him to be anonymous forever.

Blood pours freely out of the wide gash in his temple. I can't see how deep the wound is, but the amount of blood he's losing is terminal. It *has* to be. He gives one more solitary, mad bark of laughter, and then the guy topples sideways into the mountain of cardboard boxes, his body rigid and locked.

I snap out of my shock. I stand up, and I run. I don't know how long it takes me to find a way around the building. I don't know what I stand on to tear my foot open. I don't feel any pain when I stumble and fall, cutting open my hands and my knees. I don't know what I'm thinking as I careen around the corner, out onto the street.

I do experience the relief of a stranger picking me up off the ground and calling for help, though. And I do feel it. I do feel the relief of knowing that I'm not about to die.

EIGHTEEN

THE FALL

ROOKE

5 Years Ago

Goshen Secure Facility

"*Get him, Viorelli! Fucking* kill *him!*"

It's pissing down outside, raindrops hammering against the windows, the sky grim and forbidding as Viorelli circles the Russian kid, Misha, who was brought in last week. Misha made some dumb mistake, sat at a table he wasn't supposed to sit at, and

Jared has taken it upon himself to teach the newbie a lesson.

I watch. I don't get involved. Getting involved whenever Viorelli is on a rampage usually ends badly for both of us. I keep my head down and I eat my food. Everyone else stands in a circle as Misha does his best to defend himself against the fucking psychopath. They chant, they boo, they heckle. Jared's right-hand guy, Osman, grabs a food tray and tries to hit Misha with it, and that's when all hell really breaks loose. Jared turns on Osman, lunging at him with something. Something in his hand. Something sharp.

"I don't need your fucking help, asshole!" he shouts.

I don't see what happens next. The crowd takes a giant step back. The room is suddenly silent, and then Misha is shouting loudly in Russian.

"Shut the fuck up, man. Shut the fuck up, he's fine!"

My curiosity gets the better of me. I get up. I don't need to move to see what's gone down now. On the floor, Osman is laying on his back, his hands clutching at his throat, and a fountain of blood is spraying between his fingers.

"Get up, man." Jared kicks at Osman with his boot, but Osman isn't going anywhere. His hands fall limp, resting on top of his chest, his body twitching and jumping as his nervous system shuts down.

Someone in the crowd hoots, splintering away, dashing across to the other side of the room, and then everyone else does, too, screaming and shouting. The doors burst open and twenty guards storm into the room, riot shields in their hands, weapons drawn. Jared rushes forward in the melee and snatches the screwdriver by the handle, ripping it free from Osman's neck. He comes straight for me.

It's like he's seen his opportunity and now he plans

on killing me, too. I've been waiting for this moment, though, I'm ready for it. I reel back, ready to go to fucking war with him. When he reaches me, he doesn't attack, however. He thrusts the screwdriver at me, eyes narrowed into slits. "Take it, Blackheath."

In the confusion, the guards don't seem to know who they're looking for. They grab the entire block one person at a time, throwing bodies down to the ground. I can hardly hear Jared over the chaos that's unfolding around us. His intentions are obvious, though. He wants me to take the fall for him.

"You're crazy," I mouth.

"Take the fucking screwdriver, Blackheath. *Take it.*"

He really is insane. Osman probably would have taken the shiv for him. Shame he just killed him with it. A row of guards are approaching from the left. I slowly shake my head, then step backward directly into their path. Better to be bodychecked and get taken down than to be caught anywhere near Viorelli right now. As expected, the guards slam into me from all angles. I don't fight back. My body is suddenly lit up with electricity as someone applies the prongs of a Taser to my skin.

I collapse, my back bowed, my teeth grinding together. I can still see though. I watch the guards grab hold of Viorelli. He kicks and fights, lashing out wildly with the screwdriver. No chance they won't know he was responsible for the dead guy in the middle of the room now. I try to laugh as they take him down, too.

I try really fucking hard, but it's impossible.

NINETEEN

THE MUSEUM

ROOKE

"**B**oy, I swear to god, if you do not get back, I am going to Taze you in the motherfucking face. Is that what you want?"

I slam my fist against the police barricade that's been set up to create a perimeter around the museum, openly snarling. I've lost my bag somewhere along with my headphones but I don't give a shit about that right now. I give a shit about Sasha. I give a shit about nothing else. "Do me a favor, asshole. Fucking try it. You think I haven't been Tazed before?" The god's honest truth is that I've been Tazed more times than I care to remember. The first few months in juvi were tough. It goes without saying that I was fucking furious that I was in there; every time a fight kicked off or kids started causing shit, I was right there, smack bang in the middle of it all, blowing off steam. My body is well used to the rollercoaster of a two-pronged police issue stun gun. It's not a particularly fun ride, but I'll line up for that shit all day long if it means they'll give me some information about the situation inside the museum.

The cop on the other side of the barricade narrows his eyes at me. "Do *not* fuck with me. I've had a shitty morning, and this bullshit is making it even worse. I will take you into custody if that's what you want."

I don't want that. If he takes me away, I won't be able to see if it is Sasha that's being held inside the building. I have her phone number—it was inside that book she dropped back at the museum—but she's not picking up. Oscar had her home number but that's ringing out, too, so I have no idea where she is. She could be at Trader Joe's doing her weekly grocery shop. She could be at a yoga class. Or she could be kneeling on the ground with the muzzle of a gun digging into the base of her skull. The not knowing is driving me crazy.

I ran across the bridge earlier. I fucking *ran* through the streets of Manhattan until I arrived out front of the museum and I forced my way through the already considerable crowd, straining to see what the fuck was going on. I called Jake and told him to get his ass down here, but he hasn't shown up yet. I feel trapped. I feel like my hands are tied behind my back, and I can't fucking *do* anything. I don't know why I'm filled with this level of panic, but it's hard to fucking breathe around it, and I'm on the verge of losing my shit.

On this police officer.

Right now.

"Just tell me," I grind out. "Who is inside the building?"

"I *have* already told you. We do not know who is inside

the building. We're trying to ascertain that information right now. But guess what? Even when we *do* know who's in there, we sure as fuck aren't gonna tell you, kid. Now clear the barricade before I lose my goddamn patience."

Boy. Kid. If he calls me either of these things one more fucking time, I am going to destroy him. They'll need a phenomenal set of dental records to identify him by the time I'm through. I am going to break his nose. I am going to beat him black and blue. I'm going to—

"Rooke! Rooke, man, what the fuck is going on?" A hand lands on my shoulder. The contact startles me, and I spin around, ready to start thrashing whoever is touching me. It's Jake. He holds up his hands, reeling back from me.

"Whoa, whoa, whoa, dude. Chill."

"Do you know this punk?" the cop asks.

Jake nods. "Yeah. I do."

"Then do him a favor and get him out of here before he does something stupid."

I'm about to vault over the barrier and head butt the fucker, but Jake grabs me by the back of the shirt and pulls me back. I try to fight my way free, but with so many people pressing in from all sides, pushing and shoving angrily at me, it's impossible. I let him tug me back through the crowd, growling obscenities under my breath. Once we're clear, Jake rounds on me, glaring with a furious intensity. "Are you fucking crazy, dude? Trying to start a fight with a cop? You have a record, or have you forgotten all about that? Mess up like that and it won't be juvi for you. It will be big boy jail, asshole."

"*Big boy jail*," I repeat. "Yeah. Very grown up. It's not my fault that guy was being a prick. I just asked for information. He was being a cunt."

"He wasn't being a cunt. He was being a cop."

"Isn't that the same thing?"

Jake rolls his eyes. "It's their job to secure the building.

What do you think would happen if they just let every one of these gawking motherfuckers inside to take a look around? Do you think that would make the situation inside there better or worse?"

I stare at him for a moment then let out the breath I've been holding. "Okay. Sorry, you're right. What am I supposed to do, though? She could be in there."

"Who?"

"*Sasha.*" It's infuriating that he hasn't figured that out already. He knows she works at the museum.

"Ahh. Right. Yeah, well, do you *know* it's her in there?"

"No, I don't know for sure that it is. But it is."

"Why don't you just calm down? It could be some fucking dude in there for all you know. It could be—"

"There she is! Look! Over there!"

"Oh my god! She's been shot!"

"Help! Somebody, help!"

Cries go up all around us, drowning out Jake's voice. Adrenaline fires through my body, and my hands begin to shake. "What the fuck? What the fuck's going on?" I scan the area; it's only when people start rushing to the left of the museum that I see what's happening. A figure is on their knees, on the ground, leaning against an elderly guy wearing a thick blue coat. He's trying to prop the figure up, but he's struggling. Another guy in a suit rushes forward, dropping his briefcase on the ground. It cracks open, and sheaves of paper go flying, swirling upward on the wind as he helps the figure—a woman—to her feet.

She lifts her head, her face covered in blood, and it's her. It's Sasha. I was right.

"*Fuck.*" My blood drains from my head, pooling in a sickening fashion somewhere low in the pit of my stomach.

"Is that her?" Jake asks.

I nod. "I have to get to her. Shit. She's hurt. She's hurt

really bad."

"She's cool, man. Look, the EMTs have her. She's okay. She's okay."

A couple of guys rush to her, jump bags in their hands, relieving the businessman and the elderly guy of their burden. At the same time, about twenty guys with cameras all surge forward, snapping off shots and shouting out questions. The flashes from their Canons and their Nikons seem to make the dull, grey day suddenly brilliant white. Sasha flinches, raising a hand, squinting, shaking her head. She's freaking out. The police hurry in from either side. A tall blond woman goes to Sasha, talking to her as the EMTs look her over.

I want to hit pause. I want to stop everything so I can go to her myself, to push everyone out of the way, scoop her up into my arms and carry her away. She looks terrified and stunned, like she's just not able to comprehend what's happening.

"Do not do anything dumb right now," Jake warns. His fingers dig into my arm again. Now that we're clear of the crowd, it would be easy enough to shrug him off and go charging over there, but he's right.

What use am I to Sasha right now? I'm not a medical professional, so I can't take care of her injuries. I'm not a cop, so I can't question her about what's happened. Or I could, but then what? I don't have my gun. I can't storm the museum and go find the motherfuckers that have done this to her. I can't go in there and arrest them.

I am no good to her right now.

"What's the closest hospital to here?" Jake asks.

"The closest hospital?"

"Yeah, man. Think. They're not gonna keep her out here any longer than they need to, are they? They're going to take her to get checked out. If we head to the hospital, you'll be able to talk to her there."

Damn it. He's right. I wrack my brain, thinking.

"It's Mount Sinai, right?" he asks.

"No. Lenox Hill. They have an emergency department there. That's where they'll take her. Greenwich Village, just across the park." Of course, nothing is "just across the park" in New York. Central Park is massive. We'll never beat an ambulance to the hospital on foot, never in a million years. "We need a cab."

Jake's already come to that conclusion. He gestures up the street. "Traffic won't be moving here any time soon. Let's get over to Amsterdam."

******

It takes twenty-five minutes to get to the hospital. When we arrive, it's to find that the ambulance has indeed already beaten us, and that no, we aren't going to be permitted to see the patient. The nurse on the front desk says "the patient" as if Sasha is some sort of alien, some freak of nature that's under investigation by local authorities, and that we're mad for even thinking we might be able to share the same breathing space as her. We're told we can't even wait in the waiting room for her. A pair of thuggish security guards appear, hands on a pair of Glocks, and we're ushered outside the building where a crowd of news reporters are already setting up their equipment, bright LED lights shining down over the parking lot, making the grim, oppressively cold day look like it's actually seventy degrees and sunny out.

"Fuck this. There has to be another way in." I scan the perimeter of the ground floor, looking for another entrance that we might have overlooked. There doesn't appear to be one, though. Jake blows out a sharp breath down his nose, his eyes glittering with frustration.

"Dude. Do *not* go back into that building. It's asking for

trouble. Why don't you just come home with me now? We can see what happened on the news? She looked fine."

"She did *not* look fine. She was covered in blood. Jesus Christ, man—"

"All right, all right. Fuck. Don't lay me out. I'm just trying to keep you out of jail here."

I scrub my hands over my face, nodding. "Sorry. I don't fucking like this, though. I don't like not knowing what's going on."

Jake gives me a long, hard look, sizing me up. Figuring me out. "I've never seen you like this," he says. "You're freaking me out. Just take a deep breath, okay? There's nothing we can do right now. We have to be patient, and—"

I hear a burst of static behind me—the sound of a police issue radio. In juvi I learned quickly that you stopped and listened whenever you heard that sound. Frequently, it meant the guards were being informed that the governor was coming by to toss the cells. Sometimes it meant that a friend was being returned to general population. Other times, it meant a hailstorm of fire and shit was about to rain down on us and we were about to get our asses beaten.

"*...seems disoriented. Couldn't really give us a clear description. Either way, there's no one there. The place was empty. We've gutted the place from top to bottom.*"

I turn around, searching for the source of the tinny voice coming out of the radio. A few feet away, a couple of cops are standing with their backs to us, talking quietly to each other, coffee cups in one hand, Philly cheese steaks in the other. They don't even seem to notice that they're broadcasting for everyone to hear.

"*You think she's making it up?*"

"*Nah. Captain said she was hysterical. Said she killed the guy and his body was out the back of the building. Eight*

170

guys searched the area, though. There was blood there for sure, but it could have been hers. They're testing it now."

"All right. Let me know when they're taking her home. In the meantime, alert every single hospital in the city. If she thinks she hurt this guy, he might go looking for medical assistance."

My mind is spinning uncontrollably. They're talking about Sasha, of course. They have to be. And she thinks she *killed* someone? Fuck me. I'm gutted. The thought of her having to defend herself to that extent? It makes me feel like I'm about to throw up. I'm shaking, filled with an instant boost of adrenaline. I'm about to say something to Jake, but he shakes his head, a firm, immoveable look on his face. "We're not starting our own fucking manhunt, Rooke. No fucking way. We are going home. *Now.*"

I clench my teeth, hissing under my breath. The guy knows me. The guy knows me far too well.

No way I'm going home, though. No. Fucking. Way.

TWENTY

JACOBI

SASHA

"Cosmetic? It doesn't feel cosmetic. It doesn't look cosmetic, either." What a strange way to describe the injuries I've sustained. Looking at myself in the small compact mirror the nurse is holding up in front of my face, I can't seem to recognize the face staring back at me in the reflective surface. Swollen eye. Swollen nose. Split lip. Cuts on both cheekbones. The eyes are the same, though, those are definitely mine. They're filled with fury and tears, stinging every time I blink.

"Don't worry, Ms. Connor. You'll heal up nicely in a week or two. After that, no one will ever know you were hurt."

172

But *I* will. I look away from the compact, and she clips it shut, sliding it into the pocket of her scrubs. "Your ribs on the other hand? They're going to take a little while longer to heal. You're lucky. Nothing was broken, but you're incredibly bruised. Moving around is going to be pretty painful for a while now. So no driving, no running, or anything like that. The meds you've been prescribed are strong as all hell. Don't operate any heavy machinery, light aircraft, power tools—"

I hold up a hand, cutting her off. "I won't be doing any of that. I don't need the drugs."

The nurse arches a skeptical eyebrow, pursing her lips. "Mmhmm. We'll just see about that now. You're feeling okay right now because you're already doped up to the eyeballs. As soon as you get home and that morphine starts to wear off, you're gonna be in a world of hurt."

"I'll take my chances."

"You'll take your meds home with you and take them when you need to. And when you do—"

"No operating any space craft, school buses or forklifts. Got it."

The nurse nods, placing an orange bottle of pills down on the small table beside my bed. "Good girl."

"Are you done, nurse? We really need to finish our conversation with Ms. Connor." A middle aged, grizzly detective stands in the doorway of the hospital room— Detective Jacobi. He was the one to question me when I first arrived at the hospital. They let him talk to me as I was being assessed, but when he got pushy they made him leave the room. He looks frustrated, like I'm purposefully avoiding answering his questions and he's about ready to arrest me and take me down to the station. The nurse glances at me—a questioning look.

"You feel up to talking to these fools now? They aren't gonna stop coming in here 'til you've told them whatever you know, honey."

"Yes, it's fine. I don't mind." Truth is, I want to explain what happened to the detective. I've been itching to finish answering his questions for the past three hours, but instead I've been poked and prodded, examined and re-examined, and I'm beginning to feel a little violated. Or *more* violated, should I say. The nurse gestures the cop inside, and leaves, closing the door behind her.

Detective Jacobi's face is marked with a thousand lines. I get the feeling he earned each one of them working stressful, thankless cases that have soured him against the general public as a whole. He looks at me with suspicion, if not open hostility. "Where were we, Ms. Connor?" he asks, sitting on the edge of my bed.

"You were in the middle of accusing me of slitting Amanda's throat. You were implying that the death of my son might have finally caused me to have a nervous breakdown." I say this calmly, though my veins are filled with fire. He blinks, then takes a small notebook from the pocket of his damp-looking jacket; it must be raining outside.

"I didn't accuse you of anything, Sasha. I'm simply trying to record the facts. It's my job to assess your mental state."

"I thought it was the doctors' jobs to assess my mental state," I reply. "I'm sorry. I didn't realize you were a trained psychologist."

He huffs. "Why don't we start from the beginning? You tell me everything that happened from the moment you arrived at the museum, and I'll try not to say anything that might upset you. Deal?"

Right now I'm wondering where my sympathetic female police officer is. I'm wondering where my trauma therapist is. I'm wondering a lot of things. I've invested a lot of time in the CSI TV franchise; I'd never have thought this is how a situation like this would play out. Here I am though, being stared down by the most terse, unfriendly detective in New York.

I do what he wants. I tell him absolutely everything, from walking through the front door, to seeing the bastard in the ski mask for the first time, to smashing the hook into the side of his head and running for my life. I don't leave anything out. I go into explicit detail. I try not to cry when he asks me if I was assaulted sexually. I tell him I don't know, that I was unconscious for a length of time, and I have no idea what happened to me while I was out cold, and I feel an icy wash of terror settle deep inside me.

He asks more questions: my stockings were ripped in the feet, but were they ripped in between my legs? I tell him, no, I don't think so. He asks if I'm sore anywhere other than my ribs and my leg. I say yes, I'm sore everywhere, because I am. My whole body is ringing like a struck bell. Even breathing hurts at this point. Down to my toes, I feel tender and compromised, entirely unlike myself. Shifting in my bed is a monstrous task that seems incomprehensible right now.

An hour passes, and every minute detail goes down into Jacobi's notebook. He grunts every now and then, but he doesn't make any other comment until we're done. That's when he looks up at me, locking me to the spot with dark, invasive eyes and he tells me something that makes panic rise around my throat like a clenched fist.

"Is there any chance you didn't hit this guy as hard as you think you did?"

I stare at him dumbly, trying to process the question. "Yes. I hit him really hard. I mean, I...I saw the blood. There was blood everywhere. And the hook..."

"You saw the hook actually strike him?" He sounds unsure.

"It didn't just strike him, Detective. It sank into his

skull."

He grimaces, making a swift note of this. "Okay. It seems we're on the hunt for a tall, psychotic redheaded guy with a hole in the side of his head, then. He must have gotten up and run off because we couldn't locate him, Sasha. There was no body to be found."

He leaves, and I sit and stew on this information. Seriously? How can they not have found his body? He was dead when I left him. There was blood everywhere...

The nurse comes back an hour later to let me know that the doctor wants to keep me here for a couple of days for observation, and that my friend Allison is waiting for me, anxious to see if I'm all right. Another police officer comes by to tell me that detectives will be by again tomorrow to talk to me, to see if I've remembered anything else about the "incident" as they're calling it. The young kid with the bad acne scars then warns me not to talk to the press, just in case I say something that compromises their investigation. The door opens again, and I'm about to tell the person standing in the doorway to politely fuck off and leave me alone, when I see who it is and my words die on my lips.

He came.

"How did you get in here?" I whisper.

Rooke just stands there, staring at me. His jaw is clenched tight, eyes filled with a frightening calm that belies the turmoil he's clearly neck-deep in. "How bad is it?" he asks quietly.

"Nowhere near as bad as it looks."

"It looks pretty fucking bad," he growls.

"Gee. Thanks."

Rooke doesn't respond to my attempt at humor. "Who did it?" he demands.

"I don't know. Some redheaded guy. I think he was drunk or high. He didn't tell me his name."

"Describe him to me."

"Rooke, I've been through all of this with the cops. They're handling it."

"They're not going to handle it. They're going to fuck it up. *I* won't fuck it up, though."

It's weird. Relief washes over me, so intense and powerful that I feel every single rigid muscle in my body finally relax. The look on his face says it all. Rooke's going to go out there, and he's going to find this guy. He's going to make him pay for what he's done. I feel safe all of a sudden. Then, reality starts to kick in. He can't go after this guy. He can't. He's angry right now, so angry I can see every single one of the veins in his arms bulging from where he's clenching his hands so damn tight, but he's going to kill this guy if he finds him. He's going to murder him, and then what?

"Rooke. *Please.*"

"Tell me everything," he grinds out. "*Now*, Sasha."

I shake my head. "No."

"He was ginger. Did he have any birthmarks? Scars? Tattoos?"

And there it is. Tattoos. Rooke must see my expression change, because he takes one small step into the room. The tension pouring off him is like heat from a fire. It fills the small space, sucking all the air out of the room. "*Tell me,*" he says quietly.

"I don't know what it was. Something small on the back of his hand. It looked like a black smudge. It was faded and blurry, like he'd had it for a long time."

Rooke nods slowly. "Anything else? What was he wearing?"

"All black. Black jacket, black pants. His shoes...wait, his shoelaces were different colors. One was red, one was black."

Again, Rooke nods. "Okay. How tall was he?"

"About six foot, I guess."

"Did he have an accent?"

"No. He just sounded slow. Like he was really out of it. That's all."

Rooke inhales deeply. His eyes travel across my body, surveying the damage, and I suddenly feel very vulnerable. I can't decipher the look on his face. "Are you mad at me?" I whisper.

Something breaks in him. He glances away, like he can't possibly bear to look at me anymore. "Why the fuck would you think that?" he says.

"Because...you're looking at me like I'm broken. You're looking at me like you're disgusted."

"I *am* disgusted."

My heart plummets in my chest, my lungs aching painfully.

"I'm disgusted with myself. That I didn't get to you in time. I should have stopped this."

"How were you supposed to know?" He's crazy if he thinks for a second that he's responsible for any of this. Last night was the first real time I allowed him in, to connect with me. Does he think he should be following me around, protecting me from unknown assailants twenty-four hours a day, seven days a week? That's just ridiculous.

He grinds his teeth together, pressing his lips into an unhappy, angry line. He still won't look at me. "No one should have dared fucking touch you, Sasha. No one should have been allowed to fuck with you. There are consequences to an act like this. Dire, awful consequences. I'm going to make sure this guy pays for what he's done to you. I can't leave him fucking breathing. I *won't*."

"Rooke, please—" I try to sit up, to reach out to him, to stop him from leaving, but it's too late. A wall of pain comes crashing down on me and I sink back into the bed, gasping at the shock of it. Rooke hovers in the doorway, his head hanging low.

"Rest, Sasha. I'll be back for you. You don't need to worry about that."

TWENTY-ONE

ASSHOLE, BUT NOT A CUNT

SASHA

"I'm never leaving you alone again. Never. Not tonight. Not this week. You're stuck with me, sunshine." Ali takes my keys out of my hand (newly equipped with a fresh can of pepper spray) and opens the front door to my house, taking my coat and the overnight bag she brought to the hospital for me, then ushering me inside. I follow her, mute, because I don't have anything to say. She's been rambling ever since we left the hospital, and I don't have the energy to engage.

I get it. She feels bad. She shouldn't, though. When I dialed her back at the museum, the call did connect. She *did* pick up, and she *did* hear what was going on. She called the cops, and alerted them to the fact that I was being assaulted, but somehow she seems to think that she didn't do enough. It was ten forty when the EMTs drove me across the city to the hospital. It's not as if the police were the ones who saved me, but who's to say that guy in the ski mask wouldn't have chased after me and recaptured me if the cops weren't thick on the street? Who's to say he wouldn't have killed me dead for hitting him in the head with that dull metal hook?

I can't believe he's not dead. I just can't process the information. I can't believe any of it really. It's been three days since it all happened, and I can't wrap my head around any of it at all. I haven't seen or heard anything from Rooke. Luckily, I haven't seen or heard anything on the news *about* Rooke either. I'm taking that as a win.

Ali tosses my keys into the dish on the stand in the hall and ushers me into the kitchen. I sit down heavily at the counter, watching her as she hurries around the room in a flurry of activity. "What do you want, coffee or tea? I can make us some lunch, too. Oh, wait." She peers into the fridge, frowning. "Maybe not. I can call for something though. Some Thai food? Or maybe a pizza?" She'd normally give me shit for not having any food in the fridge but I guess she's giving me a hall pass in light of recent events.

"I'm not hungry, Ali. Honestly, I just want to take a nap. I feel…" I grasp for a word, *any* word, that could possibly describe what I'm feeling right now. It's like I'm snatching at thin air.

"I know. You must be exhausted by this whole thing." Ali smiles sympathetically, and I want to scream at her to get out. She won't, though. It won't matter how many times I tell her I need some time to myself, that I'm sick of being fussed over, poked and prodded and asked if I'm all right. She will ignore these comments and refuse to leave, no matter what, so there's really no point in saying them. I grind my teeth together, breathing slowly down my nose.

"I'm going to go lie down for a while. Maybe I could eat something later on."

Ali nods. She turns and starts rifling in the cupboard under the sink. "No problem, babe. I'll just do some cleaning or something. Do you have any laundry that needs folding?"

I may not keep much in the way of perishable goods in my refrigerator, but my place is always clean and neat as a pin. And I hardly have a pile of crumpled laundry that needs taking care of, either. If it makes her happy to run a duster over my shelves, though, I'm okay with it. Anything for a moment to sit alone in my room by myself so I can gather my thoughts. My injured knee spasms as I slowly climb the stairs. My ribs sing with pain every time I take a breath.

My physical hurts all seem to melt away the moment I close my bedroom door behind me. This is the first time I have been alone since I managed to run around the side of the museum. Nurses, doctors, friends—I've been surrounded by people twenty-four seven since Tuesday, and now that I'm shut inside a room on my own I feel like I can finally let go.

I climb into bed, planning on crying myself to sleep, but the moment I release my desperate hold on my emotions, allowing everything to wash over me, I'm numb. There are no tears. There's no fear or worry. There is only a cold, heavy sensation pressing down on me, weighting me to the bed.

I pass out.

I wake up a long time later, sweating, panicked and afraid. My attacker from the museum plagues my dreams every time I sleep. He holds his hands around my throat; he uses his fists to hurt me; he throws me down stairwells, and he smashes my head against marble floors. It takes a while to calm my frantic heartbeat. I'm safe now. He's gone, and I'm safe. I tell myself this over and over, and eventually I manage to catch my breath.

A large chunk of time has passed. It was morning when we got home and when I look out of the window now I can see that the light is fading in the sky, already dusk. Downstairs, I can hear talking, muffled and unintelligible. The television? Maybe the radio? As I listen, I can make out the steady rise and fall of Ali's voice, though, along with the odd word here and there, and I know that she has to be talking to someone.

"I'm sorry. She's just not...maybe in a couple of days...No, she hasn't said..."

The other voice is harder to make out. Deeper, less inflection. Definitely male. I get up and creep to the door, and then I crack it open and tiptoe out into the hallway. It's dark, apart from a misshapen chink of light from downstairs, cast upward onto the ceiling.

"Can you just tell her I'm here?"

"Next week, Rooke. She's completely...well, she's fucked. Of course she's fucked. She's been through some crazy shit, and now she just needs some time to decompress, okay?"

There's a long pause. The silence is filled with the beating of my heart and the nervous push and pull of my breath.

"No. Actually it's not okay. I'm seeing her. I will pick you up and physically move you if you don't get out of the way, Ali."

"That's pretty rude!"

"What about me makes you think I'm a polite guy?"

I almost laugh out loud. I thought the same thing about him when we had sex. There's a thick silence, and I can imagine the look on Ali's face. She's not used to anyone standing up to her like this, let alone a guy. She seems to have the ability to strike the fear of god into men, no matter who the hell they are. Rooke Blackheath isn't a man, though. He's some sort of myth that no one really believes in until they lay eyes on him for themselves.

I quickly jog down the stairs, ignoring the twinge in my knee every time I hop down a step. Ali looks like she's just been caught red-handed stealing something. And Rooke...

He's standing in the doorway. A dusting of snow rests on the shoulders of his worn black leather jacket. He's so damn tall. I don't think I've ever really appreciated how tall he is until now, with his head nearly scraping the top of the doorjamb. There's a stack of books pinned against his body under his left arm, and there's a tray containing takeaway coffee cups in his other hand. How very...*normal*. Steam rises from the cups, clouding in the entranceway. I look down at his shoes and notice that the deep reddish brown leather is darker at the toes, wet where he's been walking through the rain and the snow. I can smell him from where I stand on the third step of the stairs—notes of wood and smoke, but fresh. Cold, masculine smells that seem incredibly out of place inside my home.

I notice all of this. I take it all in, scanning the way he's holding his body weight on his right-hand side, and the creases in his t-shirt, and the way his hat is tilted at an odd angle on his head. I document it all with a fierce intensity, paying attention to every small detail, because I don't want to look at his face. I don't want to look him in the eye. I'm terrified. If I do look at him, I don't know what I'll do anymore. I don't know myself well enough anymore to trust my own reactions. This man is going to break me. I've been worried sick over him. Worried that he was going to do something stupid and get himself hurt. Now he shows up here, unscathed, looking utterly normal, and I want to throw myself at him.

"Sasha?" Ali says my name disapprovingly. I already know she's about to urge me back upstairs, away from this situation and any confrontation it might bring. I have no problem looking her in the eye, so I do that, swallowing hard.

"It's okay, Ali. You can let him in."

I'm surprised by how firm I sound. I speak in a tone that brooks no argument. Ali must be able to hear this; she holds up her hands, stepping back out of the way. Instead of talking to me, she faces Rooke. "If you upset her, I swear to god and all things holy..."

"Don't worry. I didn't come here to cause friction." He holds out the tray of coffees to Ali. "Yours is the one on the left."

She gives him a weird, curious look but reaches out and takes the coffee all the same. "I'm not gonna ask how you even knew I was going to be here, let alone how I like my coffee."

Rooke shrugs, taking a determined, bold step inside the house. "You're a good friend. That's how I knew you'd be here. Or rather I knew *someone* would be here. I honestly have no idea how you take your coffee. It's just black, no sugar."

"And the other two?"

"Have a fuckload of whiskey in them."

"Jesus Christ, she can't have whiskey. She's medicated up to her eyeballs."

I step forward, intervening before Ali can shove him back out the door again. "All right, all right. I won't drink the coffee. No harm, no foul. Rooke, come with me. Ali, I won't be long, I promise." I set off in the direction of the dining room, hurrying through the kitchen, not looking behind me to see if Rooke is even following me. I hold the dining room door open and he sweeps in quickly after me.

I close the door, planting my back against it, palms pressed flat against the wood. Rooke stands beside the dining table where we hold book club each week, where he sat and consumed nearly a full cheese board all by himself, and I have no choice now. I have to look at him. I have to see the intention in his eyes.

My heart feels unnaturally swollen inside my chest as our eyes meet. Rooke places the books and the coffees down on the table and then stares at me, unblinking, the fingertips of his left hand braced against the surface of the table. His face is a confusion of emotions. His stubble is almost a full-blown beard right now, and there are shadows under those light brown eyes of his. His mouth is twisted into a half smile, but it's kind of angry.

"You're not scowling," he says quietly.

"Pardon me?"

"Normally when you look at me, you're scowling."

"I am not."

"Okay." His voice is so deep. It's the voice of someone years older and years wiser than him. The sound of it makes my palms feel clammy. My throat feels tight all of a sudden.

"You're just agreeing with me to avoid an argument. I can tell."

"I am." His mouth twitches, and a glimmer of that wicked confidence flickers behind his eyes. I hold out my hand, eyeing the coffee he brought. "Are you going to give that to me or not?"

"No." He shakes his head slightly. "Not if you're high on pain meds."

"I'm not. I haven't taken anything. I told Ali I did just to shut her up."

Rooke smiles—a full, broad smile that makes me feel strange. "Badass. If I were you, I'd be popping those pills though. You look..." He trails off, his eyes moving over my body.

"Like shit?" I offer.

"Like you need pain meds." At least he doesn't tell me I look terrible. He said as much back in the hospital, and I'll admit that I cared.

"Sasha?" he says quietly.

I close my eyes.

"Sasha, look at me."

I open my eyes, and he's still frozen to the spot, still staring at me, still hovering like a ghost at the other end of the table. The snow on his shoulders has melted now, leaving wet streaks down the front of his jacket. "I've been worried," he says. "Really, *really* fucking worried. About you. I haven't been able to fucking think straight. I'm sorry about the hospital. I should have stayed. I shouldn't have left like that. I just...I couldn't fucking handle it."

"It's okay. I'm sorry, too."

He angles his head to one side. "Why are you sorry?"

"Because. This whole thing made you freak out. You shouldn't have been—"

"Fuck." He shakes his head, laughing angrily under his breath. "You really don't understand any of this, do you?" He gestures between us, frowning, his brow creased into deep, unhappy lines. "I *care* about you. I'm intensely attracted to you. I fucking want you. So seeing you whisked off in a motherfucking ambulance, covered in blood, and then not being able to check in with you? That's done more than disturb my thought patterns, okay?"

I rock back onto my heels. I'm a broken fucking mess. Can't he tell that just by looking at me? Why does he want me like this?

"Are you all right now?" he asks, grinding his teeth together. "At least tell me that."

"I'm fine. I'm tired. I'm still in shock, I guess. I hurt all over, but I'll be okay."

Rooke takes a step forward. He's only three feet away from me now, but it feels like he's standing right in front of me, as if there's no space between us at all. It's thrilling and frightening at the same time.

"I know this is the worst time, Sasha, but I need you to do something for me, okay?"

"I don't know. It depends what it—"

"Send Ali home. Right now. I'm going to take care of you."

"God, I can't. She'll have a fucking fit."

He takes a step toward me, growling under his breath. "It's not a request. It's what's going to happen. Either you go out there and tell her or I will. And I'll use much harsher language, I fucking promise you that."

I feel like I'm drunk. I feel like I'm out of my fucking mind. The prospect of telling Ali to go home is an awful one, but it's better than what's going to happen if I unleash Rooke on her. I allow my shoulders to sag, then I open the door.

"Wait here," I tell him. "Don't get involved."

He holds his hands up, an act of surrender.

Ali's standing in the hallway, trying to look like she wasn't eavesdropping a second ago. I can see from the look on her face that she heard what he just said, though. I don't even bother pretending with her. "I'm sorry, love. I know you want to make sure I'm okay, but—"

"Is he good to you?"

"What?"

She rolls her eyes. "Is he good to you? Does he treat you right? Is he careful with you? Do you feel safe with him?"

I'm stunned. "Yes," I say softly.

Ali just nods, looking down at the floor. "All right then. I mean, he's six foot five and he's built like a brick shithouse. If you say he makes you feel safe and he treats you the way he's meant to, then of course I'm okay with leaving. He's way more equipped to protect you than I am. Just know the intention was there, though, okay? I get points for that. And if he so much as sneezes in a way you don't like—"

I hug her, cutting her off. "Thank you."

She gingerly hugs me back. "Okay, okay. I'll be around tomorrow with some groceries for you." I wait with her while she puts on her jacket and her odd, stripy woolen hat. At the front door, she plants her hands on my shoulders and looks me dead in the eye. "I love you, kid. You know that, right?"

"I do."

"Good. Now go and get fucked by that ridiculously scary looking man. And no. I do not want details later, thank you very much. I don't think I'm brave enough to even hear about it."

Rooke's leaning against the wall when I head back into the dining room. Ali was right: he is a scary looking guy. He's certainly not someone I would ever have looked twice at before running into him at the museum. He's not all sharp edges and dark scowls, though. There's a tiny glimmer of light to him, too.

His face is a blank slate when he turns and looks at me, and I find myself trying to decide which side of him I'm about to witness now. That question is answered the second he opens his mouth.

"Strip, Sasha."

"What?"

"Take your clothes off. Now. I want to look at you."

"I don't think—"

"Good. Don't. That's the last thing you need to be doing. Now be a good girl and take your clothes off."

When I don't move, he arches an eyebrow at me. The pain in my body seems to ebb, replaced with something else, then. The faintest hint of need. "Do you want me to do it for you, Sasha?" he asks.

Slowly, I shake my head. I begin the task at hand. It takes me a long time to get undressed. Lifting my arms over my head takes work, as does bending down to slide my jeans from each of my legs. I hesitate in my underwear, unsure if he wants me to continue. When I look up at him, I see just how stupid a thought that was. Of course he wants me naked. I slide my panties down my body, kicking out of them, and then I try to unfasten my bra strap. I physically can't do it, though. My ribs thrum with pain when I reach behind me, and in a second Rooke is behind me, his breath hot on my neck as he brushes my hair out of the way with careful fingers, undoing it for me. He slides his hands over my shoulders, pushing the straps down, his chest pressing up against my back. Slowly, he takes my bra from me and allows it to drop to the floor.

"On the table," he whispers into my ear. "Lie on the table. I need to see you properly."

I'm past the point of arguing. He is so undeniably in control of this situation that I'm willing to do whatever he tells me to right now. I don't even have the energy to ask why. The polished wood is cold underneath my skin. Rooke stands to the side of the table, waiting patiently as I scoot back and lie down. Once I'm in place, he begins to walk around the table, inspecting the myriad of green, blue, and yellow bruises that cover my body. He starts at my neck, angling his hand for a second, then placing his thumb against one of the bruises on my throat. He matches up his hand exactly to the spot where the guy in the museum held me by the throat, and a cold, hard fury flashes in his eyes.

Next he moves down to my arm, doing the same thing, angling his hand until it matches up with the bruises. I understand what he's doing, then. He's figuring out how my attacker assaulted me, how he held me down and pinned me, how he dragged me, how he hit me, how he abused my body.

I feel small. I want to climb down off the table and end this macabre reliving of my attack in the museum, but Rooke is so focused, so single-minded right now that I know he won't let me. He needs to do this. Like he said, he needs to see.

The process takes a long time; I'm covered in bruises, cuts and scrapes. When he's done with my front, he makes me roll onto my stomach and he goes through the same thing on my back.

Once he's finished, he doesn't say anything. He gets me to turn over, and then rather than holding his hands to my injuries, he places his mouth to them instead. It's like he's saying a silent prayer as he moves across my body, kissing and stroking, working his way down from my neck, over my collarbone, over my ribs, my stomach, my thighs.

This shouldn't be sexual. I am a broken, beaten, hollow shell of a human being, but the way Rooke touches me has a dominance to it. It's as though with every kiss and every touch of his hand, he's removing the violence from my body, replacing it with something much deeper. A connection between the two of us, set in place over and over again. By the time he turns me onto my back and begins caressing my broken skin there, I'm panting, my breath coming in short, sharp blasts, my head swimming.

This man has such a control over me. Such a heady, delirious power. My body responds to him in a way it would never respond to anyone else. It's incredible and it's frightening, and I don't know how to act. He lifts me up into his arms, and he carries me upstairs.

My breath catches in my throat when he almost takes me into Christopher's room. "No. Not that one. There…" I point to my bedroom door, and he heads into the room without another word. Setting me down gently on the bed, he stands back and begins to undress. Shoes, first. Shirt. Ripped jeans. He's not wearing any underwear again. He has the type of body I didn't actually think existed in the real world—packed muscle on top of muscle that he must have worked impossibly hard for. His tattoos are everywhere, over his chest, his stomach, his shoulders, spiraling down both his arms, his hands, up around his neck. He's a work of art, a masterpiece of his own making. I allow myself a minute to take him in, too intrigued to be embarrassed by my open curiosity. He must know what I'm doing because he just stands there for a moment, shoulders back, hands by his sides while he allows me to inspect him.

"You're quite something," I whisper

"So are you," he replies. "You didn't need a liter of ink and a thousand needles to accomplish it, though. You just...*are*."

"You'd still be incredible without the ink."

He shrugs. "Maybe you're right. These tattoos *are* me in a way, though. Everything I've done. Everything I've been through."

I bite the knuckle of my index finger, frowning a little. "Are you going to tell me what they mean?"

Again, he shrugs. "Maybe one day. For now..." He climbs up onto the bed, and a thrill of nerves races through me. His cock is hard already, brushing up against his belly, and he's staring at me like he's staring down the barrel of a fucking gun. Unafraid, though. Unwavering, and unashamed. Kneeling next to me, he takes himself into his right hand, palming himself, working his hand up and down the length of his erection, his gaze drinking me in from head to toe.

"Open your legs for me, Sasha."

There is no way to say no to that. I don't think I would,

even if I could. I open my legs, exhaling down my nose, trying not to panic too hard. This is still so, so new…and after everything that's happened in the past few days…this is probably a horrible idea. I should be in therapy or something, not about to have seriously intense sex with this crazy-hot man. Do I stop myself, though? No, I don't. I need to feel something other than scared, or sad, or pissed off. I need to feel *this*. I need to feel his hands on my body, making me forget…

Except he doesn't touch me. He takes hold of my hand and guides it down…

"I told you that you would touch yourself to make me happy, didn't I? Make me happy, Sasha. I need to know how you please yourself. I need to see you come by your own hand."

This is not what I had in mind. The way he just spoke has made me break out in goosebumps, though. He really does want to study the way I touch myself, as if it's of the utmost importance that he understands how I like to come when I'm alone. "Okay." I'm breathless, the word barely there, but Rooke hears me just fine. He sits back on his heels, gently guiding my legs even further apart as I slide my fingers down over my pussy. I'm wet already. More than wet. I'm so turned on that I'm surprised, and maybe a little embarrassed. "God…"

"Don't do that," Rooke rumbles, his voice low. "Don't ever be ashamed of your body. Especially when I can see how turned on you are. Do you have any idea what that's like for me? Do you have any idea what that does to me?"

I bite my lip. He reaches out and takes my other hand, wrapping it firmly around his cock. He's so fucking hard, it feels like it must actually be painful for him. I squeeze very gently, and his head tips back, his eyes shuttering closed.

"Fuck, Sasha. *Jesus*."

Growling, he removes my hand, replacing it with his

own. "I can't do it," he says. "I can't even have you fucking touching me right now. I'll end up hurting you."

My eyes practically roll back into my head. How can he say things like that to me? The words just trip off the end of his tongue like they don't matter, but they have a profound effect on me. He can't have me touching him? He'll end up hurting me? A statement like that should make me scared, especially after everything that's happened, but the prospect of him losing control because of my touch, being rough with me, his hands hard on me, his teeth, his mouth, his body... It makes my head spin.

Slowly, I work my fingers over my pussy, rubbing in small circles over my clit. Rooke watches, fascinated. "Your body is perfect," he says. "Your hands are the sexiest fucking things ever. I can't stop staring. Slide your fingers inside yourself for me, Sasha. Show me. Show me how you fuck yourself."

I never use my fingers to fuck myself. I always use my vibrator. It feels strange to be exploring my body, performing acts for the first time while Rooke watches on. I carefully do as he's asked, and I slip my index finger inside first, followed by my middle finger. Rooke's eyes are glazed over, filled with lust and need. He bites down on his bottom lip, groaning as I begin to pump my fingers in and out of my pussy.

"Fuck. Seriously. *Fuck.* Make yourself come for me. I want to see the moment when you tumble over the edge. I want to watch your body shake. I want to see your back arch. Your toes curl. Come on, Sasha. Do it for me." As he talks, he works his fist up and down his cock, his grip getting tighter and tighter. The muscles in his arms are straining, right along with the muscles in his shoulders. His breath is coming out in short, sharp blasts. He's so turned on right now. I can see the strain on his face. He wants to fuck me. He wants to slam himself inside me and make me scream, but he's holding back. He just spent thirty minutes worshipping my body, massaging me, grieving over the pain I've suffered. He's playing it safe.

I'm not normally the type of girl to take charge in the bedroom, but I need him to realize something. I need him to realize that I want him to be a little rough with me right now. I am so sick of people walking on eggshells around me. I am so sick of people looking at me with pity in their eyes. I may be bruised and I may be covered in cuts and scrapes, but I am *not* broken. I reach out and I place my hand over Rooke's, my fingers curling around his cock. He shudders the moment I connect with him, a dark, sinister look forming in his eyes.

"*Sasha...*"

"Rooke. Don't. Please. I need you to..." I don't know how to finish the sentence. I need so much from him. I should never have allowed him past the wall I so carefully constructed after Andrew left, but now that I have it would be an impossible task to try and go back. He told me I was his, and every part of me responded to that statement. I *am* his. He *is* my gravity. Every second spent away from him *is* a second wasted. When I was laying on my back in the museum, dazed and hurting, my head was filled with thoughts of him. If he turned around and walked out now, I would be devastated. I knew it would be like this. I railed against the idea of forming any sort of connection with him, because I knew *this* was how it would be.

"Tell me," he says. "Tell me what you need."

"Just...I need...*you.*"

"I'm an asshole but I'm not a fucking cunt, Sasha. I'm not going to fuck you like this. I won't."

"Please. I need you to. I want you to. I want you inside me. *Right now.*"

I can see how hard it is for him to stop himself from

acting. I squeeze, tightening my hand around his, and he growls, the sound resonating deep in his chest. "If you don't let go, Sasha..."

Screw this. He's been pushy and arrogant the entire time I've known him, and now he's turned into a gentleman? No. Just *no*. I move quickly, propping myself up on an elbow so I can lean into him. Maybe he isn't expecting me to act so boldly, considering my battered state. He doesn't react until it's too late, though, and his rock solid erection is sliding into my mouth.

"Jesus fucking Christ," he groans. "*What...the...fuck?*"

Pleasure swells inside me. I've taken him by surprise for once. His thigh muscles tense as I work my mouth up and down his shaft, my eyes fluttering closed as I enjoy the taste and feel of him. I'm good at this. I know I am. I know, because Rooke's whole body is shaking, trembling uncontrollably. He fists my hair suddenly, snarling like a caged animal.

"You're playing with fire. Do you want me to fuck your mouth? Do you want me to? Because I'm three seconds away from me losing my shit, and then there's no turning back. There's no stopping once that happens."

I look up at him, up the length of his insanely sculpted body, and I just look at him. I don't need to speak. Rooke bares his teeth in response, gripping hold of my hair even tighter.

"All right. I want to feel your tongue, Sasha. I'm not going to be careful. I'm going to fuck your mouth, and you're going to take it. All of it."

Taking all of Rooke into my mouth is going to be a challenge for sure, but I'm so turned on right now. I'm ready for whatever happens next. I close my eyes, but Rooke gently taps my cheek with the tip of his index finger. "Eyes on me, princess. Don't look away. I wanna see the look on your face at all times. I want you to watch my dick sliding into your mouth. I want you to *see* the moment when I come, as well as feel it. As well as taste it."

God. I've read about this kind of thing at book club—guys talking dirty, taking control of their women—but I had absolutely no idea just how heady being on the receiving end of that kind of dominance would be. It's addicting. It's strange and scary, but it's also incredibly hot at the same time. Rooke rocks his hips back, sliding himself out of my mouth. Holding onto my hair, keeping me in place, he thrusts into my throat again, until I can barely fucking breathe.

"Shit! Holy fuck," he gasps. "I'm so fucking deep." Again he repeats the action, withdrawing, then thrusting back into my mouth. "Don't stop teasing yourself, Sasha," he commands. "I want your legs open wide for me. I want your fingers in your pussy. *Now*. Do it for me. Don't make me ask you again."

I am his to control. I might as well be a puppet on a string. I have no free will left now. All I have is the intense desire to please him, and I will do that by any means necessary. Rooke's gaze is cast down between my legs, watching me as I fuck myself with my fingers. I can't take my eyes off his face, though. His mouth is open, lips parted slightly. His brow is slightly furrowed, and there's an expression of grim concentration on his face. He continues to thrust himself deep down into my throat, one hand tangled in my hair, refusing to let me move, and I can feel him getting harder and harder with each and every movement he makes.

"Goddamnit," he groans. "You're going to kill me, Sasha. You're fucking going to kill me with that mouth of yours."

I sweep and swirl my tongue, running it over the head of his cock, and he shudders again, jolting violently. "Holy. Fucking. *Shit*." He wants to come. I want him to so badly.

The taste of him is dizzying; I can't seem to get enough. Rooke finally locks eyes with me, stroking his free hand down the side of my face. "You're so goddamn perfect," he growls. "You're mine. You're fucking mine. I won't let anything else happen to you. I won't ever let anyone else touch you. I promise. Fuck, I'm getting close..." His head rocks back, and I moan. He's so fucking hot, I can't contain myself anymore. I pump my fingers in and out of my pussy, cold, spiraling pins and needles working their way through my body. I can feel it building inside me. I know I'm going to come if I keep on doing what I'm doing, and in this moment nothing on this earth could make me stop.

Closer...

Closer...

Closer...

I want to close my eyes. I want to sink into this euphoria, allow it to overwhelm and encompass me. Rooke told me not to, though. I keep my eyes trained on him as my climax slams into me like the bullet from a gun. I cry out, moaning, thrashing on the bed, and Rooke reacts in kind. "Fuck. That's it, baby. That's it. Come for me. Come all over your fingers for me."

His movements quicken, his cock driving deeper and deeper into my mouth, and then there are fireworks going off in my head and he's coming, too, so hard that he roars, his head kicking back, his back curving to extreme degrees as he flounders in his orgasm. I swallow him. I don't want to spit out the come he leaves in my mouth. It's part of him, a vital part of him, and I want it inside me.

"Holy shit." He swallows thickly, releasing his grip on my hair. I lie back on the bed, still staring up at him, completely stunned by the fury of what just happened between us. Rooke looks like he can't really believe it either.

"Give me your hand," he whispers. I hold up my left,

but he shakes his head. "The other one."

"That one's covered—"

"*Give it to me.*" His eyes are stormy, dark and dangerous. He's not to be messed with right now. I slowly raise my right hand, conscious of the fact that my fingers are slick and wet with the evidence of my own orgasm. "You think you can just swallow me and there wouldn't be consequences? There are consequences to every action you make, Sasha. This is what happens when you swallow my come." He sucks my fingers into his mouth, first the index finger and then the middle finger. His eyes close as he licks and sucks, taking care to clean each of my fingers. If I'd read this in a book, I might have accepted that it would be hot and moved on. But let me tell you now: Rooke Blackheath sucking your slick, wet fingers after you just made yourself come with them is not something you can move on quickly from in real life. It's the most erotic, sexual thing that has ever happened to me, and I fucking revel in it.

"Your pussy is mine, Sasha," he says quietly. His eyes glitter, a small, perilous smile playing around the corners of his mouth. "Don't ever deny me. I'm going to want to fuck and lick and play with it every day. If you try and stop me, there will be consequences to *that* action, too."

TWENTY-TWO

THE RITZ

ROOKE

"I can't tell you something I don't know, man. Come on! *Please*! This is fucking crazy, Rooke. You *know* me. I deal in prescription meds and pot. I don't get caught up with crazy dudes that break into museums."

Mike Maurizio, my sometimes friend and drug dealer, flinches as I raise my fist in the air. My knuckles are killing me. I shouldn't have used my hands on him but I lost my temper. It's been a long-ass time since I've done that. They teach you an awful lot of anger management techniques in juvi. I didn't think I was paying much attention at the time, but in hindsight some of those techniques must have worked their magic on me, because it's been years since

I've really lost control.

Mike hasn't put up much of a struggle as I've thrown him around the dingy basement of his mother's walkup. I start to feel a little remorseful as he tries to back away from me, hands raised. "You may not work with people like him, Mike, but you know fences and you like to run your mouth. The cops said this guy wanted to steal something valuable from the museum. Something he could sell to make a profit. Guys like that usually have a buyer already lined up."

"I read the papers, too, dude. That guy was fucking crazy. He hadn't thought any of it through. Why do you think he would have had a buyer lined up?"

This is a really good point. I'm just bullshitting Mike at this stage, trying to scare him into spilling anything he might know. It's a futile task, I'm aware, but I'm at my wit's fucking end. I combed the city while Sasha was in the hospital, looking for the redheaded motherfucker that hurt her, and I haven't been remotely successful in finding him. I've found pimps and hookers, plenty of meth addicts and shady pawnbrokers, dealers, thieves, and con men, but I haven't found a ginger guy with a hole in the side of his head.

I wanted to ask Sasha for a more detailed description of the bastard earlier, but I took one look at her and knew she wouldn't approve of this. Her beautiful face was black and blue. Her lip was swollen and angry, and she seemed completely worn out. Asking her to talk about what happened some more was the last thing she needed. She probably didn't need me coming in her mouth quite so violently, but shit. She took over. I could easily have not touched her. I could have left her well alone, but I could tell that would have made things worse. She needed the release.

I grapple hold of Mike by the collar of his shirt, jerking

him toward me, almost tearing him off the sofa he's sitting on. "Tell me where you'd take something you wanted to sell, then. Something rare. Something easily recognizable."

"I don't know. The Ritz, maybe? Arnold's been paying out a lot for things recently, not asking as many questions as usual. And even if he hasn't bought anything, he'll probably have a better idea of who has." I let go of Mike and he runs his finger around the inside of his shirt collar, scowling. "Didn't need to be so damn rough, man. Now my mom's gonna be asking what the hell I've been up to again. I got enough going on without you showing up here like a crazy person, thumping me in the face for no reason."

"Do you have any pot?"

"When do I *not* have pot?"

"Point." I slump down onto the sofa next to him, holding my head in my hands. "Sorry, dude. Feeling a little mentally frayed right now."

"I'm mentally frayed every day. I don't go around hitting people." He's salty, and I don't really blame him. Thanks to all the drugs he's done over the past fifteen years he has a five second memory, though. All I have to do is sit here long enough and he'll forgive me. Rummaging around in a small wooden jewelry box resting on the arm of the sofa, Mike takes out a joint and sparks it, sending a plume of thick smoke up in a cloud over our heads.

"You're so ghetto," I inform him. "Haven't you heard of a bowl before?"

He holds onto a lungful of smoke; his body starts to jerk and he releases it, coughing. "Haven't you ever heard of asking nicely, asshole? I would have given you that information without you having to wale on me first."

I take the joint he offers me and I take a deep drag on it. "Have you ever...just...lost your fucking mind? Like, completely just lost it. Like you have no idea where it went, or how to get it back?"

"Only once. At summer camp. My cousin Brenda. She kept flirting with my best friend Damien, and dude. I wanted her bad. She was the first kid in our year to get boobs. Not ittie bittie tittie committee boobs." He cups his hands in front of his chest, squeezing imaginary flesh. "Real *boobs*."

"Urgh. Gross. Your cousin?"

"Hey, when you're twelve years old, stuff like that doesn't matter. Not even for a minute. You know, Brenda turned into a grade-A bitch. I'd probably still fuck her now if the opportunity presented itself, though."

******

I'm pretty fucking high by the time I leave Mike's. The Ritz is actually a small jeweler's shop below a bed and breakfast in Harlem; both the jeweler's and the bed and breakfast are run by the same guy—a short, overweight Armenian guy named Arnold. Every time I say his name, I think of that *Hey, Arnold!* Cartoon character with the football-shaped head. In reality, Arnold from the Ritz looks nothing like the fictional character, but I can't seem to shake the association.

A couple of blocks away from the shop, I check the antique Rolex on my wrist, a gift given to me by the daughter of one of our clients who died last year. The previous owner of the watch had been coming to the antiques store for years—years longer than I've been working there—and he bequeathed it to Duke in his will. Duke took one look at the cracked tan leather strap and the dull shine to the face and handed it over to me without a second thought. The piece must be worth about fifteen thousand dollars, but Duke's tastes run a little more expensive and shiny.

It's eleven fifteen. Technically Arnold should be closed

203

by now, but when I round the corner onto 125th I'm hardly surprised to see light still blaring out into the darkness, escaping between the cracks in his shutters. I don't knock on the door. I make sure to ring the bell—one short, sharp blast to make sure he knows it's one of his regulars.

Inside a rabble of dogs start barking; they slam their bodies into the reinforced door with the steel bars, snarling like savages. After a few moments, Arnold's very round, non-football-shaped head appears on the other side of the glass. "You know, where I come from, it's considered very bad luck when a crow appears in front of your house," he says. I hear him perfectly, even over the racket the dogs are making.

"Good thing I'm a rook and not a crow, then."

Arnold waves off this comment, unlocking a series of deadbolts on the other side of the door. "Rook. Crow. They are one and the same to me. What are you doing here so late?" He kicks at one of the dogs, shooing it back so he can open the door. For all their ferocious barking and snapping, they run at me, jumping up at me as soon as they can wriggle through the gap, licking at my hands and panting.

"I'm looking for someone."

"I don't deal in people. I deal in *things*. Things are easier to control. Tea?"

"No, thank you." I slip into the shop and Arnold begins the laborious task of closing all the deadbolts again. The inside of the shop smells like cinnamon and cloves, like the little black cigarillos Arnold smokes. The counters are cluttered with contraband probably not seen during regular opening hours: guns; knives; a set of knuckle dusters. A solid brick of gold rests on top of a stack of invoices like it's a common paperweight.

"Are you sure you won't take some Lapsang Suchong?" Arnold mumbles, hobbling around the counter.

I wrinkle my nose in answer.

"All right. If you change your mind, you keep it to yourself. It'll be too late by then."

"I'll be fine."

Arnold measures loose tea leaves into a silver strainer with shaky gnarled hands. "Who is this person you're looking for?" he asks bluntly, still going about his task.

"A deadbeat. The guy who broke into the museum the other day. You know who I'm talking about?"

"I know someone broke into the museum the other day. I don't know anything else, I'm afraid."

I don't know if I believe him. He's looking down, focused on not spilling tea leaves everywhere, and I can't get a gauge on him without looking him directly in the eye. I stoop down, leaning heavily against the counter. "He hurt someone. A friend of mine. What would you do if someone hurt one of your friends, Arnold?"

"I would kill them of course," he says mildly. "I understand your need to find this person, Rooke. That doesn't change the fact that I can't help you. I wish that I could. If I could tell you a name or an address, then you would be happy, and I like to make you happy. Especially when it's so late at night and I'd like to finish my inventory and go to bed. But since I haven't any clue who this person is, I regret that you're going to have to leave my shop an unhappy man. That pains me, it really does."

Hurting Arnold isn't really an option. Not if I don't want to get myself kneecapped and dumped in the Hudson. Besides, the guy is ancient. It would feel wrong hitting him. At least Mike could have fought back if he'd had the fucking stones to.

I don't owe Arnold anything, and you'd think that would put me in his good graces. However, if you owe Arnold something, you're in his debt in more than one way. You don't just owe him money. You owe him your fealty, you're at his beck and call. You owe him a favor, and boy does he call in those favors. If you *don't* owe him any favors, there's a power imbalance in the relationship as far as Arnold is concerned. For some reason, he's less likely to help you out if he feels like you're his equal, which means I am shit out of luck on that front.

The only way I'm gonna get a guy like Arnold to help me out is if I have something to pawn with him, or outright sell to him at a discounted rate. I immediately think of my watch but then change my mind. I'm sentimental over the thing. I have no idea why, but giving it up, even when I got it as a gift, feels wrong somehow. I have nothing else of value on me, so where does that leave me?

Arnold finishes the ritual of his tea making and lifts the comically small tea dish to his mouth, blowing on the pale liquid inside. "Your mother came here yesterday," he says softy. "She was looking for you."

"My *mother*?"

Arnold tips his head to one side, indicating that he was just as surprised as I am now. Most people come to know Arnold through dodgy dealings and underhanded mischief. That's how I came to know him for the second time in my life. The *first* time I came to know him, he was my father's antiques dealer and a family friend. I spent summers here, cataloguing the estate sales that came in and dusting high shelves that had never been dusted before. Then came high school and all of the chaos that followed with puberty, and Arnold just kind of faded from the backdrop of our family life. He was a friendly uncle who simply...disappeared.

The second time I came to know him, I was beaten black and blue, and a cracked-out junkie was trying to split my head open with a tire iron over a bag of money I was transporting for Jericho. Car money. Mob money. That is to say, *Arnold's* money. Every blood-stained, tainted dollar bill that passes hands in the New York underground eventually makes its way back to him. It's beyond weird that my mother would come here looking for me. I haven't mentioned Arnold to her in years. She has no idea that I'm still connected with him now.

"She brought me this tea," Arnold says. "She was wondering if I knew how you were supporting yourself these days. I told her I hadn't seen you in a very long time, of course. She was...*dubious*, shall we say."

"Does she know what you do here?"

Arnold gives me a sharp, chilling glance. "Does she know that I sell jewelry? That I provide bed and breakfast services to those in need of it? I assume she knows. The sign above the door clearly states these things."

"All right. That was a stupid question. I'm sorry."

Arnold grunts in agreement. "Your mother is an interior designer. She cuts the crusts off her sandwiches. The thread count on her bed sheets runs into the thousands. How would such a woman know anything of the shady dealings that occur here after the sun goes down? I thought you perhaps might have mentioned something to her..."

The way he trails off at the end of his sentence is a suggestion. A deadly suggestion. If he thinks for a second that I've been running my mouth off, or even accidentally uttering his name in circles where it should never be uttered, I am a motherfucking dead man. I shake my head, laughing under my breath. "I'm not that careless, Arnold. You know I'm not."

He stares at me for a second, and then nods once, short and sharp. A decisive nod. "True. Better this is brought to your attention, though. Better you're aware of a potential problem on the horizon now rather than later."

"Potential problem?"

Arnold, master of saying very loud things with the quietest of gestures, taps the pad of his index finger against the rim of his cup. "Well, of course. She is your mother, jan. And is it not always a son's duty to look out for the welfare of his mother?"

TWENTY-THREE

HAPPY BIRTHDAY

SASHA

Two Weeks Later

Fourteen days. Fourteen days can change so much. Every day, Rooke has stayed with me, taking care of me just like he said he would. He occasionally goes to work and Ali comes over. The second he's home, he makes her leave and we fall into bed, clawing at each other's bodies like lunatics, kissing, licking, stroking, sucking... I become intimately acquainted with every single part of his body, and he with mine. He tells me what he wants, and I obey him without question. If he says he wants me on my knees, I am there. If he tells me to stay still, I am frozen to the spot. If he commands me to finger myself while he watches, I do it without blushing. I am unafraid. At night he holds me in his arms, and I sleep. I don't dream. The nightmares leave me when I'm securely nestled with my head on his chest. I keep the door to Christopher's bedroom locked, and Rooke doesn't ask questions.

He accomplishes the impossible: for a very, very brief moment in time, against all the odds, I am strangely happy. A day soon comes, though, where he simply can't. I lie to him. I tell him Ali is coming over, and he goes to work, and I prepare for the pain I'm about to suffer. Even more than Christmas, I dread December the eighth. I fear the date creeping up on me more than I fear the anniversary of the accident. I fear it more than anything else in the world. On this day eleven years ago, I was laid out on my back in the hallway at home, screaming in agony as my little boy made his way into the world. Today is Christopher's birthday.

There are a few things people don't tell you about childbirth. Midwives, doctors, new mothers themselves... The first thing they don't mention is the tearing. You can literally feel it, your body splitting in the most terrifying way as a child the size of a bowling ball makes its way out of your vagina. The second thing they don't mention is your overwhelming need to poop all over yourself. Andrew always said he knew about that part, they'd covered it in the birthing prep classes we'd attended, but I never could recall it. Maybe I blocked the information out, blotted it from my memory, deeming it too distressing to process at the time. I was certainly surprised by that turn of events when I was in labor, that's for sure.

The third thing people tend to gloss over, or skip entirely when dealing with soon-to-be mothers, is the panic. You're so excited when you see that little pink cross develop on the pee stick you bought at the all-night pharmacy at 3 a.m. It's a hell of a lot of fun buying tiny little socks, and onesies that say, "Mommy's little angel" on them. Putting the crib together and decorating the nursery is so exciting that it's almost too much to bear. But the delivery part? The pushing? The urge is so strong, so powerful, so undeniable that it takes you by surprise. I had no idea my body could demand something from me in such a way. An addiction is hard to overcome, but with the right support and a healthy dose of mental fortitude, it can be overcome. Not this, though. It's as urgent and vital as breathing. When those contractions hit me, coming on impossibly fast and strong, I had to push. I had to bear down, to expel the tiny human being from my body, and I had no choice in the matter. A crippling panic hit me, then. I wasn't ready. I wasn't prepared. I was going to be a horrible mother. I shouldn't have been in charge of bringing another life into the world.

Everyone said how awful first time labors were. They were the longest, most painful, hardest, most difficult labors of a woman's life. They weren't supposed to sneak up on you when you were least expecting them, an entire month before your due date, just as you're getting ready to meet your friend for coffee, and they definitely weren't meant to escalate into full delivery in less than thirty minutes.

I didn't have time to get my overnight bag. My overnight bag wasn't even packed properly. Andrew was on a flight to San Antonio and wasn't picking up his phone. And the ambulance? The ambulance wasn't supposed to be stuck in three feet of snow eight blocks away, unable to reach me.

Giving birth to my son was perhaps the most frightening experience of my life. More frightening than being assaulted at the museum. Then, I was only afraid for my own life. Being alone and trying to make it through that experience was scary because it wasn't just about me. What if something went wrong? What if he was breach? What if he had the umbilical chord wrapped around his neck, cutting off his oxygen supply?

I endured that brief moment of insanity, pain and worry with a strange kind of clarity that made me realize nothing was ever going to be the same again once it was over, one way or another. And I was right. Nothing ever has been.

I start drinking at 7 a.m. I polish off an entire bottle of Malbec, drinking from the bottle as I sit on the bottom step of the stairs in my pajamas, staring at the parquet flooring in front of the front door. My cell phone starts ringing at eight—a Texas number. Andrew, calling to check in on me, no doubt. I don't know anyone else in Texas, and who else would be ringing today of all days anyway? He must have snuck away for a moment, ducked out the back door, away from his new wife, into the yard or something. His finger is probably pressed into his ear so he can hear better as he waits for me to pick up. Has he thought about what I'm going to say when I answer? Does he have a script prepared and ready? *Hi, Sasha. How are you? Keeping well, I hope...*

I doubt he's gotten that far to be honest. He's been calling on this day for years, and I never pick up. He just does what he thinks is the right thing by calling, and I do what I think is the right thing by ignoring my phone at all costs. The system works well for us both.

I open a fresh bottle of vodka at 9 a.m. The hallway is swimming by the time I'm a couple of inches down the bottle. Doctor Hathaway would lose his mind if he knew I was doing this again. I can hear his disapproval ringing in my ears as I place the neck of the vodka bottle to my mouth and I take another long, deep drink from it.

"You lost your child, Sasha. Is drinking going to bring him back? You already know how destructive this behavior is. Why continue walking in a direction when you know it's taking you further from the direction you're meant to be heading in?"

But fuck that guy. The thing about therapists is that they've often stood ankle deep in misery. They get their feet wet just by observing their clients' pain and suffering. They usually have stable, happy, healthy families, though. Framed pictures of their dorky kids on their desks. Wives or husbands calling when sessions run over to see how long it will be until they're home. They don't know what it's like to be immersed in misery, for the surface of the water to be miles overhead and for you to be so fucking tired that it's only a matter of time before you sink and drown. Hathaway doesn't know that walking down the wrong path is the only thing that keeps you alive sometimes, irrespective of how unsafe and fraught with danger that road may be.

By midday, I'm so fucked that I can't even lift the nearly empty bottle of vodka to my mouth anymore. I lay flat on my back on the floor where I gave birth, and I laugh at the way the room is pitching from side to side. My ears are ringing like crazy. At some point, I think I'm going to throw up. I roll onto my side, my body bowing as I retch, but I don't remember if I'm sick or not. I pass out. Slipping into the oblivion seems like the smartest option for me right now. A dull thudding sound half wakes me some time later, the sound of my heart maybe, slamming in my chest, struggling to function under the stress of all the alcohol pumping around my body, but I ignore it. I fall back into the darkness. I slip, slide, tumble, fall…

Breaking glass.
Ice cold air, hitting the bare soles of my feet.
Hands on me, turning me over.

Voices, frantic, calling my name.

"Sasha? Holy fucking shit. What have you done?"

Andrew, not in Texas... Andrew, showing up in my life again after all this time, shouting at me, so, so disappointed all over again.

"Open your eyes, baby. Come on, open them up for me. Come on. Can you sit up? Oh, god...what the...*fuck*?"

I groan, trying to free myself from the hands of my ex-husband. Who the fuck does he think he is, breaking in here, trying to tell me what the fuck I should do? How dare he come back here? How dare he—

My stomach heaves as he turns me over. Bright flashes of light explode behind my eyes. I try to open them, and everything is blurry, distorted, bent out of shape. Andrew's face doesn't look right. His hair is dark. His eyes are—

Rooke.

Oh god, no. Rooke has broken into my house, not Andrew. Rooke is bent down, frantically working over me, trying to get me to sit up. I can't fucking breathe.

"Goddamnit, Sasha," he hisses. "*What have you done?*"

******

"Makes a change from our regulars. I've had to pump the stomachs of a bunch of frat kids over the past week, but not a thirty-year-old housewife. Do you think she drank on meds? She's pretty bruised up. Looks like she's been cage fighting with Tyson or something."

I can hear the nurses talking outside my cubicle. I can hear a number of disturbing things—the sound of a heart monitor, the sound of a child crying somewhere in a distant room, a man and a woman arguing loudly in Russian somewhere closer—but the nurses talking about me is the most upsetting thing to reach my ears.

"Who knows? I wouldn't be all that surprised if she just drank herself this way though. Happens more often than you'd think. Husband's cheating, spends too many late nights at the office 'working'. Doesn't pay her any attention. Kids are ungrateful little shits, running riot all the time. A vodka soda seems like a good idea. Then a second sounds like an even better idea. Suddenly you're passed out in your hallway in a pool of your own puke and your nephew's breaking down the door to scrape you off the floor."

Ha. *Nephew*. I close my eyes, hoping to drown out the sound of the chatter, but it doesn't help. It feels like my veins are filled with ice water. I'm chilled to the bone, and yet my skin is slick with sweat. I don't know how long I've been here or what really happened to land me in the hospital, but I have a pretty decent idea. I do remember Rooke lifting me from the floor and carrying me in his arms. I do remember the sound of broken glass crunching under his boots.

Then...

Blackness.

I open my eyes, slightly freaked by the memory of the nothingness that took hold of me. The curtain surrounding my bay twitches slightly, and half a face appears—one blue eye, and one nostril and some bright pink lipstick. The eye goes wide, and the curtain falls back into place.

"She's *awake*," the nurse hisses. "Shit, you don't think she heard...?" There's a scuffling sound, and the curtain opens fully, revealing a tall guy in his forties wearing a white lab coat and a checked button-down shirt. He looks pissed. The two nurses follow him into the bay, eyes cast to the floor, their cheeks rosy. Looks like they just got busted gossiping about me.

"Good evening, Ms. Connor. I'm Doctor Elias Soames. This is Nurse Wheatley and Nurse Diddick. I'm sure you're acquainted with them by now."

"You could say that." My throat hurts when I speak, raw, like I've been throwing up for hours and hours. Doctor Soames must see me wince, because he reaches into his pocket and produces a slim black penlight and leans over me.

"Open for me," he says. I open my mouth, and he frowns gently as he inspects me. "Yes, unfortunately your throat is a little enflamed. Not uncommon when you've had your stomach pumped. Tell me, how are you feeling?"

"Like I just got run over. And then backed over."

"Well, I suppose that's what you get when you drink the well dry. Your blood alcohol level was dangerously high, Ms. Connor. Is this something that happens regularly?"

Oh god. This can't be happening. I want to pull the sheets over my head and hide myself away but that doesn't seem like a particularly adult way of handling the situation. "No," I say. "It doesn't. Today's just...just particularly hard for me is all."

Soames nods in a businesslike manner. "Okay. I'm going to have to take your word for that. Please know there's help available here if you need it, however. All you have to do is reach out. Now, there's a young man in the waiting area that's been asking to see you for the last six hours. We advised him he'd be better off going home and waiting for you to call, but—"

"It's fine. You can let him in." I'd love for them to send Rooke away. I'm so humiliated right now. What did I look like, sprawled out on the floor like that? And in a pool of my own vomit, no less. Perfect. It would be so much better if I could just hide here for another few hours, then go home and hide in my shame for a couple of days before I see him again, but if there's one thing I know about Rooke Blackheath, it's that he's a stubborn and persistent man.

So long as I'm here, he won't just go home. He'll raise hell until he's either been arrested or he's laid eyes on me, and I don't want him getting into trouble. Not because of me.

Soames shoots an acidic glance at one of the nurses, who scurries off. The other nurse looks lost for a moment, and then she turns tail and bolts, too. Soames shakes his head ever so slightly. "Please accept my apologies on their behalf. Idle chit chat is more rife in this hospital than the common cold. They'll be getting a stern talking to, I promise."

"It's okay. I'm sure they're just saying what everyone else is thinking anyway."

He collects my chart from the foot of my bed and makes a few scribbled notes on it, then replaces it. "We'll keep you here for another hour or so. Once your fluids are back up, you'll be free to go home. Might I make a suggestion, Ms. Connor?"

I have a feeling I'm not going to like this suggestion.

"Don't let what other people think affect you," he says. "There are seven and a half billion people in this world, and every single one of them has an opinion. The only opinion that should matter to you is yours. And your beau's, of course."

I give him a weak smile. "So *you* don't think he's my nephew, then?"

Soames shakes his head. "A nephew wouldn't look quite as terrified. Only a great deal of love can make a man panic like that." He turns, about to leave, but then he appears to think twice about it, hovering at the edge of the curtain. "I dated a woman who was older than me once. *Significantly* older. Everyone said it would never work. They gave us six months. A year, tops. I'm glad to say they were all very wrong."

"You made it work?"

He smiles. "We've been married fourteen years now."

He leaves just as Rooke arrives. Soames was right: he does look panic stricken. He's pale and drawn, and his usual arrogance has fled him. He barely even sees the doctor as he moves past him. Sitting on the edge of the bed, Rooke interlaces his fingers together in his lap, staring down at his hands. He sighs heavily. "I've been thinking," he says. "While they were treating you this whole time, I've been sitting in the waiting room, thinking."

"Sounds stressful," I whisper.

"Yeah. It was. See, we've been almost living together for the past two weeks, and I've felt shitty. I know something I shouldn't know. You're going to be mad when I tell you what it is I know, and you're going to tell me you don't want to see me again."

Dread sinks through, heavy as a stone. What is he talking about? There's only one thing he could possibly have found out that would cause me to react like that, though. I know as much already. I just don't want to admit it to myself, because that will mean there will be no more sanctuary in Rooke. He's been separate from anything related to my past this whole time. That has been a blessed relief. When I look at him, I haven't seen someone who feels sorry for me, someone who's potentially judging me as a bad parent. He's just been a guy, and I've just been a girl. Now, though...

Rooke lifts his right hand and slowly spell-signs Christopher's name.

"How do you know how to do that?" I ask in a flat voice.

"You can learn anything on Youtube. Google told me the rest. About you. About the accident. About you losing your son."

A heaviness hangs in the air. You could cut through it with a goddamn chainsaw. Neither of us says anything for a while, which gives me time to compile my thoughts. He's right: my immediate response to the fact that he knows about my son is to scream at him. Tell him he has no right knowing about this. Tell him that I want him to go, to leave my life and never call me or show up on my doorstep again. Maybe that's what I would have done a couple of months ago. Even three weeks ago. Since I met him, though, things have been different. He's challenged me so many times to approach my life in another way. To move beyond what I think I should or shouldn't do. And more than that. He's shown me that other people aren't necessarily always who you think they are. *They* don't always conform to society's idea of who they should be, or how *they* should act. I count to ten very slowly in my head. I've only reached seven when I feel his fingers tracing down the side of my face.

"I'm not saying you should have told me. I'm saying you *can* tell me," he whispers. "*Anything.* I told you the worst thing about me when I would never normally breathe a word about my extracurricular activities. I wanted you to know the darkest part of my life, because I already knew about yours and it didn't feel right. Unfair, somehow. But you listened to me, and you didn't turn me away. I knew you wouldn't, because this isn't something you turn your back on, Sasha. There's nothing that can turn this off now. This thing between us...you're afraid of it. The moment you stop fearing this and you accept it, you'll be able to see just how fucking beautiful it is. And the moment you accept it will also be the moment you don't have to carry this shit on your own anymore."

I know I'm about to cry. The second I open my mouth and try to speak, my throat will close up and I'll choke on the words. I still try, though. "It's not that easy. It's not something I can just hand off to someone else, so they can carry half the load for me, Rooke. This is ingrained deep inside me now. It would be like trying to give away half of my soul."

"I'll take a part of your soul," he says quietly. "Give me the wounded part. Give me the part that hurts you every time you breathe. Give me the part that feels so heavy you just don't think you can carry it anymore. I'll take care of it for you."

I feel like I've been struck with something hard and blunt. Rooke just stares at me with a solid, steady look on his face, and I can feel my eyes stinging, my throat closing up. He means it. I read it on every line of him; he would carry my pain if he could. I have no idea why, but he would. Even Andrew couldn't do that for me. I suppose it makes sense that he couldn't—he had his own pain to carry, after all. Kika, Kayla, Ali and Tiffanie all tried to help with the load, but they all soon bowed under the pressure of that kindness. Something in the way Rooke's so fixed on me right now, the tight clench of his jaw and the set of his shoulders, tells me he could do it though. If I let him, if I knew how, he would carry every single hurt I possess, until I barely even felt them anymore.

"I can't do this," I whisper. "It's too much."

"It doesn't have to be."

"You don't understand."

"I can try. You could *let* me try. What have you got to lose?"

"EVERYTHING!" I take a raw breath in and I choke on the air flowing into my lungs. God, I can't cope with this. It's too hard. It's too much. I cover my face with my hands, embarrassed that I'm suddenly crying.

"Why would you lose everything?" Rooke asks.

"Because. If I trust you, if I make myself vulnerable, I have to let down the walls I've spent so long constructing. And if it doesn't work out between us, if I trust you and you let me down, or if I fuck things up, there's no way I'll

220

be able to put that wall back up again. No way in hell. It took too much to build it the first time around. I have nothing left, Rooke. Seriously. I have nothing left."

*****

I hate being carted out of the hospital in a wheelchair. It magnifies my humiliation to unbearable degrees. It feels like everyone is looking at me, watching, judging me. Rooke's been quiet for a long time. He's simmering; I can feel the annoyance and disappointment rolling off him like heat from a sidewalk in summer, and it's making things really uncomfortable. I told him he didn't need to stop and drive me back to my place, and he just grunted. He spoke to the nurse about what care I might need at home—lots of water, lots of rest—and then he pointedly ignored me.

It's raining outside. Big, fat, heavy droplets of water that explode every time they hit the sidewalk. The sky looks grim and serious, much like Rooke as he helps me to my feet and returns the wheelchair to an orderly by the door.

"Wait here," he says. He doesn't look back at me as he jogs off into the rain, presumably looking for a taxi. I watch him go, his hair instantly wet as he crosses the blacktop, and I can't help but look around, searching for an exit from this situation. If I slip away now, it's unlikely he'll follow me home. After picking me up off the floor and getting me to the hospital, he shouldn't want to see me ever again. Me vanishing would be the perfect way out for him.

He's disappeared. I crane my neck, trying to spot him in the increasingly hard rain, but he's the one who's vanished. *He's* the one who's ducked away in the dusk.

I step back, away from the curb, as a black sedan rolls up in front of the hospital entrance. The window buzzes down, and then Rooke hops out of the driver's seat and comes around the vehicle to open the passenger door for me.

I just stare at the car and at him, processing the fact that he has a car. "You borrowed this?" I ask.

He cocks his head, looking at the car. He's tired, though. He's not really seeing it. "In the most illegal sense of the word, yes," he confirms.

"What does that mean?"

"I stole it from one of your neighbors." He slams the door shut on me, cutting off my horrified gasp. He climbs into the driver's seat and slams his own door, clipping his seatbelt into place. Rooke holds onto the steering wheel with both hands, eyes directed straight ahead. "Aren't you going to put your seatbelt on?"

I continue to stare at him with my mouth open.

"Jesus Christ, Sasha." He leans over and grabs hold of my seatbelt, yanking it across my body, fumbling as he tries to drive the metal clip home. I snatch the seatbelt away from him, ripping it from his hands.

"Seriously? You're seriously worried about me buckling up when the car we're in is fucking *stolen*?"

"I was joking. Fuck. This is Jake's car."

"Who's Jake?"

Turning on me, his eyes are blazing, filled with fire. "Jake is my roommate. I've lived with him for the past four years. You'd know that, but you don't ask pertinent questions about who the fuck I am or about my fucking life. You just focus on the stupid shit that doesn't matter to anyone but you. But you're going to, Sasha. I'm not going to let you panic your way out of this one. I'm done, okay? I'm done standing back, allowing you to fuck this up, waiting for you to figure this shit out on your own terms. If I have to force you to see this, I will. Do you think I won't lock you in a basement and fuck you stupid until you can finally see how important this is? Do you think I won't hold you hostage until you admit how you feel? That you're in love with me? That the way I touch you turns you on beyond words? I've been to jail, Sasha, and it's literally the worst place on earth. It stinks, you're worried about getting ass raped twenty-four fucking seven, and the food is enough to make you puke three times a day. I despised it there, but I'm willing to risk going back if it means you'll quit this shit and just behave. Do you hear me? Do you understand?"

At what point do I give in? He speaks these words of truth to me, and I'm blinded by them. I can't see which way to run, or which way to turn. I'm turned around, lost, and so afraid of the consequences of really allowing myself to fall for him that I push and shove against the very idea of it like a little child, refusing to accept the inevitable. There are a thousand ways to get hurt every time I step foot out of my front door, though. My heart is a resilient muscle now. It's taken such a beating, had so many experiences at fighting to heal itself over and over again, when I thought there was just no way I would ever recover from the pain I was in, and yet each time I've found a way back, to heal, to recover and to keep on stepping through that front door.

If he hurts me, I can get over it.

If my heart gets broken again, what's one more fracture amongst a spider's web of scars?

Rooke presses his lips together, nostrils flared. He swallows, and his Adam's apple bobs, shifting the ink on his neck. There's a wild and untamable light in his eyes that reminds me of a storm out at sea—distant and far away, but obviously savage and dangerous in nature. He doesn't speak. He doesn't move the car. He waits.

After a long time, I take a deep breath and I close my eyes. "Okay, Rooke. *Okay*. You win. I'll tell you everything you want to know."

TWENTY-FOUR

LET GO

ROOKE

Once when I was fourteen, I walked in on Sim and Richard. They were fucking. Or rather, they were having *intercourse*. My mom was laid out flat on her back, eyes vacant and staring up at the ceiling, and my dad had this look of concentration on his face that made him look pained. They didn't see me standing there in the doorway of their bedroom until Richard finished his perfunctory thrusting and collapsed onto the mattress. Sim turned her head, and there was a brief moment where we were connected, she was seeing me and I was seeing her, her pale pink silk nightgown still rucked up around her hips like a rape victim, and she looked exhausted. Beaten down. She looked so much younger than she did during daylight hours, when she was rushing around, cleaning, talking on the phone with her friends and telling me to keep my feet off the furniture. She was someone I didn't recognize, and for a heartbeat in time I felt sorry for her. Then, the anger crept in around her eyes again, her mouth pulling down into a grimace, and she was back. Sim. My mother, annoyed and disappointed in me for the fifteenth time that day. Except this time she was embarrassed, too. It took me a while to figure out why: that having someone witness the mechanical, unpleasant nature of the love making she shared with her husband meant someone else knew there was no actual love left in her marriage.

I vowed back then that when I had sex with a woman, I would dedicate myself to her enjoyment. I would make sure she *wanted* me to be on top of her. I would make sure she was dizzy with wanting me and everything I had to offer. I swore I would know how to please her.

Did that mean I went out and I fucked a bunch of women to gain experience? Yes. Did that mean I got my ass beaten by seniors in high school when I screwed their cheerleader girlfriends? Fuck yes. Nearly every day of the week, before I was packed off to juvi. Don't get me wrong, I wasn't unsafe or stupid. I had a condom in my pocket at all times; I knew that it actually had to get used instead of just sitting there. As a result, while my stupid friends (Jake include) were all filling prescriptions for antibiotics to clear up their chlamydia and a colorful array of other nasty STIs, my dick was in perfect working order. When I got out of juvi, I fucked my way across New York, learning about a woman's needs. It's a thing of beauty, a woman's body. Far more delicate and fragile than any clock or car engine I've worked on. I know how and where to touch, though. Where to lick, where to kiss, where to excite.

Sasha and I sit in silence as I drive her home from the hospital. Side streets whip by in a blur. Yellow taxicabs weave erratically through the traffic. The rain comes down so hard it's next to impossible to see out of the windshield. My mind wanders as I go through the motions of shifting gears—where I'm going to kiss her first. Where I'm going to touch her. How many times I'll make her come. How many times she's going to scream my name. I have a solid plan by the time I pull up outside my place.

Sasha squints blearily out of the window, looking up at the building beside us. "This isn't my house," she says.

"I know. This is my house. I know you're tired. I know you're sick. It's time you came here, though. You'll be comfortable. You'll be taken care of. Don't even think about arguing with me, okay?"

She looks stumped for a second, then shakes her head. "I wasn't going to."

Well there's a surprise. "All right then." I get out of the car and I take my jacket off. By the time I'm around the other side of the car, I have it held out for Sasha to shield her from the rain. I can feel water trickling down my back, in between my shoulder blades as I walk her slowly to the house.

"Which apartment is yours?" she asks. Her hair is wet. Despite the shadows under her eyes, as well as the slight bruise there too, she looks fucking phenomenal. I find this is when people are at their most captivating. At least their most honest. She's not wearing a lick of makeup, she's getting soaked regardless of my best efforts, and she's leaning against me for support. I want to scoop her up and crush her to me, hold onto her forever.

"I don't have an apartment here," I tell her. "It's all mine. The whole building."

"*What*? The whole...?" She looks up, eyes taking in the

first floor, then the second, then third and the fourth. "What the hell, Rooke? How can you afford this?"

"I told you. I'm a spoiled little rich kid. My parents gave it to me as a living inheritance."

She blinks, seeming to try and take in the information. "Wow. And I thought my place was overkill. So...only two of you live here?"

"Only the two of us. And don't worry. I'm on the top floor. Jake's two floors down. Sound doesn't travel well at Chez Blackheath."

"Oh god," she groans. "I just got off an IV drip. My leg was nearly broken recently and you're going to make me climb four flights of stairs?"

"Nope. I'm going to carry you."

"Like hell you—"

I cut her off when I bend and pick her up quickly, lifting her into my arms.

"Rooke! *Put me down!*"

"Quit. Let's just get inside. You can pummel me to death with your girly fists then. Right now I'd appreciate it if you'd stop hitting me." She stops slapping her hand against my chest long enough for me to fish my keys out of my pocket one-handed.

"Take them. Open it," I tell her.

She reaches down and takes the keys from me, and then she's opening the door, pushing it open, and I'm taking her inside. The house is warm. For a second I consider sinking down onto the bottom step of the stairs and just holding her in my arms while we both thaw out. She's shaking, my leather jacket half draped over her body, her shirt plastered to her chest. Her jeans are drenched too. It would be better to get her into a hot shower and fast.

I climb up to the first floor, and that's where Jacob meets us. He's hurrying out of the living room carrying his guitar case and a mountain of sheet music, a bagel stuffed into his mouth. When he sees us, he puts down the guitar case, pins the sheet music under his arm, and he removes the bagel from between his teeth.

"We've talked about this," he says, pointing at Sasha. "No roofied girls in the house, Blackheath."

"Shut up, asshole. This is Sasha."

Jake rolls his eyes. "Of course it's Sasha. Who else would it be?" Holding out a hand, he gives her one of his super awkward, super shy smiles. "I'm not going to ask why he's carrying you like that," he says. "I probably don't want to know."

"You definitely don't," she says quietly, shaking his hand. I'm glad Jake hasn't put his foot in it. I texted him and told him I was going to be at the hospital, and I also explained why. He's a smart fucker. He knows I'd kick his ass if he embarrassed her.

"I have a gig tonight. I won't be back until late. It was nice to meet you." He gives me a strained look as he slips by us and jogs down the stairs. He hasn't said anything about how impractical my relationship with Sasha is since the shit that went down at the museum. He's a stubborn guy, though. He probably thinks this is crazy. He probably thinks I should have dropped Sasha off at home and left her ass there, never to speak to her again.

******

SASHA

He carries me up the next flight of stairs, bypassing the living room, straight to the bedroom. He takes me inside and places me carefully down on the bed. I look around, surprised.

"What is it?" he asks.

"I don't know. I just...I figured your place would be..."

"A disgusting frat house?"

"Yeah. I guess. I definitely didn't think it would be this clean."

"I'm twenty-three, not a barbarian."

"Actually, you are kind of a barbarian."

He smirks, that terrible, reckless "fuck me" smile of his that makes my toes curl inside my shoes. "You fucking *love* me this way," he informs me. "You love the danger. If I didn't scare you a little, you wouldn't be interested. You can't deny that."

He's right; I can't. I don't like to admit to something like that, though. It makes me seem as though I'm not quite right in the head. After all, what kind of woman willingly wants to be a little afraid of the guy she's sleeping with? What kind of woman wants to feel like her entire life might spiral out of control any second now because the guy she continually allows into her bed is a criminal and a thief?

"Now that you have me here, trapped in your bachelor pad, what are you planning on doing with me?" I ask.

Rooke arches his left eyebrow, his head turned to one side. "You know exactly what I'm planning on doing, Sasha. You know, there will come a time when I fuck you and you aren't fresh out of the hospital, though, right?"

His comment is like a punch in the gut. I have been hospitalized more than any one person should be over the past couple of weeks. I want to defend myself, to explain to him that this isn't normal for me. I went five years without seeing the inside of a hospital before the incident in the museum. I hadn't even been to see a general practitioner in all that time. I plan on saying all of this, but Rooke's phone buzzes in his pocket before I can form the words. He pulls out his cell and quickly reads the message he obviously just received. Frowning, he puts his cell back into his pocket.

"What is it?"

"Nothing. Just work."

"Work? At this time of night? I had no idea watch making was such a demanding job." I realize I've made a mistake as soon as I finish speaking. A hard, blank look forms on Rooke's face.

"Not that job. My *other* job."

My cheeks flush scarlet. "Ah. The…"

"The car-boosting job, yeah."

"Aren't you going to reply?"

He looks at me, his gaze steady. Unshakeable. "No. I'm not in a position to take this particular job."

"Why not?"

"Because it would require me leaving you right now, and I'm not going to do that."

A pleasant, strange sensation coils deep in the pit of my stomach. What the fuck is wrong with me? I'm excited and giddy that my boyfriend is turning down grand theft auto work in order to care for me, because I drank myself stupid and needed to get my stomach pumped. There is something very, very wrong with this scenario. Rooke smiles, an almost, kind-of-there smile. "You're taking this very well," he says.

If only he knew how well…

"I'm clearly disturbed," I tell him.

Rooke shakes his head. "If you were disturbed, you'd be telling me to take the job. You'd be telling me you'd come along for the ride."

I stare at him, unblinking. Was that an idle, off-the-cuff comment, or was he making a veiled suggestion? I narrow my eyes at him, trying to decide. "That really *would* be crazy."

"Yeah. Only a really badass woman would go on a

boost with her insane boyfriend."

"Do you want to take the job, Rooke? Are you asking me if I'll come with you to steal a car right now?"

He laughs, picking up a small silver pocket watch from the desk by his window. He opens it and glances at the face, then he lifts his head and looks me dead in the eye. "Yes. I am. What do you say, Connor? Are you in, or are you chicken?"

No. No fucking way, Rooke. That is categorically the most stupid, erratic, dangerous suggestion anyone has ever made to me. I work at a museum, for crying out loud. I am a curator. I go to bed at ten thirty every night. I'm not that kind of woman. I'm just not...

These are the thoughts that stream through my head, making their way to my mouth, ready to be spoken, but when I open my mouth an entirely different string of sentences come out. "I'm not chicken. I'm brave enough. I'll do it. I'm just kind of sick, in case you hadn't noticed."

Rooke snaps the pocket watch closed. "You're right. You *are* sick. And I'm just screwing with you. I am never going to be the reason you find yourself in danger, Sasha. *Never.*"

I'm kind of relieved he wasn't serious. I'm also kind of shocked at myself. What the fuck was I thinking? "Does that mean you're going to stop working for these people altogether?" I ask.

He goes very still. He doesn't say anything for a long time. And then, very quietly, he says, "Are you *asking* me to?"

"No. I don't know. I don't think I am." I've never really asked myself this question. I've known he's involved in illegal activity for a while now. Why hasn't it crossed my mind that I should ask him to stop? Why haven't I asked him whether working in Williamsburg at the antiques shop is ever going to be enough for him? Perhaps it's because I look at him, even now, and I see his tattoos and the quiet hum of anger that always seems to be there, regardless of his mood, and I know there's no way for this man to live a normal life. One where he wakes up and goes to work to mend watches, comes home, runs errands, takes the trash out, watches TV or reads, and then falls asleep at ten thirty like I do. There's a darkness inside him. The night owns him, or at least it owns a decent-sized chunk of him. There will always be a side to him that needs rebellion and destruction. The real question is, can I accept that? Can I make my peace with it? And if I can, then how does that kind of chaos fit into *my* life?

"You're overthinking it," he says under his breath. "I can see it on your face. You're worrying. You're trying to paint pictures in your head. Don't do that."

"How am I supposed to stop?"

"You just...*let go*."

I just let go? He has no idea how impossible it would be for me to do that. I've been fighting for control for so long now that relinquishing it goes against every single instinct I possess. The way he says it makes it sound so easy, though, like it should be as simple as breathing.

It never will be for me. It really never will be.

"You're repressed," he says. "You hold back. You come between yourself and what you want all the time when you overthink shit, Sasha."

"I do not."

"You do. Take right now, for example. You're watching me. Checking me out. You want me, but you're not going to do anything about it, are you?"

I have been watching him. I'm not some crazed, drooling idiot who can't keep her emotions from her face, but Rooke picks up on everything, and I mean *everything*. If there's anything I've learned from spending every day with him for the last two weeks, it's that he's so perceptive to changes in my mood. He reads me like a book. Often he knows what I'm feeling or thinking before I even do. It's both frustrating and amazing to be so in tune with another person like that. I sigh, frustrated. "What am I supposed to do? Climb up into your lap and demand you to fuck me?"

"Yes. That's exactly what you're supposed to do. Better yet, don't make the demand. Take what you want, Sasha. Just fucking *take* it."

Just like back in the antiques store, he gives me a look that poses a question: *Are you brave enough? Will you accept the dare?* He just loves to push my buttons and fuck with me. I'm incapable of backing down when he does this and he knows it all too well. Bastard.

I don't know where to begin, though. He's so fucking full of himself. Trying to wrestle power from him seems like it would be a fruitless task. Still. Maybe it's worth a shot. Maybe he's right, and I do manage to talk myself out of the things I want purely because I'm worried what he will think or feel.

"C'mon, Sasha. Show me. Show me what you've got." His voice is laden with sex. His eyes have taken on that predatory intensity he gets just before we fuck, and I can feel myself instantly getting wet.

"All right. Fine. But don't say you didn't ask for it."

His smirk is phenomenal. "I'm ready for you, Connor."

"Stand up. Take your clothes off. Strip, then lie down on the bed."

He's not even remotely embarrassed. He gets to his feet and undresses without saying a word. His lack of embarrassment is understandable then. He has to know that he is just...fucking...*ridiculous.* He looks like a professional athlete. He looks like he's spent years training and sculpting his body to look like this. He's breathtaking.

His cock is growing harder and harder by the second.

He hasn't touched himself, but he's obviously getting more and more turned on as he lies himself down on the bed. I'm doing that to him. I'm responsible for his excitement, and that in itself is a heady, powerful thing. I've never felt this way before. I've never felt like a *sexual* being.

"I would never have expected you to hand over the reins like this," I tell him.

He looks amused. "Why not?"

"Because. You love being in control. You love being dominant. Ordering me about in the bedroom is your favorite thing to do." Over the past two weeks, he has done nothing *but* order me around in the bedroom. To see him hand over his control so easily is really surprising. He arches his back, his chest raising a little as he stretches. I've never seen anyone so comfortable in their own skin. His confidence has been a huge turn on since day one. I love watching him when he's naked. It feels wrong that I even get to, though, like I'm going to blink and he's going to vanish any second, a brief, hazy figment of my imagination.

"You're a grown-ass woman, Sasha. You can handle the responsibility. I have faith in you," he says.

It's a good thing he has faith in me, because personally I'm freaking out a little. It's easy being submissive. Being submissive means everything is taken care of. All you have to do is commit and hand over your will. Being in charge of a situation like this is a huge responsibility. What if I can't turn him on the way he turns me on when we have sex? What if he's bored in the first ten minutes and decides I'm too vanilla for him?

There's a lot going on in my head as I get up from the bed and slowly take my own clothes off. Rooke watches every movement I make with complete focus. He barely even blinks as I kick out of my jeans, carefully slipping the straps of my bra down over my shoulders, wriggling my hips as I remove my panties.

"Your body is incredible," he says quietly. "Watching you strip is the sexiest thing in the fucking world."

That agent of self-sabotage in the back of my head wants to downplay this compliment. She wants me to blush and tell him he's being silly. She wants me to say something self-deprecating, telling me that I'll look stupid if I don't. I'm learning a lot about this bitch in the back of my head, though. She doesn't want me to be happy. She's the voice of negativity, of scorn and of derision. She doesn't lift me up. She doesn't make me free in any way. Listening to her only ends in me feeling damaged and unworthy of love and respect. I trust Rooke. He's incredibly smart and he knows his own mind. He doesn't say things flippantly. He's direct, and he's honest. He wouldn't say something like that if he didn't mean it.

So fuck it. I choose to bask in the warmth of his admiration, instead of shield myself from it. Life is too fucking short. Drawing my shoulders back, angling my chin a little higher, I smile. "Thank you."

Rooke props himself up on one elbow. His eyes are shining, a huge grin of his own spreading across his face. He begins to clap. "Yes. My girlfriend is a motherfucking *boss.*"

My cheeks redden, an out of control burn spreading down through my body. "Is that what I am? Your girlfriend?"

He nods sagely. "I'm afraid you don't get a choice in the matter."

"Wow. Most guys avoid that word at all cost."

"Most guys are fucking idiots, Sasha. *Idiots.* They're too afraid of what they'll be losing if they commit themselves to one woman. I'm very aware of what I'll be losing if I *don't* in this particular instance."

He constantly surprises me. I'm constantly wondering

what I did to invite this strange, wonderful, out-of-this-world man into my life. We do not work on paper. In real life, our lives have slotted together so perfectly that I can hardly seem to remember what being without him was like. I've known him less than a month, and I'm infatuated with him. No, it's way more than that. Far, far beyond infatuation. I'm just too scared to admit the true depth of my feelings, even to myself.

I climb up onto the end of the bed, and Rooke lies back, no longer leaning on his elbow. I'm no longer worried about this. With a few words, he's set my nerves to rest. Now, I just want to make him feel as amazing as he makes me feel. "Don't touch me," I tell him. "Do *not* touch me until I say you can." He places his arms at his sides, watching me as I slowly crawl my way up the bed. His eyes are on fire, his lips parted. His cock is fully erect now, straining against his belly. I hover over him, straddling him, our bodies only a couple of inches apart. Rooke bites his lip as he looks up at me—I can tell he likes what he sees. I can also tell that he's struggling not to touch me already. His shoulders tense as I lean down, skating my mouth over his. My nipples graze his chest, and I shiver, a wave of sensation relaying all around my body. I want to lower myself, to grind my whole body against his, but if I do that it will be a very short step to sliding down on his hard-on and fucking him like a wild animal. I don't want this to be over that quickly. Now that I'm feeling a little calmer, I want to draw this out. I want to tease him. I want him to be begging me to let him come by the time I'm through with him.

I inch down a little, so that my breast is frustratingly close to his mouth. "Open," I command.

Rooke gives me a savage, entertained smile that lets me know I'll probably be paying for this at a later date. I'll take his punishment gladly, though. I plan on earning it.

"Lick," I tell him.

His tongue darts out between his lips, and he does as I've told him. He runs the tip of his tongue over the erect, tight bud of my nipple, and I have to suck my bottom lip into my mouth. He's so fucking hot. It's not just the way he looks, or the way those light brown eyes of his remain trained on me as he swirls his tongue around my nipple. It's the fact that this monster of a man is going against his very own nature in order to please me right now. That's what's driving me insane.

"Bite," I tell him.

A wicked glimmer flashes in his eyes. "How hard do you want it?" he asks slowly.

"As hard as you think I can take."

"Careful, Connor. I know a lot about the human pain threshold. You can take way more than you think." There's a challenge in his voice that makes the hairs on the back of my neck stand up.

"Do it. I can take it. *Bite.*"

Rooke growls, a low, rumbling sound of frustration. Carefully, he fastens my nipple in between his teeth and he gradually, slowly bites down. The pressure is pleasurable at first. I can feel the need building between my legs, my pussy getting wetter and wetter. The pain intensifies as he applies more and more pressure, until I'm arching against his mouth and I'm gritting my teeth together. I've never had anything pierced before, but I imagine having my nipple pierced would feel very similar to this. The pain shuttles through me, a stabbing hurt that is mirrored in my other breast, and down the backs of my legs, into the soles of my feet.

"*Ahhh!*"

Rooke doesn't stop. He continues to bite down while I ride the wave of sensation. It's dizzying. I can stop it at any time, I know I can, but that only makes it harder to say the words. He thinks I can take this, so that's what I do. I take it. When he finally stops, I'm holding my breath and my eyes are screwed tightly shut.

"Fucking beautiful," he whispers. "You're so fucking beautiful."

"Suck," I tell him.

My nipple throbs when he takes it into his mouth. The ache is bittersweet, half tempering the sharp, stabbing pain from his teeth a moment ago, but introducing a new, burning pain now. It fills my head, sends me spiraling down a deep, dark well of sensation. I gently rock back a little, so I can feel his cock between my legs, rubbing up against my pussy. I'm so ridiculously wet, and he's so ridiculously hard. Rooke hisses, sucking in a sharp breath, his body jolting underneath me.

"*Fuck.*" His voice is strained. I reach down between our bodies and I close my hand around his cock, guiding it so that it slides against my clit as I begin to rock against him. His eyes roll back into his head as he releases a jagged sigh. "You're going to fucking kill me," he says.

"No. I'm going to sit on your face and you're going to make me come with your tongue," I reply. I let go of him, moving up his body before I can change my mind. I've become accustomed to just how much he loves to eat my pussy over the past few weeks, but I've never done this before. I've always been on my back with him down between my legs. I kneel over Rooke's head, and he groans, swearing under his breath. I swear I could come just from hearing that sound. The second his tongue touches my clit, my back is bowed and I'm regretting the position. It feels too damn good. Too perfect. I'll climax so quickly like this, I know it. I wind my fingers into his hair as he licks and sucks. He reaches up and takes hold of me by the thighs, pulling me down harder onto his mouth. He's breaking the rules, but it feels too good. I let him get away with it.

"Fuck me with your fingers," I pant. "*Right now.*"

He snarls as he obeys. I feel like I'm swimming with sharks right now. Trying to tame a lion. Going head to head with a predator that is way, way stronger than I am, easily capable of destroying me. It's thrilling and terrifying all at once. Rooke slides his fingers inside me and the fire that's burning in the pit of my stomach rages out of control.

"Jesus. Holy shit." My mind shuts down. I rock against his mouth, taking my pleasure, just as he told me to. When he slides his hand back a little, his fingers teasing, playing over my ass, I can't cope anymore. I reach back and place my hand over his, holding it in place, letting him know what I want.

I want him inside me there too.

Rooke rumbles beneath me, a sound of extreme need. He's gentle as he pushes a finger into my ass, but I can tell it costs him. He wants to be rough with me. He wants to flip me over and fuck me so hard right now, but he has himself on a leash.

With his tongue on my clit and his fingers in both my ass and my pussy, my body feels like an Edison bulb, a flow of electricity charging and snapping through a filament that loops and arcs through my body. "Shit, Rooke. Shit!"

He would be swearing too, if he wasn't busy with his mouth. I'm on the brink of coming when I tear myself away from him. I need him to be inside me. I *need* it more than anything.

I shift back and sink myself down onto his erection, doing my best not to cry out. Having his fingers inside me is one thing, but his cock? I don't know if my body will ever be able to take him easily. I'm always going to need to be seriously turned on before he tries to fuck me. Rooke bares his teeth as I rock back and forth, taking my pleasure from him here too.

"Damn, Sasha. You're so fucking wet. I can feel you all over me," he hisses. "Such a fucking turn on."

I know it's just a matter of time now. I'm edging closer and closer to a cliff face, toward a fall that is inevitable for both me and for the beautiful man beneath me.

I stretch it out though, delaying, teasing, tormenting... Every time Rooke is about to come, I hover over him, so that only the very tip of his cock is inside me, and I command him not to. He has remarkable self-control. He wants to physically own me. He wants to turn me over and fuck me like a freight train. He wants to coax my orgasm out of me just as badly as he wants to come himself, but each and every time I tell him no, he curses and grits his teeth, head back, chest proud, muscles in his throat working over time, and he beats it back.

When I do finally allow him to come, he roars at the top of his lungs, his fingers digging into the mattress, his body flexed and bowed, and I can do nothing but come right along with him. Watching him lose himself like that would make me come on the spot, no matter what.

My orgasm winds me, knocking the air right out of my lungs with its ferocity. I collapse on top of him, panting, hyperventilating, and Rooke wraps his arms around me. His whole frame is twitching and shaking, his eyes closed, his lips slightly parted. I want to stay like this forever, staring at the blissed-out pleasure on his face, him still inside me, his come slick on the inside of my thighs, his sweat and my own, so salty on my lips.

We fall asleep, tangled up in each other. I don't know how long we're unconscious for, but when I wake, Rooke is sitting on the end of the bed. His face is in shadow, and I find myself wanting to trace my fingers down his creased forehead, down the bridge of his nose, over his lips, his chin, down his throat. He's carved out of stone. When you look at him, there's no real visible softness to him. He's a hard man to study without feeling a faint glimmer of panic sparking in your gut.

His tattoos are a warning. Mother Nature made the most dangerous of all her creatures colorful, patterned and hostile, a caution against attack, violence or consumption. Whether he meant to or not, Rooke has accomplished the same thing with his ink. Fucking with him is unsafe and ill advised. To interfere with him is to invite turmoil and anarchy to your doorstep. I've seen the way people look at him. They see the tattoos, as well as his formidable size, and they shrink back into themselves, looking quickly away before he can notice them noticing *him*.

I've seen past the ink, though. I've moved beyond the way he looks, the way he holds his body, and the way you feel nailed to the wall when he looks at you. He's shown me a softness I would never have expected from him, and it's turned a tide in my heart. I think only he would have been capable of such a thing. His mouth twists into a very small, quiet kind of smile.

"I've never had anyone here before. You're the first."

This surprises me. I would have thought his bedroom had a revolving door on it, given how confident he seems with women. I really don't like thinking about that, though. Even more surprising. I was never jealous with Andrew. I never worried about him flirting with other women at work, or some pretty young thing taking a shine to him. I just accepted that he was with me and that was that. If he wanted to go off and cheat, then that simply meant our relationship was broken beyond repair and I was better off without him anyway.

With Rooke, the idea of his hands on another woman's body makes me feel physically ill. Even thinking about him with girls in the past makes me seriously uncomfortable.

"Why?" I ask. "Why have you never brought anyone here?"

"Because. This is my space. I can think here. I can be real. Having someone else here compromises that."

"Then why did you bring *me* here?"

His smile turns crooked. "Because you're part of me, Sasha. It doesn't matter where I go with you. I can always be real. And so can you." He pauses. "Tell me about him. Tell me the parts you miss the most."

He's talking about Christopher. I told him back in the car that I'd answer his questions, tell him anything he wanted to know. That doesn't make this any easier, though. It doesn't make my chest any less tight as I shift on his bed. I gather his bed sheets around me, covering myself, and I hug my knees to my chest.

"He was small for his age," I say quietly. "His arms and legs always kind of looked too long for his body. All the other kids in his class were in the middle of growth spurts, but he seemed content with being small. He loved to play. He loved animals. He wanted to be a vet."

I look down at my hands. I haven't used them to sign in so long. It feels wrong to even be considering doing so right now, but slowly I begin to make the shapes that come rushing back to me. Monkey. Elephant. Duck. Mouse. Tiger. Dinosaur. All of Christopher's favorite animals. Rooke watches intensely, taking everything in. Signing takes precise movement and practice. It's strange to watch Rooke use his huge hands, hands undoubtedly intimately acquainted with violence, to mimic my movements. There's an unexpected grace to him that makes my heart burn painfully in my chest.

I'm struck with a strange and saddening realization: Christopher would have really loved Rooke. Just like the man sitting in front of me, my son had a way of knowing how things worked, especially people. He would have been able to see beyond Rooke's gruff, frankly frightening exterior and see the man beneath.

Rooke would have made him happy.

TWENTY-FIVE

THE NURSE

ROOKE

JERICHO: Asked around. Might know something about the guy from the museum. Come by after nine.

Mother. Fucking. Asshole.

I've been staring at Jericho's text all night while Sasha has been sleeping, and I've been trying to decide what to do. I meant what I said to her. I promised her I would kill the fucking guy who broke into the museum and put her through hell, and I intend on following through with that promise. I just didn't know if telling her what I am planning was for the best, though.

There's no way she would let me go. No way in hell.

Laying in bed next to her is such a fucking gift. I listen to her breathe through the dark hours of the night, and I think. I think really fucking hard. There's a smart way to handle this, and there's a dumb way to handle it. I asked Jericho weeks ago to help me find the fucker from the museum, and now he thinks he might know where he is. Okay. So do I go over there, guns blazing, demanding Jericho hand over the information so I can find this evil son of a bitch and shoot him in the back of the head? Or do I wait? Ask Jake what to do? Go and see Arnold, maybe see if he can find me some backup?

I lie there and I stew. At dawn, Sasha rolls over onto her side so that she's facing me, her dark hair a mass of loose curls arranged madly around her peaceful face, and I just stare at her. She is so unexpected. Never in a million fucking years would I have imagined her into existence. I haven't spent a great deal of time picturing what the woman I would fall in love with would be like. Honestly, a part of me just assumed I never would allow myself to do something so fucking stupid as fall in love. Now that she's here, naked in my bed, her hands curled into fists like she's trying to fight off demons in her sleep, I'm undone. I'm not thinking rationally. I want to protect her so badly that I can't seem to focus on anything or anyone else, and my blood feels like it's constantly on a low simmer as it travels through my veins because I can't seem to keep her from harm. Harm caused by other people, as well as harm caused by herself.

I stroke the wild strands of her hair out of her face and I study every line of her, committing them to memory: her high cheekbones; the slight, gentle upturn to her nose; the thick, dark lashes that rim her eyelids; the swollen pout of her lips. I try not to see the fading bruises, or her spilt lip. Seeing them only makes me fucking crazy. She's so fragile.

So breakable. I'm determined to make sure nothing ever happens to her again.

At five forty I climb out of bed, careful not to wake her. It's still dark outside, the world shrouded in shadows. When I look out the window, I find everything masked in a thick layer of white, so much snow for as far as the eye can see, buildings, cars, mailboxes all buried and hidden. That will make life harder for me, but not impossible. Quickly collecting some clothes from my walk-in, I gather everything I need together and I bundle it under my arm, then I stoop down beside Sasha and I reach underneath the bed. My go-bag is right where it always is. Right next to it is a smaller black leather bag. One I don't normally take out very often. I grab both of them by the straps and I make my way out of the bedroom, holding my breath, hoping Sasha doesn't wake up. She doesn't even stir. Downstairs on the ground floor, I put on my jeans, thermal shirt, down jacket, a rain jacket, and my thick waterproof Sorels, and I check inside my bags. My tools are inside my go-bag, every one of them where they're meant to be. I take the small leather pouch containing my throwing knives and I slip it into my back pocket. From the other bag, I remove the Browning Buck Mark that I've had ever since I got out of juvi. The gun is small. Nothing special. There are plenty of far more impressive, flashier, more theatrical pieces out there that I could have bought, but I didn't want to draw attention to myself. Gang bangers go for big guns. They go for bling—a weapon that, in their eyes at least, reflects their status. Gun dealers talk when they sell a piece like that. They keep tabs on people, and they show an interest. I wanted something average and unremarkable that would get the job done. Something that wouldn't have people following me in order to see what I was up to twenty-four seven.

The clip is full. The safety is on. *For now.* Outside on

the street, Jake's car is missing. He took it with him when he went to play his gig last night, and he hasn't brought it back. Could be he got snowed in somewhere. Could be he hooked up with a groupie and got his dick wet. Either way, I can't borrow his ride.

I turn my keys over in my pocket as I hurry down the street. Cold. *So* fucking cold. I don't seem to feel it, though. I'm numb from the pores of my skin down to the very basement of my soul. By the time I find a cab and make it across to Jericho's place, the sun is a brightly burning disk of silver in the sky, hovering just above the buildings on the horizon.

The garage isn't open. I hammer my gloved fist against the shutter, and Raul eventually appears, his mouth set into a grim, downturned expression.

"You're late. We thought maybe you changed your mind."

I don't say anything. I slip silently past him, gritting my teeth together. Inside, Jericho is standing over the auto repair pit with a pair of bolt cutters in his hand. The front of his shirt is drenched in blood. His eyes are filled with murder when he lifts his head and looks at me.

"Have you been dealing with my problems for me, Jericho?"

He grips a toothpick between his front teeth, grimacing at me. "No, no, Cuervo. This is one of *my* problems. I'll happily deal with yours, too, though. I'm on a roll."

I don't look down into the pit. It would be ill-advised. It's been a long time since I've seen a dead body—not since I left juvi—and looking a dead man square on the eye right now would only make me question what I have to do next. I don't care who's down there. Jericho's business is Jericho's business. I need to concentrate on handling my own. "You know where he is?" I ask.

Jericho tosses the bolt cutters over in his hand and spits his toothpick down onto the mess he's made in the pit. "I do. Margot Fredricks. You know who this is?"

"I've heard of her. She's a nurse or something." When you're in this line of work, sometimes you get hurt. *Often*, you get hurt, and you can't just walk into the hospital. Get patched up like a civilian off the street. People ask questions about gunshots. They want to know how you ended up with five stab wounds to your torso. They call the cops when it looks like you've broken eight bones in your hand because you've beaten someone half to death. So people like Margot exist. People with medical training, who'll take money under the table in exchange for treatment.

"My friend here was holding out on some information that I wanted quite badly," he says, gesturing to the pit. "He was being stubborn, and I was getting a little carried away. He needed stitching back together while I continued my conversation with him, so Raul took him over to see Margot last night. She had another patient, it seems. A man with a head injury. Some ginger guy with a bad temper."

"He tried to start with me," Raul adds. "He was fucking crazy. When I saw the tattoo on the back of his hand, I knew he was your guy."

Why the fuck didn't I think of that? I should have. I knew he was hurt. It makes sense that this motherfucker would look for help. "What's Margot's address?" I growl.

Raul looks to Jericho, who nods. Reaching into his pocket, Raul then produces a slip of paper and hands it to me. "I don't know if you'll get much sense out of him. He was rambling all kinds of madness before he got rough with me. After I hit him in the head a couple of times, he stopped rambling altogether."

I grunt, slipping the paper into the back pocket of my

jeans. "Thanks. Did Margot tell you who he was? Did she know his name?"

Raul nods just once. "Casper. She said his name was Casper."

******

Margot Fredricks is a short, slim woman in her late forties. She looks stunned when she opens the door to me, like she was expecting someone but it wasn't me. She glances up and down the hallway littered with used hypodermics and discarded baggies, nervous. Twitchy. "Can I help you?" she asks. She has the haunted, bone-weary look of someone who has to ask this question to dangerous strangers at least five times a day.

"Jericho gave me your address. He said you had someone here. Someone I'm looking for."

"I don't know any Jericho. And I live here alone. I'm afraid you must have the wrong apartment."

I take a step forward, narrowing my eyes at her. "Look at me. Do I look like the kind of guy you should be lying to right now? I'm not in the mood to be fucked with. Invite me in."

She looks flustered. There's a hard edge in her eyes, though. She's used to being threatened. She's used to dealing with people like me. Only the left-hand side of her body is visible. She's holding the door half closed, the edge of the wood jammed up against her chest. On the other side of the door, I hear the familiar sound of a gun being cocked. "I think you should leave now. I don't like being bothered unexpectedly by strangers who don't have an appointment."

I'm not leaving. No fucking way am I leaving. I take another step forward, so that I'm only a foot away from her now. "And I don't like hitting women," I say quietly. "I think it's a cardinal fucking sin to hit a woman, in fact. That doesn't mean I won't kick down this fucking door and force my way into your apartment, though. It doesn't mean I won't make a bully of myself to get what I came here for. Do you understand what I'm saying, Ms. Fredricks?"

"You think I don't know how to defend myself?" A low tapping sound rings out into the hallway—the gun she's holding in her hand behind the door, rapping against the wood.

She's brave, I'll give her that. Really brave. Still. I came here for a very important purpose. I'm not leaving until it's taken care of. "Step away from the door," I tell her.

"Are you deaf? You need to leave. *Now*."

"Fucking move, or I'm going to move you myself."

Margot's a smart woman. She registers the tone in my voice, and she knows what's about to happen: I am about to really lose my fucking temper. I am about to *really* lose my shit, and she is standing directly in the path of the storm. She makes a frustrated, angry sound as she moves back, allowing me inside. "Tell Jericho he's not welcome here anymore. Tell him not to send anyone else here again. I'm done dealing with his—"

"I'm not a fucking errand boy. Tell him yourself." I should be a little more mindful of the fact that this woman has a gun, but I'm too lit up with anger to really pay her any attention. She's not going to shoot me. She operates an illegal hospital from her apartment. She needs the income and badly, or she wouldn't be taking such a huge risk. She doesn't want the cops here any more than I do. I tear through the apartment, moving from room to room. There's medical equipment everywhere. A gurney in the hallway. A row of IV stands in the living room. Even a heart monitor balanced precariously on top of the television.

"No! Don't go in there, that's a sterile—"

I force open a door, charging inside. Inside, the space is immaculate, spotless, and smells heavily of disinfectant. I was expecting a bedroom, but this room could easily be an OR in a hospital. It's fully stocked with yet another heart monitor, what looks like a respirator, metal stands, with blue sheets of paper covering surgical instruments. No people, though. No redheaded Casper.

"Are you happy now? What the fuck is *wrong* with you? I told you there was no one here!" Margot is a ball of fury as she barrels into the room behind me.

"Where is he?" I demand. "Where's Casper?"

"I'm not telling you shit, asshole. You've no right to barge in here—"

I move swiftly. I'm not even thinking. I close my hand around Margot's throat, and I take three giant steps, forcing her to move with me until her back is pressed firmly up against the wall. Her eyes are wide. She swallows, and I feel the movement of her throat beneath my hand. She's stunned. Paralyzed, a rabbit trapped in headlights. I lean a little closer to her, so I'm all she can see, smell and hear. I need her to understand me. She needs to really believe the words that come out of my mouth next. "Do *not* test me. Do *not* open your fucking mouth again unless it's to give me the information I am looking for. Do you understand?"

She nods.

"I am looking for a man named Casper. He *was* here. I know he was. *Where. Is. He. Now?*"

"He left," she whispers. "After that other guy Jericho sent over nearly fucking killed him last night. I don't know where the hell he went, but he was furious."

I loosen my hold on her neck. Looking down, I see something has me struggling to put a leash on my anger: a pair of beaten, tan leather shoes. The right shoelace is red. The left one is black. I growl under my breath. "What time did he leave?"

"About three."

"Where did he go?"

"He didn't say. He was ranting and raving about finding another doctor. I told him not to go, that he needed to rest, but he wouldn't listen. He just kept on and on about this doctor."

"Why would he need another doctor if he was receiving treatment here?"

"How should I know? He had a serious head injury. Nothing he said made sense. He was going nuts about finding another doctor from the moment he staggered through the damn door."

I let her go. I can see she's telling the truth. She really doesn't know where he's gone. At this point, if she did know, I'm pretty sure she'd tell me whatever she knew just to get me to leave.

"*Fuck.*" I scrub my hands through my hair, trying to remember how to breathe. He was here. He was *just* fucking here. I should never have waited. I should have left the house last night, the moment Jericho sent that message over. So fucking stupid.

I turn around and Margot's arms are raised. She's holding her gun in her hands, the gun I've been ignoring until now, and she looks pissed. The weapon is pointed right at my head, and her finger is hovering over the trigger. "I really am going to have to ask you to leave now," she hisses.

"Fine. Fine. It's okay. I'm go—" Something occurs to me, then, stealing my words. Something hits me in the gut with the force of a battering ram, and I'm nearly bent double with the force of my realization. "The other doctor," I say. "Was he talking about someone in particular? Did he mention a specific doctor by name?"

Margot's brow creases, like she can't imagine how this could possibly be relevant information. "I don't know.

Yeah, I suppose he did. Clark? Campbell? Carter? I can't remember."

Ahhh, fuck. Dread cycles through me, chilling me to the bone. "*Connor*?" I ask.

"Yeah, that was it. Connor. He said he was going to find Doctor Connor. Now get the fuck out of my house.

TWENTY-SIX

SURPRISE VISITOR

SASHA

Waking up alone is never fun, especially when it's in someone else's bed. Rooke left me a note telling me to stay at his place and wait for him, but honestly it felt weird being there without him, like I was intruding or something. I take one look outside and decide trying to walk anywhere is out of the question, so I call a cab and wait by the front door for thirty minutes until the guy eventually shows up to drive me home.

I'm not in the mood to make small talk, so I sit in the back seat in silence, watching the world slowly crawl by, everything white, everything silent and peaceful, the sound of the city somehow deadened by the snow, and I keep my thoughts to myself.

My heart sinks in my chest when I get out of the cab and see the broken pane of glass in my front door. I forgot Rooke had to smash the window to get in yesterday. If I'd remembered, I would have called someone, had them come over and at least board it up until it could be replaced. As it stands, my place has been open and unprotected for close to twenty-four hours. Anyone could have let themselves in and helped themselves to whatever they wanted inside.

I take out the pepper spray Ali bought me just in case. No sense in calling the cops just to see if someone's inside. The front door is set back from the road in such a way that it's actually really hard to see, so it's unlikely anyone's noticed the broken glass, anyway.

I unlock the door with my key despite the yawning hole in the window and I let myself inside. "Hello? Is anyone here?" The house is freezing cold. There are papers scattered all over the floor in the hallway; the wind must have blown them from the phone stand. A strange rushing sound is coming from the kitchen. I'm careful as I walk through the ground floor, checking in the living room and the dining room to make sure I'm alone before I head to the back of the house, toward the sound.

The cold tap is running, water rushing like crazy out of the faucet. A soaking wet tea towel is on the floor, along with a clear glass bowl full of murky water. I know I'd thrown up when Rooke found me. The hallway floor was clean just now. Rooke must have cleaned up the mess and left the tap running when the ambulance showed up for me. Luckily the sink was empty, otherwise it would have flooded and water would have been pouring out over the tiles for the last twenty-four hours. I turn the tap off and head back through the house, looking for signs that someone might have been in here.

There are none. Nothing has been moved. Nothing's

been stolen. Apart from the stack of paperwork from the museum that's now on the floor in the hallway, everything is as it was left. I call out, checking upstairs as well, can of pepper spray clutched tightly in my hand, but there's no one there, either.

My cell phone starts ringing. It takes a long time for me to find it at the bottom of my purse. It's Rooke. I miss the call, but my cell starts ringing again almost immediately. I pick up, and loud street noises blast down the line.

"Sasha? Where are you? Are you still at my place?"

"No, I'm at home. What's wrong? Has something happened?"

"The guy who attacked you at the museum. Casper. His name is Casper. He's looking for you. Does he know where you live?" The words are jumbled, all running together. It's hard to make out what he's saying over the sounds of the city in the background—car horns blaring, sirens wailing. My limbs suddenly feel very heavy. I can't seem to move, like my feet are cemented to the ground.

"I don't know. I don't think so. He could have found out, though. There are ways to do that, right?"

"Yeah. There are. Don't stay at the house. Leave. Go somewhere safe, somewhere with a lot of people. Text me and tell me where you go. I'm coming to you." I can tell he's trying to sound calm, but there's a clear edge to his voice. He's worried, and if Rooke is worried then *I* ought to be terrified.

"Okay, I'm going. I'm leaving the house now." I hang up, panicked. Casper. How did he find out the guy's name? Is that where he went this morning? To go look for this guy? My stomach rolls. Good god, please don't let him come here. I can't take it. I can't handle seeing him again. Not alone. God, not even with Rooke. It takes a monstrous force of will to make myself move. Once I convince my body to cooperate, I'm suddenly galvanized and running, hurtling down the stairs, charging toward the front door.

Nearly there.

Only a few more feet.

I step on a piece of paper and skid, but I manage to keep my footing. My heart is a trip hammer in my chest, thundering, racing out of control. Glass crunches under my feet as I reach the front door, then I'm racing down the steps of the brownstone, my lungs prickling from the cold.

I slip again, only this time it's on ice. I stumble, scrambling to grab hold of something, to remain upright, but there's nothing. I clutch at thin air, and then there are hands on me, clawing at me, grabbing at my jacket. I scream, alive with fear, alive with terror, trying to rip myself free of the person who has just caught me and stopped me from falling over. I can't, though. He has me tight. He pulls me up, presses me tight against his body. A familiar smell washes over me, a smell that hits me like a wall of pain. It's not stale coffee and cigarettes though. It's Tom Ford aftershave. It's seven years of marriage and a dead son. It's deceit and disappointment and cheating. It's my ex-husband.

******

"What are you doing here, Andrew?"

I still haven't regained myself. I can't slow down my erratic pulse; my heart seems determined to burst its way out of my chest any second now, and no amount of deep breathing appears to be helping. Andrew stands in front of me on the sidewalk, looking very much like himself, which is to say smug, arrogant and pathetic all at once.

"Why do you think I came?" he says, frustration thick in his voice. "You didn't respond to my letter, and then boom! I see you on national fucking news, the victim of a serious hostage situation. You didn't think I'd be worried? You didn't think I'd want to know that you were safe? Goddamn it, Sasha. I come back here and the house is wide open. I was about to call the cops when you come flying out of the place like a goddamn lunatic."

I press my fingers into my forehead, closing my eyes. "I don't have time for this, Andrew."

He gives me a hurt, wounded look now. The same one he gave me the night he told me he had fallen in love with someone else and he was moving to Texas to start over. Like *he* was the kicked puppy, and I had no right feeling sorry for myself. "I know you might not believe it, Sasha, but I do still care about you. You were the mother of my son."

I choose to pretend he didn't just say that. I pull my jacket tighter around my body, scanning up and down the street. There are no signs of the guy who attacked me at the museum. That means nothing, though. He could be hovering in a doorway somewhere, ready to come at me the moment I walk by. I am really unhappy about Andrew being here, but damn. Walking with him to find somewhere safe to wait for Rooke is better than walking there alone. I look at him, holding eye contact, probably the longest I've done so in three or four years. "Do you really want to make sure I'm all right?"

He has the audacity to look stung. "Yes! Of course I do. Jesus, I'm not a monster."

He *is* a monster. He went and had another son and called him Christopher; it doesn't get any worse than that. I just raise my eyebrows. "I need to get to Ali's place. Will you come with me?"

Doubt flickers across his face. Ali tore him a new one when he left New York. I can imagine how unappealing the thought of seeing her again must be. "Seriously?" He shoves his hands into his pockets, letting his head tip back as he groans. "Fine. But I'm not going inside."

"I didn't ask you to. Come on."

I don't explain why I'm still limping a little as I attempt to speed walk away from the house. I don't tell him who I'm texting as I message Rooke and give him Ali's address. I tell him nothing. If I did tell him that we're probably in danger right now, he'd undoubtedly bail and run away all over again. That's just how he handles his shit.

TWENTY-SEVEN

ESCALATE

ROOKE

I get the address. It's close to Sasha's place, within walking distance, so it shouldn't take her long to get there. Jake calls me as I'm burning across the city in a stolen Nissan Skyline. Not the most inconspicuous car I could have taken, but fuck. You do what you gotta do.

I almost don't pick up the phone, but some sixth sense tells me I ought to. I make a habit of never ignoring my gut. My friend sounds stressed the fuck out when I hit the green answer button. "Rooke? Where are you, man?"

"Running errands." *About to fucking kill a man.* "What's up?"

I swing the car through a left-hand turn, trying to

force myself to slow down. If I get picked up now, I'm in serious shit. "Well. A guy showed up at the house. He was asking for you. I let him in, and then he proceeded to beat the shit out of me. He's currently holding me at gunpoint. He says he'd like it if you came home now."

"*What*? What guy?" A rolodex of potential assholes spins wildly before my eyes. It could be one of many people, but now? Today? The timing is off. This has something to do with Casper. Has to. Jake makes a hawking spitting sound, then a pained grunt echoes down the phone.

"He says...his name is Jericho."

What the fuck? *Jericho*? I only left him a couple of hours ago. Why the fuck would he be at my house, assaulting Jake? "Put him on the phone," I snarl. "Put him on the phone *right fucking now*."

There's a rustling sound, and then a familiar, heavily accented voice in my ear. "Cuervo. I am not a happy man. I had to drive over here. You know how much I hate to drive."

"Explain what's happening. Explain why you're at my house, laying hands on my friend." I have never fucked with him before. I have never screwed with his shit. He's made a big fucking mistake screwing with mine right now. I don't care how crazy he is; I don't care how many people he's murdered. He is going to fucking bleed for this.

"Oh, you know. It's all a coincidence really. I love a good coincidence."

"Jericho—"

"See, you came to the shop before, and I was busy, was I not? I was in the middle of something. I was working on a guy in the pit. He told me something very interesting after you left. He said he knew you. Said you spent time together in juvi over at the Goshen Secure Center. Imagine how upset I was when he said you were released early…for working with the cops."

"What the fuck are you talking about? I've never worked with the cops. Never."

"Well, that's unfortunate, Cuervo. This kid seems to think you did. He knew an awful lot about you."

I haven't seen anyone from Goshen since I left the godforsaken place. I have no idea who the hell he's talking about. It was a long time ago now. Five years, to be precise. I've made an effort to forget the thieves, racists and petty criminals I shared such a cramped, closed space with back then. People were in and out of there every other day. There's no way anyone would specifically remember—

My hands reflexively tighten on the Skyline's steering wheel.

Oh.

No fucking way.

God, you have got to be kidding me.

I grind the name out through my clenched jaw, shaking my head. "Jared Viorelli. *Jared fucking Viorelli.*"

"Ahh, so he was telling the truth. You *do* know him."

"Yeah, I know him all right. He's a fucking liar, Jericho. I never worked with the cops. I refused to take a fucking shiv from him after he stabbed someone in the neck with it. The guards found it on him. He was transferred out and sent to Edgecomb." Goshen was bad, but at least it was a juvi facility. Edgecomb, on the other hand, is not. It's a full-blown correctional facility, and Jared's stay there would have been un-fucking-pleasant to say the least. "Why the hell are you listening to that guy?"

Jericho is silent for a moment. "People are often most truthful when they're having their fingers cut off, my friend. It takes concentration to lie convincingly when you're about to lose a thumb. Jared was *very* convincing."

"He's a fucking psycho. If I was working for the cops, why wouldn't they have shut you down by now? I've been running cars for you for years."

Jericho doesn't say anything. He's quiet for a long time. Far too long. "You'd better come home, *hijo*. I need to look you in the eye."

"Fuck you. I can't come home. You know I can't. I'm in the middle of something."

"Then your friend dies. Just as a precaution, you understand." He hangs up.

I can't let Jake die. No fucking way I can let anything happen to Sasha either, though. I message her, asking if she's safe, asking her if she can sit tight for a couple of hours. I hate doing it. I hate trying to prioritize my friend and the woman I'm in love with, but it has to be done.

Sasha: I'm okay. At Ali's now. I wasn't followed.

Me: Are you sure?

Sasha: Positive. I had someone keeping an eye out.

I don't know what that means, but I don't have time to ask questions. It takes me thirty minutes to redirect and head back home. Traffic is a nightmare, but the Skyline's aggressive and so am I. I bully my way through the city, not caring about the cops anymore. Let them try and pull me over. Just let them fucking try.

There are no cars parked out the front of the house, but no surprises there. Jericho isn't stupid. He must have parked his ride a few blocks over. I let myself into the house, ready to fucking destroy the man who's harmed my friend, and I'm immediately met with four guns pointed directly at my head. Seems like people are really determined to use me as target practice today. Jake is sitting on the middle step of the staircase, head hanging loose. He looks up and his face is a mess. Nose broken.

Black eye. The works. Jericho is leaning against the bannister, typing something on his phone. He doesn't look up. Doesn't need to. Why would he when he has four of his guys, mean looking motherfuckers, pointing their weapons at me?

"Nice place you have here, Cuervo." He tap, tap, taps into his phone. Sniffs. Puts the phone into his pocket. "I'm glad you made it back here before I got bored and broke both this bitch's hands." I see Jake's guitar laying shattered in pieces on the floor. Jericho must have figured out pretty quickly that he was a musician. Broken his instrument to fuck with him. Better that he did break the guitar than Jake's hands, though. I would never have forgiven myself if he lost his ability to play.

My hands are itching by my sides. I haven't felt like this in a really, really long time. Not even when I kicked the shit out of that tweeker who was trying to steal my payday. I want to hurt the fucker. I want to damage him, tear him apart, fucking rip him limb from limb. The odds are stacked against me, though. I have to try and play this smart.

"How many cars do you think I've brought you over the years, Jericho?" I ask quietly.

A look of confusion flashes across Jake's face. "Cars? You actually know these guys?" It shouldn't really be a huge shock to him that I do. He knows about my checkered past. He knows that I'm hardly a model citizen. I get up and randomly vanish for hours in the middle of the night. I come home bloody, bruised and manic three nights out of the goddamn week. He's a little naïve, though. Clearly more than a little. I give him a warning look. A *keep-your-fucking-mouth-shut* look. Jericho shrugs, looking down at his hands. He's changed his shirt from earlier, but his hands are still covered in blood. There's a good chance a lot of it is Jake's but I'm betting Jared

Viorelli's DNA is still caked around his fingernails, too.

"I couldn't count, *hijo*. It's been a while. I don't exactly keep a record of these things, y'know?"

"Well I've been keeping track. It's forty-three. Forty-three cars. How many do you think I'd need to hand over to you for the cops to make an arrest? Three? Five? Ten, maybe? It sure as fuck wouldn't take forty-three. That asshole played you. And now you're burning bridges. Now you're making enemies. Now, I am seriously fucking pissed."

Jericho frowns, both of his eyebrows banking together—a strange look on his normally stoic, expressionless face. "I am enemies with everyone in this town, Crow. And all business relationships end sooner or later. It's just a matter of when. And where. And how. I'll admit...perhaps I overreacted a little in this instance."

"*Overreacted?* Let's go ask Jared if you *overreacted*. I'm going to fucking kill that son of a bitch."

"I'm afraid that's impossible. The matter has already been taken care of."

I take a step forward, my pulse throbbing at my temples, and Jericho's guys, guys who have opened up the garage for me countless times, all raise their guns an inch higher, bristling, baring their teeth.

"Calm the fuck down," I hiss. "I'm not insane. I assume you've destroyed every stick of furniture in the house? Did you find anything to prove Viorelli right?"

Jericho slowly shakes his head. "I found a hundred and sixty-three thousand dollars underneath your bed, though. Saving for a rainy day, *hijo*? You know, squirreling away that amount of money might look suspicious to some people."

Jake looks absolutely stunned now. A hundred and sixty-three grand is a shit load of money. I get that. "Does it matter?" I roll my shoulders, cracking my neck. "If you're going to kill me, can we get on with this? If not, let Jake go. He's hardly—"

In the time it takes me to pause between words, the strangest thing happens. Jake, sitting on the step with his mouth hanging open one second, does the unthinkable: he gets to his feet.

The next three seconds are a blur. Somehow, from somewhere, Jake has a gun in his hand. A deafeningly loud shot rings out, and then one of Jericho's guys is on the floor, laying in a pool of blood. A moment passes. Jake stares at the gun in his hand, and Jericho and his boys stare at the guy on the ground, their eyes made of glass.

"What the—"

I react. I have no choice. I'm reaching for the gun I've been carrying around all day, the one I'm meant to use on Casper, and then it's in my hand, and I'm pulling the trigger. A pop of light bursts, white and red, and then another, and then another. They're not all from my gun. I lunge, driving my fist into the throat of the closest guy, who's spinning around, about to fire on Jake. He staggers away from me, the back of his head hitting the wall behind him. The cramped space inside the hallway is a confusion of moving bodies. I can't tell who is who. Someone shouts, a sound of pain, of surprise, and then there's the sound of another body hitting the floor.

Another gunshot.

"*FUCK!*"

I don't know where the cry comes from. It could be Jake. It could be any of the other men. Everything turns gluey, time slowing, my vision tracking wildly through the smoke and the arms and legs, and I see Jericho, raising his hands, aiming, about to shoot.

I beat the bastard to it.

I fire, my arm kicking back, and Jericho slams into the bannister, crying out.

It's as though reality snaps back into place, time racing to catch up with itself, then. Everyone is turned to Jericho, who is sagging in a heap on the floor, releasing strained, agonized gasp after gasp as he clutches at his chest.

Two of his men are dead on the floor. The other two are staring down at their boss like they can't comprehend what just happened, or what they should do next. And Jake...

Jake has been shot, too...

He holds one hand to his stomach, and blood is pouring out from beneath his fingers, thick rivulets of crimson fluid trickling from his body. My arm is still held out, gun in hand. Jake holds his out in his other hand, too, a look of cold fury in his eyes.

"Get the fuck out," he hisses.

"You're going to fucking pay for this, *cabron*," one of Jericho's guys spits. Alfonse. I think his name is Alfonse. His sister brings him his lunch at the garage every day. He stoops, reaching for Jericho, but I block him.

"Don't think so, asshole." If Jericho makes it out of here, Jake and I are fucking dead. Alfonse and the other guy will shoot us both in the head as soon as they make it out of the door. If we have their boss and he's still alive, there's a chance they'll back off and wait to see what happens.

Alfonse spits blood at Jake. "Better leave the state, fucker." He points his gun at Jake, then at me. "We got you pegged."

"Go," Jericho gasps. "Go. He won't kill me."

He's mighty sure of himself right now. I don't really see that I have much of an option. Hardly going to contradict him right now, though. Alfonse and his friend step over the bodies of their dead friends, and they leave.

So fucking surreal. Once the door closes behind them,

the three of us just exchange looks. *How did we get here? That was really fucking unexpected. Where do we go from here?*

Common sense returns pretty damn quickly, though. I stride over the dead men in my hallway, and I grab hold of Jericho by the throat. He grimaces up at me, baring his teeth, his gold grill spackled and stained with blood. I don't try and hide my fist as I pull it back. "Guess it's time for *you* to arrepiente, motherfucker."

My right hook knocks him clean out.

******

Blood in the snow.

God knows how there aren't cops lining the street yet, but the place is deserted. A woman walking her dog watches me carry Jericho down the steps from the house and doesn't bat an eyelid. Jake's bleeding out all over the place; he needs a doctor and fast. The Skyline's right where I left it, parked directly in front of the house. Jake opens up the rear passenger door, and I bundle Jericho into the back. I almost drop his unconscious body when I see what's already taking up space on the other side of the console.

A head.

A severed fucking head.

Jared Viorello's lifeless eyes stare up at me, his neck a mangled mess. He was obviously balanced upright on the seat, but the movement of me shoving Jericho back there jostles the car and the head topples over, revealing blood and sinew, bone and tendons.

"Fuck. *Me.*" I give Jericho one last push and slam the door closed. On the other side of the street, Jericho's heavies are leaning against the railings of a tall walkup. Alfonse points his fingers at me—a makeshift gun—and fires. "One hour. If he's not back at the garage in one hour, you're fucking dead men," he shouts. "Your girls. Your families. Your friends. *All. Fucking. Dead.*"

Three seconds later, Jake and I are burning through the snow in a stolen Nissan with an unconscious gang leader and a decapitated murder victim as cargo.

"How bad is it?" I try and pull Jake's hands from his stomach, but he holds them there tight. He's ghostly pale and shaking.

"About as bad as you'd expect," he says evenly. "I've been shot in the stomach. I'm probably fucking dying. Go on. You can say it."

"Say what?"

"I should never have grabbed that guy's gun. I should have sat fucking still. I should have—"

"Shut the fuck up. Right now. Shut the fuck up. This is on me, not you." I punch the steering wheel, growling under my breath. This is not good. This is seriously not fucking good. "Don't worry. I'm gonna get you fixed up."

Margot is the last person who will want to see me right now, especially after this afternoon's encounter, but there aren't any other options. Jake passes out on the journey to her place. I park in the underground lot beneath her building, and then I drag Jericho's still lifeless body out of the backseat and I heft him into the trunk. Skylines aren't known for their roomy storage space; it takes three attempts to get the damn thing to close. I take off my jacket and I throw it over Jared's head, still on the back seat, and then I'm carrying my best friend to the elevators. His gunshot wound seems to have stopped bleeding now, and I'm fairly sure that's not a good thing. He's probably just out of blood.

On the fifth floor, I stand outside the door I practically hammered down only a couple of hours ago, and I do it all over again. I smash my fist against the wood until Margot opens up. She takes one look at me and shakes her head.

"Oh no. No way. *You have got to be fucking kidding me.*"

TWENTY-EIGHT

THE BRIDGE

SASHA

A watched pot never boils. How many times have I heard this during my lifetime, and why do I keep on staring at this damn cell phone? I physically cannot stop myself. He hasn't called. He hasn't texted. It's been three hours and I haven't heard from him at all.

"For crying out loud, Sasha, quit bouncing your knee. You're making me nervous." Ali puts the third cup of coffee she's made for me down on the coffee table, shooting a hateful sideways glance at Andrew in the process. He's standing at the window, looking out onto the street, his back to us, but I'm pretty sure he must be able to feel the fire and brimstone Ali is sending his way. He hasn't said more than three words since we got here.

"Are you going to tell me what's going on?" Ali hisses. "What the fuck is *he* doing in town?"

"I can hear you, y'know. I came because I was worried about Sasha. Is that a crime?"

"A bit late to be showing your sensitive side now, isn't it?" Ali snaps.

My head is spinning and I feel sick to my stomach. I am going out of my mind with worry. "Stop! Just stop. Please. Jesus wept. You're driving me mad. Can you both please just...*not*? The deafening silence was better than you two bickering."

Ali sits down, dealing me a cool look. She's just trying to protect me, I know, but I'm wound too tight right now. I shouldn't have snapped. I should be keeping my head but it's so hard when—

My cellphone bursts into life. I nearly drop it in my haste to answer, adrenaline firing like gasoline through my body. "Hello? Rooke, god, where are you?"

"Ms. Connor?" The voice on the other end of the line does not belong to Rooke. It belongs to someone much older, far gruffer, if that's humanly possible. The hope that just flooded my body disintegrates in a heartbeat. "Ms. Connor, this is Detective Jacobi. You may remember we met at the hospital recently?"

Jacobi. How could I forget? I can't hide the disappointment in my voice. "How can I help you, Detective?"

"I thought you'd like to know that we've apprehended the man who broke into the museum and assaulted you. His name is Casper Reins. An ex-Marine. He was found wandering the streets in the early hours of the morning, disoriented and badly injured."

I lean forward, elbows on knees, pressing the phone

against the side of my head, unable to blink. "You found him? He's in custody?"

"Yes. He suffers from severe schizophrenia. And you were right. You hit him pretty hard by the looks of things. He was admitted to Mount Sinai this morning."

"Am I in trouble?"

"No. No. You were defending yourself. And he admitted to killing the security guard. There's still some paperwork that will need to be—"

He talks on the other end of the phone for a while, but who knows what he says. They have him. The cops have Casper. The relief I experience is crushing. I can hardly catch my breath. No more worrying that I'm going to wake up in the middle of the night and he'll be there, standing at the foot of my bed. No more looking over my shoulder.

So, then, where is Rooke?

"Ms. Connor? *Ms. Connor*? I didn't quite catch that."

I must have asked the question out loud. "I'm sorry. Nothing. I can come by the station in a couple of days? Would that be okay?"

"Fine. Just, please, don't talk to the press until we've made an official statement."

"I won't." I hang up and immediately check my phone. No missed calls. No messages. I close my eyes.

"Would someone please tell me what the fuck is going on?" This is Andrew's best, most authoritative voice. His investment banker voice. His *I-earn-six-figures-even-in-Texas* voice.

Ali clears her throat. "Sasha's dating a twenty-three year old ex-con with a penchant for romance novels."

I could kill her.

"What? Is that true?"

I open my eyes, and Andrew has finally turned away from the window and is looking at me like I'm a stranger. I am a stranger to him now. We shared a past once upon a time, but now we're both different people. We don't recognize each other anymore. I'm suddenly struck by the awful realization that I never loved him. "That…that is so reckless, Sasha," he chides. "Honestly, I knew you were struggling, but that is ridiculous. How can you—"

"Fuck you, Andrew."

"Pardon?"

"I said, fuck…you…Andrew. Leave. Now." He blinks, his eyelids shuttering, as he clearly tries to process what I'm saying. "Go back to Texas, go back to Kim. Go back to your new son, who I will refuse to call Christopher until the end of time. *Go.* I don't want you here. I don't ever want to see you again."

Ali makes a choking sound when I mention his new kid. She jumps up out of her chair, her arms lifted as if jumping into action but she doesn't really know what she's meant to be doing. "*You have another child?*"

"You've changed," Andrew whispers. "Are you still drinking?"

I cross the room and I slap him across the face. I'm done exchanging words with this man. I'm done looking at his face. I am done breathing the same fucking air as him. If he won't leave, then I will. I turn, and I leave. Ali calls after me, but I don't stop. I leave her apartment, and my body feels so much lighter. Andrew has had that coming for a very long time, and the knowledge that Casper is in police custody is almost enough to make me weep. My ribs, my face, my leg…everything feels almost back to normal. All I need now is for Rooke to show up and I'll really believe that this nightmare is on its way to being over.

I'm in no hurry to get home. When it snows like this in New York, the city continues to throb and hum, always moving forward, surging to the beat of a persistent drum. The drumbeat slows a little, though. People seem a little more aware of their surroundings. Of the other people on the street. Of the smoke and the steam, and of the cold, the way it makes you feel alive.

I walk slowly, remembering the times I walked back from Ali's with Christopher. I always wondered how he perceived the world without all of the chaotic noise; it seemed to me even back then that life would feel so much calmer without the sirens, the screeching of tires, the thump of helicopter blades and the chatter of street vendors. He would watch, studying the streets and the houses around him so intensely. He really looked at people, at their faces and their hands. He saw way more than most people.

God, I miss him.

I'm almost home when a silver Audi pulls up alongside me. I don't think anything of it at first, but when the window buzzes down and a dark-haired guy leans out, I see that his shirt is flecked with blood and I really do start to think.

"Ah, Ms. Connor," he says in a heavily accented voice. "You are far more beautiful than the photograph on the back of your book, hermosa."

******

ROOKE

Jericho is gone.

It's not hard to pop open the trunk of a car from the inside, and he's worked around cars forever. If anyone's escaping from the luggage space of an automobile, then it's that man. I curse as I slam the trunk closed. There will be hell to pay for what happened this afternoon. He's not going to catch me sleeping, though. No fucking way. If he hasn't already bled out and died in a snow bank somewhere, if he has somehow made it back to the garage, I'm going to be ready for him.

ME: Are you still at Ali's?

There's no read receipt from Sasha. No little bubble that shows she's typing. I have this sick, twisted feeling in the pit of my stomach that tells me I need to find her. *Now*.

When Ali opens the door at the address Sasha texted me earlier, I can see from the look on her face that all is not well. "Where is she?" I demand.

"I don't know. She had a fight with Andrew and—"

"*Andrew?*"

"Yeah. He showed up. Wanted to make sure she was okay after everything with that guy. Oh, the cops phoned they caught him. He's in the hospital."

What the fuck is happening right now? I was meant to deal with Casper. I was meant to dole out justice to him, and now the police have him? Well, fuck. And on top of that, I just played a part in killing two gang members, my best friend is potentially bleeding to death in a sham hospital right now and I don't know where my girlfriend is.

"When you see her, tell her I'm mad at her," Ali calls after me as I leave.

"Nope," I mutter under my breath.

When I head back out onto the street, a police cruiser is pulled up next to the Skyline and there are two officers standing next to the vehicle, peering in through the windows. One of them is talking into his radio. My face is a blank mask as I casually leave Ali's apartment building and continue walking down the street right past them. It's only after I'm around the corner that I allow myself to be pissed off that my ride is gone. And then nearly half a block later when the dread begins to sink in. Jared. My fucking jacket's hiding his dismembered head on the back seat. Great.

I call Sasha, but her cell just rings out. I call her again, the cold stabbing at my lungs, my feet freezing from the snow. Eventually she picks up. Only it's not her that answers.

"You're too late, Cuervo."

An indescribable fear claws at me from the inside. "What have you done?"

"Nothing. Yet. But by the time you get here, your pretty little girlfriend will be long gone."

"Jericho, let me speak to her. I need to talk to her."

"I needed for you to not shoot me in the chest and cram me in the trunk of a shitty sports car, but look how that turned out. We don't always get what we need, huh, Cuervo?"

"What are you going to do?" Bile is rising up the back of my throat, burning, searing, making my throat close up. I will fucking kill him. If he hurts one hair on her head... If he so much as looks at her wrong...

"*Rooke!*"

I hear Sasha's panicked cry on the other end of the phone; she sounds terrified. God, I want to go back. There was a point this morning, just before the sun came up, when I was laying next to her, naked, stroking her hair. I made a decision. Instead of staying in bed and enjoying those quiet moments with her, I chose anger. I chose retribution. I chose revenge. And now, it looks as though that decision is going to get her killed. If I'd stayed in bed with her, I would never have been at the garage. Jared wouldn't have been able to tell that stupid, outrageous fucking lie, and Jericho would never have come to find me at the house.

A chain of events was triggered by the decision I

277

made. A chain of events I will never be able to undo. The dye is cast. The wheels to my destruction are in motion. If she dies...

"If you'd like a little wager, of course that could always be arranged."

A roaring silence sweeps through me. Jericho and his wagers. He always honors his bets, but it's never a fair call. "What are you suggesting?"

"Well...let's see. You shot me in the chest. I could shoot your girlfriend in the chest, too. See if she lives."

"Or?"

"Or I could shoot her in the chest and push her off the Brooklyn Bridge into the East River and forget about seeing if she lives. I did some research on your pretty museum curator a few weeks back, Cuervo. Did you know she's already taken one nosedive off this bridge? A miracle, they called it. No one survives the fall. She was in her car, though. Must have cushioned the blow a little. What do you think will happen to her without it?"

God. He's got her on the bridge. I'm not that far away, but how long will it take him to follow through with his threats? He can't push her. Damn it, he can't. She's not meant to die that way. She went through the trauma of it once already, only to make it through alive. Jericho is right; it was a miracle she survived. She won't be that lucky again.

"So. Your call, Crow. You decide which one it's going to be. Heads, I just shoot her and leave her on the walkway. Tails, I shoot her and into the water she goes. It's really up to you. I'm hoping you choose heads, though. Who knows? Maybe you'll make it here in time to save her life. Maybe someone will find her and call an ambulance."

"I'm not choosing, motherfucker."

Jericho makes a disappointed sound. "Ahh, that's a pity. You know how I like a good bet. Never mind, though.

It's getting late, and I'm strangely feeling a little lightheaded."

I hear the gun go off. I hear the scream.

The line goes dead.

******

I'm running. My feet can't keep up with my desperate need to go faster. I slip and slide in the snow. Car horns scream at me as I blindly careen across streets lit up with headlights. I have to get to her. I have to get to the bridge.

The bridge...

The bridge...

The bridge...

My heart is fit to explode by the time I reach my destination. Which side are they on? *Which side?* How far across are they? Jericho wouldn't have ditched her body into the water. No, he knows I'm coming for her. He's certifiably insane, but he's also a pragmatist. If he can dispose of both Sasha and me at the same time, he'll wait. It's cleaner. Neater. Less mess to take care of.

The snow is falling so fast that, instead of melting instantly as it normally would on the bridge, it's still thick on the ground. A high snow bank has even mounted up alongside the walkway. Nighttime has closed in, and a ribbon of yellow light heads in one direction across the bridge, while a banner of red flows in the other.

"*SASHA!*" I can't see her. I can't fucking see her anywhere. She has to be here. There are too many people around. Jericho would never shoot someone in public, then dump them over the railings. Too risky. Too dangerous. Too—

"*Rooke!*"

There they are. Just Alfonse and Jericho. In between them, leaning against the barrier, Sasha is pinned, wrestling like a wild animal, trying to get free. "Rooke, don't! Don't do it!"

She has to recognize the wild, frayed look in my eyes. I feel reckless, like I can't trust myself not to make the wrong call right now. My fists have never let me down before, but this situation is different; I can't go in there, throwing punches. Carefully. That's how I need to approach this. Even though every fiber of my being is filled with rage, I have to proceed carefully.

"Record time, Rooke. You're a little out of breath, no?"

"And you're looking a little pale, boss. You need to take a knee?" I shouldn't antagonize him. Alfonse sneers. When I look closer, I see he's holding a knife casually against Sasha's side, out of sight from the passing cars. Sasha's eyes are wide. She looks so scared, but she doesn't appear to be hurt. The gunshot I heard on the phone must have been theatrics on Jericho's part. Her hair floats up on the wind, whipping around her face. Her jacket is dusted with snow, thick on her shoulders. They've been standing out here for some time.

"I'm not an unreasonable man," Jericho says thoughtfully. "I'm a good Catholic. I believe in forgiveness, when it is sought out in earnest. What do you think, Rooke? Do you think you can convince me that you are sorry for how things played out earlier? That you truly feel bad for what happened to Michael and Mateo?"

"I doubt it." I'm not playing games with him. He has no interest in making me beg for Sasha's life. If I know him at all, he wants me to make him an offer—to trade my own life for hers. If that is what he wants, then he can have it. What is my life worth without her? Absolutely nothing. I'll gladly hand myself over so long as he lets her go. He can shoot me in the gut and let me tumble into the icy water below if that's how it has to be. I don't trust him to let her live, though. I need to see her walk away from this.

And that means I'm probably going to have to fight.

Jericho points at all the traffic whipping by in a blur and pouts. "What do you think, *hijo*? Do you think any of them will stop to help you? Do you think they can even see us standing here on the bridge with all this snow in the way? It's dark. It's cold. Everyone wants to get home to their families, to their dinners and their warm beds."

"Don't you think this has gotten a little out of hand?" I sigh, shaking my head. "Let Sasha go. She hasn't done anything. Let's just hit the re-set button. I'll go back to boosting cars for you. You'll stop trying to murder the people I care about. Sound fair?"

Jericho just laughs. "No such thing as a re-set button in our world, Rooke. We all have excellent memories and suspicious minds. Every time I look at you, I'm going to be wondering if you're betraying me. I'll feel the burn in my chest from where you shot me. And every time I look at you, I'll see this beautiful little treat here and I'll be sad that I didn't kill her. Or at least fuck her."

"Still time, boss," Alfonse says, sneering. "Rape the bitch. Make him watch. It'll serve him right for killing our boys." He's trying to make me react, and I want to. Really fucking badly. Losing my head right now would be disastrous, though. Instead, I slowly turn my head to look at him, sending him a look laden with promises.

I am going to hurt you.

I am going to rip out your tongue.

I am going to make you bleed.

I am going to make you wish you were never born.

I am going to fucking end *you.*

Alfonse obviously isn't taking me seriously. He laughs, pressing the knife closer to Sasha's side, and she freezes, going absolutely still. My beautiful, precious, broken Sasha. She looks like she's prepared for what comes next. She's afraid, but there's also a weary, resigned look in her eye as she stares at me. It's as if she's telling me it's all right, that she's okay with whatever comes next. It's *not* all right, though. I am *not* okay with whatever comes next.

I don't make plans. Ever since my eighteenth birthday, I have refused to look beyond the next few days of my life. The unknown has always held an appeal to me, and besides…what's the point in looking to the future when your freedom could be snatched away at any moment? Things have been different with Sasha, though. I've allowed myself to peek beyond next week. Next month. Next year, even. I've allowed myself to imagine a life with her, and it's a good life. I won't give it up. I fucking refuse. I'll give up working for New York's underground elite. I'll give up the money. I'll give up the thrill and the adrenaline. I'll give it all up before I sacrifice the chance to make her happy.

Sasha locks her eyes onto me and doesn't look away. A plan forms in my head during the brief moments we're staring at each other. It's a horrible plan, but it's going to have to do. I left my gun in the Skyline. I do still have the throwing knives I took from my go-bag earlier back at the house, though. I'm just going to have to hope that my aim is good.

"Rape isn't always the answer," Jericho says chidingly. "And god knows where her cunt has been, anyway. This one looks a little…used." He traces a hand down Sasha's cheek, and she flinches, disgust written all over her face. I have napalm for blood, and it's burning me up. I've never known such rage. He shouldn't be touching her. He shouldn't be talking about her. Still, I don't give the bastards what they want. I breathe through the insanity my anger brings, and I form the shape with my hand. A shape I know Sasha will see, that will mean something to her.

She showed me this shape in my bed last night. She

had her arms wrapped around her knees, her hair a dark, curling waterfall of chocolate and cinnamon and honey around her face, framing her sadness. Dinosaur. Elephant. Monkey. Bird. But not just bird. *Duck.*

I hold my index and middle fingers together, then tap them against the pad of my thumb. I don't hold my hand up to my face. That would be too obvious. Sasha sees, though. The years of raising a son and speaking sign language with him has made her perceptive to even the slightest hand movement. She looks at me, shocked; she understands what I want her to do, but she doesn't look happy about it. She slowly shakes her head, tears welling in her eyes. I stand firm. She's scared, I know, but she's braver than she realizes. She can do this.

Jericho leers at Sasha, grinning sadistically. "I could carve up her face. Maybe that would soften the blow for you, Cuervo. If she's disfigured, maybe you won't give a shit about her anymore."

"I'm going to use that blade on *you*," I say darkly. "I'm going to cut your fucking dick off and toss *that* in the river. Then I'm going to let Sasha drive that knife up in between your ribs, and I'm going to fucking smile as she gets to watch you die. How does *that* sound?"

"Sounds like you're dreaming to me, my friend."

"I guess we'll see, won't we?" I move quickly. Neither Jericho nor Alfonse are ready for the knife that I send hurtling through the air. The flash of silver turns end over end through the falling snow, and then it's sticking blade first out of the side of Alfonse's neck. Sasha does as I motioned to her and ducks; she doesn't need me to yell out the command. Jericho releases a howl of rage and grabs at her, but he's a forty-five year old loser who drinks and smokes too much, and I spend three hours a day boxing and sprinting up stairways. My body slams into his before he can even reach her. He impacts against the high metal railing behind him, and then I'm pounding my clenched fists into his face, over and over again, not stopping when I break his nose, or even when I feel his eye socket shatter. I don't stop until small fragments of bone are actually flying into the air, and Jericho is making a sickening gurgling sound at the back of his throat.

"Rooke? Rooke, stop, *please*." Sasha's hands are on me. She's gripping at my shoulders, trying to pull me away from the body on the ground. She screams. When I turn around, Alfonse has her by the throat and he's hoisting her up so that her feet are kicking in thin air.

Not. Fucking. Happening.

I charge at him, but I don't crash into him the same way I just did with Jericho. That could end up with Sasha getting hurt. I take hold of the knife that's still embedded in the side of his neck, and I yank it free from his body.

"Fuck! You fucking—" Alfonse's words are cut short by the blood that's filling his throat. He's a huge fucker, though. He's not releasing Sasha, and he's not going down. I take hold of him by the neck, and then I'm driving the blade back into his body. His ear this time, though. I slam the point directly into his ear. It's like turning off a light switch. One second his face is a rictus of rage, the next it is blank and he is slumping to his knees.

"Oh my god. Holy shit. Oh my god." Sasha covers her mouth with her hands. She's in shock. Her skin is white as chalk, and her fingers are trembling. She looks up and down the bridge, tears streaking down her cheeks. "What...what do we do..." she stammers. "I don't know what we're supposed to do..."

I make her sit down, and I go about fixing the situation. The lighting here is so dim. The snow bank forming a barricade between the bridge walkway and the road below is really high. I don't think for a second anyone just witnessed what went down, but I'm careful as I pick

Alfonse up by his arms and I push him over the railings. Sasha screws her eyes shut as I dispose of Jericho in the same way.

"This can't be happening. This can't be happening. This can't be happening." She chants this over and over again as I sit down onto the snow beside her. There's blood everywhere. I put my arm around her and draw her to me, clenching my jaw.

"It's okay. It's okay, baby, it's over now. I promise. It's all over now. We can't stay here, though. We have to move. Can you walk?" If she can't, I'll carry her. I just need to get her off this godforsaken bridge. She nods, though. Gets to her feet.

It takes a long time to get back to my place. When we arrive, it's to find that the road is choked with fire engines...

...and my entire house is engulfed in flames.

TWENTY-NINE

FELT AND SEEN

SASHA

"**A**re you sure you're ready to be back at work, dear girl?" Oscar Blackheath is looking particularly handsome in a blue pinstripe shirt and bowtie today. I can't stop staring at him. He is Rooke's *grandfather*. It just makes no sense. I turn the words over and over in my head, trying to understand how this sweet old man is in any way related to the man who I left sleeping in my bed this morning.

"I'm sure. I think it's important I get back to it. I'm bored at home anyway. And I can't go around jumping at shadows forever." This last statement is really true.

Rooke's been working every day at the antiques store, trying to maintain a sense of normalcy in the face of all the attention he's been receiving from the cops and the fire department.

Honestly, he should be receiving more attention than he is. He told me what happened there with the man who kidnapped me and dragged me kicking and screaming to the bridge. He told me about the two dead bodies that should have been discovered inside the building, but weren't. He has no idea what happened to them. No idea whatsoever. It's a mystery that haunts every waking moment of my day. I know it's bothering Rooke, too. He's as stern and stoic as ever, but I can see the firm set of his jaw every time his cell rings. He's just waiting. Waiting for something to happen that spells disaster for him and for me.

"Good. Well I can't say I'm sorry you're back. This place has been terribly dull without you, my girl." Oscar scratches at the back of his head, making a non-committal grumbling sound. "I would invite you to have lunch with me, but I'm afraid I have a prior engagement. Honestly, I'd like to cancel but—"

"Daddy, there you are."

Oscar looks like he's been shot through with a thousand volts. He leans back and steps out of my office into the hallway, turning to face a tall, severe looking woman with a very frosty expression on her face. Her dark brown, almost black hair is pulled back into an immaculate bun. Her eyebrows are perfect. Her dress is Gucci. Her bag is Prada. Her shoes are Manolo Blahniks. She struts down the hallway towards us with a swanlike grace that makes me think she must have been a runway model at some point in her life. "I've been looking all over for you," she says, giving Oscar an air kiss in the general vicinity of his weathered cheek. "The porter on the second floor said you were in your office, but when I got there the place was deserted."

"Yes. Well. I have to stretch my legs every once in a while. Don't want to fossilize and join the rest of the dinosaurs just yet." Oscar looks perturbed for a second, then smiles grimly. "Simone, this is a very dear friend of mine, Sasha."

The woman turns her frigid gaze to me, and I want to hide under my desk all over again. As soon as I see the color of her eyes, it hits home. Simone. Oh god. She arranges her mouth into what might generally be described as a smile. "Ah, yes. *Sasha*." She offers me her hand to shake. Her fingers are freezing. "I believe you know my son."

A lot is being said in those few short words: she knows I am *fucking* her son. My cheeks flush, wildfire spreading across my face. It's my first day back, and I am sure as hell not prepared for this. Meeting Rooke's mother isn't something I'd planned on any time soon. Meeting his mother without him is just plain terrifying.

"I do," I agree, trying to keep my chin held high.

Simone hovers a hand just above Oscar's shoulder, her smile broadening slightly. "Daddy, could you do me a favor and give me a moment alone with Sasha? I would just like a brief word with her before we head out to lunch."

He looks guilty as hell as he shuffles off down the hallway. "Be nice to her, dear. I rather like her. If you eviscerate her with that sharp tongue of yours, I shall be most displeased."

The sound of Simone's laughter is like the ringing of a tiny silver bell. Once he's gone, she enters my office and the space suddenly feels claustrophobic. She points at the overstuffed armchair in the corner of the room, eyebrows halfway up her forehead. "Can I sit?"

"Of course. Please."

She folds herself neatly into the chair, purse rested carefully on her lap. She rifles around inside the black leather bag, a gentle crease marking her brow, until she finds what she's looking for. She then holds a single silver key out to me, perfectly manicured nails flashing under the overhead lights. Even fluorescents can't make this woman look bad.

"My son rarely answers his phone when I call him, Sasha. I was wondering if you might give this to him. Not that it's much good to him anymore. I believe his house is missing a front door these days?"

"And windows. And stairs. And a few walls, actually."

She shrugs her shoulders in a prim fashion. "Once the insurance adjustors have closed their case on the house fire, I'm sure they'll renovate very quickly. These things can take time, though."

"Mmm." I slip the key she just gave me into my pocket.

"Thank you for allowing him to stay with you in the interim. I hope he isn't making a nuisance of himself?"

"He's not seven years old, Ms. Blackheath. He's an adult. We're dating. He's definitely not making a nuisance of himself."

That seems to knock her calm exterior a little. "Yes. Well. I didn't mean to sound obtuse. Forgive me. I suppose mothers always think of their sons as little boys, no matter how old they are."

Or how tall they are. Or how many tattoos they get. Rooke looks every bit as dangerous as he is. She can't have missed that.

"Anyway. I don't want to keep you. I just wanted to return that key. It was very nice to meet you. Maybe soon, Rooke will bring you to the house and you can meet me and my husband in a formal fashion." She gets to her feet. Brushes down her dress. "In the meantime, please ask him to call me. He missed our breakfast a few weeks ago, and I was beginning to wonder if he was still alive. I paid him a visit, but unfortunately he wasn't home at the time. Please tell him that I hope the housekeeping I tended to on his behalf last week was not out of line." Tipping her head to one side, she suddenly bears a more than startling resemblance to her son. He often wears the same, casual sideways tilt of the head. "It really was a pleasure," she says.

Her heels sound like gunfire on the tile as she saunters off after Oscar.

******

"Housekeeping?" Rooke frowns at the key I hand over to him when I get home. He's fresh out of the shower. Beads of water run down his back, over his shoulders, down his arms, over his chest. I put up a valiant fight, but in the end I can't help myself. I feel like a teenager as I check him out. His tattoos are complex, interlinking, weaving all over his body. They're mostly black, with a subtle touch of color here and there that accents the artwork. His body is out of this fucking world. He was smiling when I came in, a highly suggestive smirk on his face, but now he seems to be preoccupied.

"I had no idea she had a key," he says quietly. His frame locks up unexpectedly, then, all expression sliding from his face. "*Fuck.*"

"What? What is it?"

"Housekeeping? *No fucking way.*"

"I'm afraid you're going to have to tell me what you're talking about."

"Housekeeping. People like Jericho use a housekeeping service. The Barbieris, too. *She* set that fire at the house. *She* had those bodies moved."

"*What?*"

He sits down heavily, pressing the heels of his hands

into his eyes. "God. It all makes sense. It all makes such perfect sense. I can't believe this. She must have done something about the car, too."

"What car?"

"The one I stole and was driving across town. The one with Jared Viorelli's—" He almost says something, then appears to think better of it. "Never mind. Fuck. My mother disposed of two bodies and committed arson. My world just shifted on its axis a little."

"Does this mean we can stop worrying?"

"Yeah. Yeah, I guess it does."

"Then take me upstairs. I'd like some attention from you now please."

A shadow falls across his face. He's been quiet ever since the bridge, and it's been obvious why. He hasn't needed to explain. It seems as though that might have changed now, though.

"Sasha..."

"Rooke, it's okay. I don't need to hear it. I don't need the get-out-of-jail free card from you. Not now. Not ever."

He cups my face in his hands, leaning down so that his forehead is pressed against mine. "But you should have one. You saw some shit on that bridge. I'd love to say that's not who I am, but it would be a lie. That's *exactly* who I am. The man who will kill without a second thought in order to protect you. Does that make me the guy who will lose his shit if someone is rude to you? Yes. Does that mean I might lay someone out for looking at you? Most definitely, yes. I am not an easy human being to be around, Sasha. This is the moment where you get to tell me that you'd like to walk away."

Do I? I guess I have asked myself this question a number of times over the last seven days. Truth be told, I've thought about it endlessly, and I keep coming back to the same answer. No, I do not want to walk away from this.

Watching Rooke beat a man to death was frightening, but he did it to protect me. I must have gone slightly mad over the past few weeks, because something that should have terrified me and made me want to run for the hills actually ended up making me feel safe and protected. How fucked up is that?

"Like I said. You can keep your card, thank you very much," I whisper.

Rooke closes his eyes, blowing out a deep breath. "Thank fuck for that. I was trying to figure out how to stop myself from kidnapping you and it wasn't looking good."

The kitchen door opens and Jake appears, shoulders stiff, body braced, a cup of coffee in one hand and a bottle of painkillers in the other. He takes one look at us and pretends to scowl. "Jesus. How's a guy meant to recuperate with this shit going on? You're about to fuck again, aren't you?"

"You're not even meant to be out of bed," I remind him.

"Yeah, yeah. Save it for when I've had three of these and I don't know my own name," he says, holding up the pain meds.

I try not to laugh. "I'm glad he's getting better," I whisper into Rooke's ear. There was a second, just after Rooke brought him back here, when things were not looking good. Jake's temperature was through the roof. He was delirious, ghostly pale and couldn't stop throwing up. That lasted for forty-eight worrying hours, and then we woke up the next morning and his fever had suddenly broken and he was asking for food.

Rooke, my raven king, wraps his arms around me and whispers back to me. "Me too. But he needs to hurry the fuck up and leave so I can fuck you on the table." He pauses, then says, "Also, I have something I want to show you."

I've heard this before from him. His show-and-tell sessions nearly always end up with me on my back and his head between my legs; to say I'm a fan of them is an understatement. "Is that so?"

He treats me to the same arrogant, cocky smile he gave me the very first time I saw him in the hallway at the museum. "Dirty girl," he whispers. "This is different. I can show you right now if you like?"

"Okay. Sure."

Carefully, Rooke raises his right hand, palm facing me. He looks me dead in the eye. He seems to be holding his breath. Painfully slowly he lowers his middle finger, and then his ring finger, until he's only holding up his thumb, his index finger and his pinkie.

My breath catches in my throat.

"I learned this earlier this morning," he whispers.

My eyes are stinging so badly that I know I'm going to cry. There's no avoiding it. The last person to sign this to me was Christopher, right before he died. Carefully, I mirror the shape he's made with his hand and I press my fingertips to his, index finger-to-index finger, pinkie-to-pinkie, thumb-to-thumb.

Rooke huffs heavily down his nose. He kisses me softly, his lips skating across mine, nudging me with the tip of his nose. "Glad you didn't leave me hanging, Connor," he whispers softly.

I try not to let the moment overtake me entirely, but it's difficult. The love between us is fire and ice. It's loss, and it's redemption. It's pain, and it's comfort. It is everything. Having him actually tell me how he feels, especially the way he just did, is something I will remember forever, but in the end the truth is that I already knew. Some things are felt and seen long before they're put into words, after all.

After so long, my heart is finally healing.

For the first time since I surfaced the frigid, cold waters of the East River five years ago, I feel like I can finally breathe again.

FAQ WITH THE AUTHOR!

1)   Will there be more from Rooke & Sasha in the future?

I really hope so! I have a number of other projects in the works right now, but I have absolutely LOVED writing about these guys. Reach out and let me know if you're interested in what happens to them, and I will try and make it happen!

2)   Does Rooke stop stealing cars?

Hmm. Well, who knows? He's in love with his lady, but she didn't ask him to quit... Would you have asked him to end his life of crime?

3)   Will Sasha ever have any more children?

She definitely never planned on it. Recovering from the heartbreak of losing a child is impossible. Now that Rooke is in her life, though, it's up in the air. She's happier than she ever thought she could be again. Perhaps that might make her reassess her previous decision.

4)   The Barbieri family has also featured in your Hell's Kitchen series (co-written with Lili St Germain) and Chaos & Ruin series. Are you going to write something to tie all of the stories together in the future?

Good question! I would love, love, love to write something to tie everything all together. It really depends on the directions each storyline veers off into, though. Lili and I are writing the second instalment in the Hell's Kitchen series right now, and let me tell you...these Barbieri boys are insane in the very best way.

5) What are you working on next?

As I just mentioned, I'm currently working on Tribeca with Lili, but I'm also working on another co-authored project with Jonny James, who just so happens to be the model on the cover of this book!! If you want to keep up to date with Road to Ruin, you can join my newsletter right here: http://eepurl.com/IzhzL

6) Did the Bleeding Hearts Book Club continue?

Sasha loved her romance novels. There's no way she closed the club down. She definitely continued. I'm not sure if Rooke would have carried on attending. Although, he did find it kind of hot haha!

If you would like to join the real Bleeding Hearts Book Club, you can do so searching for the group on Facebook!